DEFENDER OF WALLS

KINGDOM OF WALLS BOOK ONE

TANYA BIRD

CHAPTER 1

The rain fell hard, blinding Blake as she dashed between fat sequoia trunks. No birds took flight. They knew better than to inhabit trees that side of the wall.

She stopped in the tall shadows at the edge of the borough, gaze sweeping the length of the wall. Any closer and the defenders would see her. Her eyes fell to the mud separating forest and stone. It had once been covered in grass, before the rain had arrived and never left.

Catching her breath, she eyed the defender strolling atop the wall, bow slung over his shoulder. A corpse hung beneath him—a warning to the merchants.

She needed to find Kingsley before the dogs arrived.

Her feet were soundless as she made her way through the trees towards the shaft, praying her brother was still inside the borough. Ears straining, she could hear nothing over the thudding of her heart. While she knew every inch of the merchant forest, the tunnels that ran beneath it were another matter.

A shift in the breeze made her turn, and she glimpsed Kingsley crouched ten yards away. She checked her surroundings before making her way over to him. He had removed the shaft cover and was preparing to enter the tunnel. His eyes snapped to her as she stepped into sight, hand going to the knife concealed beneath his shirt.

'What the hell are you doing here?' he whispered, looking around.

Blake closed the remaining distance between them, tucking wet hair behind her ears. 'Saving your life. There are dogs in the borough. We need to go—now.'

Kingsley glanced in the direction of the village. 'I'd rather be mauled by a sniffer dog than slowly starve to death.'

When he went to move, Blake grabbed a hold of his arm. 'You don't know what's waiting at the other end.'

'Food. Food awaits me.' He tapped her nose like she was ten years old instead of twenty. 'Now piss off home before the dogs find *you*.'

She peered into the narrow shaft, barely wide enough to fit his frame. Every time he entered the tunnels, she wondered if it would be the last.

'One lamb will feed us for a month,' he said, reading her expression.

Blake could not ignore the twist of hunger in her belly at the mention of meat. 'When the rain stops, we'll be able to buy everything we need.'

'You sound like Father.'

'Good. One of us should.'

Kingsley's mouth flattened into a thin line. 'Tell me another way to feed my family and I'll stay.'

'You could fish.'

'Fish?' He raked a hand through his unkempt hair. 'I can stand on that beach all day alongside every other desperate merchant, but I'll return home with nothing to show for my efforts. Get me a boat, and then we'll talk about fish.' He lowered himself into the shaft and looked up at her. 'Go help Mother with dinner.'

There was no food for dinner, but saying that would only prove his point, so she kept quiet.

He exhaled when she did not move. 'Do you know how hard it is watching you shake dust from the barley bag into the soup pot? Adding a carrot doesn't make it a meal.'

He went down onto hands and knees. The tunnel was half his height, so he would need to crawl the entire way.

'Be careful,' she said.

'Replace the cover, and don't linger.'

Then he was gone from sight, leaving her staring into empty darkness.

Blake did as she was told, covering the entrance with dirt and leaves. The network of tunnels, built and maintained by the merchants, connected the borough with both the noble and farming boroughs. While many knew of their existence, only a handful were brave enough to enter them. The consequences of being caught were displayed on every wall, making even the most desperate of men think twice.

'What are you doing?' came a male voice.

Blake shot to her feet and found a stern-faced defender standing five feet away. She reprimanded herself for not hearing him approach. His eyes were on the ground she had just covered, hand wrapping the hilt of his sword.

'Mushrooms,' she said, hoping to divert his attention. 'I was hunting for mushrooms.'

Hazel eyes travelled up to meet hers, pupils rimmed with gold that shone as bright as the sun she barely remembered. The man's hand slackened around his weapon.

'Optimistic,' he said, looking around.

'And subsequently disappointed.' She took in his tall frame and covering of lean muscle, wondering if she could outrun him. Defenders were notoriously fit.

He let go of his sword. 'Not a good time to be wandering around the forest by yourself.'

'Why's that?'

'There are dogs in the borough.'

'How are they at finding mushrooms?' She had no idea why she said that. Everyone knew defenders were stripped of their sense of humour within the first few months of training.

'My men are looking for tunnel shafts. You wouldn't know anything about that, would you?'

His men? Her eyes moved over the expensive uniform, pausing on his gold cloak pin.

He was a commander.

Her eyes shot up to his. She was fairly certain she was standing before the warden's son—Commander Wright. 'I know nothing of the tunnels.' She was a superb liar when she needed to be.

He looked down at her mud-soaked skirt. 'When was the last time you ate?'

'This morning,' she lied. If he thought her starving, he might think her desperate enough to brave the tunnels.

His face suggested he did not believe her. 'What did you have?'

'Fish.' It was feasible for those with enough coin and the patience to wait at the port all night for the boat to come in.

The commander let out a resigned breath, like he had just lost a battle with himself. 'Follow me.' He stepped past her.

'Where?'

He glanced over his shoulder. 'When a defender tells you to follow, you follow.'

'Am I under arrest?' She bit the inside of her cheek.

'Tempting,' he said under his breath before walking on.

Blake brushed a hand over the weapon concealed beneath her skirt. She was not a violent person by nature, but every woman in the borough had to be able to protect themselves if needed. She glanced a final time at the shaft before following him.

They had only gone ten yards when the commander stopped and crouched in front of a tree, foraging around its roots. Blake stood a safe distance away, watching him.

'Come here,' he said, drawing his dagger.

Blake's hand went into the pocket of her skirt, where the seam opened, providing access to her own weapon. 'Why?'

He looked up, gaze falling to the pocket where her hand was hidden. 'Because I want to show you sonmething. And hands where I can see them.'

She withdrew it, squinting against the rain as it fell

heavy once more. 'If I'm not under arrest, I'd like to go home.'

His attention remained on the tree. 'See these wood shavings?' He picked some up and sprinkled them to show her. 'That's how you know where to find them.'

'Them?'

'Aureate grubs. Few people realise you can eat them.'

Her eyebrows rose. 'That's what you wanted to show me?'

He traced a finger up to the hole in the trunk and began carving into it, revealing a fat grub the size of her small finger. He pulled it out and rose to show her. It wriggled in his open hand. 'You can eat them raw.' He held it out to her.

She laughed because she did not know what else to do. 'I'm not eating that.'

'Maybe not today, but you will when you're hungry enough.'

What did he know of hunger? The defenders might have been the lowest form of nobility, but they were still nobility. 'I'd quite like to see *you* eat it though.'

She expected to be reprimanded for the smug suggestion. Instead, the commander returned his dagger to its sheath, then met her gaze as he tossed the grub into his mouth, chewing as if it were the most normal thing in the world to eat food meant for lizards. Swallowing, he said, 'They're a good meat replacement.'

'So are eggs and milk, but I can't remember the last time I saw a chicken in the borough.'

'That's what happens when you eat all your laying hens.'

'So *that's* where we went wrong.' She knew better than to argue with a defender. 'I'll be sure to mention that to our local hen thief next time.'

Nothing changed on his face. 'Did you report the thief to a defender? We're not mind readers.'

'If I knew who took them, I would have dealt with the matter myself.'

He crossed his arms. 'And done what exactly?'

Nothing legal came to mind. 'Requested the hens be returned.'

Amusement passed over his face. 'Next time report it. Consequences serve as valuable lessons for future thieves.'

Blake nodded, knowing she would do no such thing. As much as she despised thieves, she did not wish anyone to lose a limb over a chicken. That was why merchants preferred to deal with such matters themselves. A broken nose would heal; a severed hand would not.

The commander looked like every other defender from a distance. They all had similar physiques, cropped hair, and neatly trimmed beards. But up close, she noted distinct features: generous lips, high cheekbones, and thick eyebrows that made his expression appear even more serious, if that were possible. There was colour in his face despite the absence of sun. He was definitely getting meat from somewhere.

'You should go,' he said.

She really should have. 'If you shut the tunnels, they'll just dig new ones. You know that, right?'

He watched her.

'No one is going to stand by while their family slowly

starves,' she went on. 'Not when there's meat on the other side of that wall.'

He did not appear moved by her little speech.

'How do you know there's anything left on the other side of that wall?' he asked.

'Because *you're* clearly getting food from somewhere.'

His eyebrows rose with the smallest hint of surprise. 'What's your name?'

Why had she not left when she had the chance? Now he wanted a name. 'It's *merchant* if your kind need something and *boor* if you don't.'

He stared at her for the longest time before speaking. '*Name.*'

She swallowed. 'Blake.' No chance she was willingly handing over her family name. Luckily, he did not push for it.

'And what does your father do?'

'My father's dead.' If she was expecting any form of sympathy from him, she did not get it. 'My brother runs the business,' she continued. 'He imports cloth.' It was a family effort, but the success and spoils of businesses always belonged to the head of the household. With her father gone, that was Kingsley. Never mind the fact that most of their income came from the private clothier work her mother did.

He finally looked away. 'Go home, *boor*, while the dogs are still leashed.'

That time she listened. But as she turned away, the ground shifted, making them both look down. It trembled for a few seconds.

'What was that?' Blake could not keep the fear out of

her voice as she looked in the direction of the shaft. A long ditch now ran between the trees, reaching all the way to the wall. It took her a few seconds to realise what it was.

The tunnel had collapsed.

Kingsley.

Her feet were moving then, pounding the earth as she ran towards the hole where the shaft had been moments earlier. 'Kingsley!' Collapsing to her knees, she began clawing at the mud, dragging up enormous handfuls of debris and clay and throwing it aside. 'Kingsley!'

A large hand clamped around her arm, pulling her to her feet and away from the ditch.

'You need to leave.' The commander spoke the words calmly but firmly into her ear.

She struggled against his grip. 'My brother's down there.' It was a dangerous confession, but a part of her hoped he might help.

The commander spun her around, forcing her to look at him. 'My men are coming. If you stay, they'll hang you alongside him.'

Every second they stood there talking was another second her brother was without air. Panicked, Blake reached into her pocket for her knife, but the commander caught her wrist in a vice-like grip, dipping his head so he was eye level with her.

'You can't help him. Go home to your family. They're going to need you.'

Her breaths came fast as she tried to process the words being spoken at her. Yes, her sisters would need her. Her mother needed her.

The sound of dogs barking made Blake jump. She glimpsed them through the trees.

'Run,' growled the commander, releasing her with a hard shove.

Blake staggered backwards, struggling to draw breath as the dogs tugged against their restraints, closer now. Regaining her balance, she took off at a run towards the village.

CHAPTER 2

If a defender stood a chance of surviving Chadora's savage coastline, he needed to have been raised on the horror stories passed down from predecessors. The stories were lessons for future defenders, a historical narrative of how to return alive instead of being eaten by small fish or washed up on the rocks days later.

As part of a defender's training, they would descend an eighty-foot cliff face to the turbulent sea below, plunge into the icy water, then navigate the sharp rocks and violent currents all the way to the flat rock half a mile offshore. The distance was manageable for a fit man, but being a strong swimmer was no guarantee. The sea fought intruders, lifting them high before sending them crashing down again.

Harlan had completed the swim more times than he could count, because the warden insisted on pushing his only son harder than any defender before him. Perhaps he felt the need to prove that Harlan was worthy of his position. Heaven forbid Shapur Wright was accused of favouring blood. It was not enough that Harlan had reduced crime in the merchant borough, and done so without losing any men under his command.

His father liked to keep him slightly off balance at all times.

As Harlan dragged himself up onto the rock the morning after the tunnels collapsed, he could feel his father's sharp eyes on him from atop the wall. He was certain the man's vision could penetrate even the thickest of fog. He had made it to the halfway point. Now he had to make it back to the wall.

Resting too long was a sign of weakness, so Harlan fought the urge to sit and catch his breath. He blinked against the water spraying him from the south and raised his arm to inspect a gash above his elbow. He had known the rock was there, but there had not been a damn thing he could do to avoid it when that wave hit.

He walked to the edge of the rock and dove in. The water roared in his ears. Clean strokes, powerful kicks, carefully planned breaths, and an ability to read the water. Those things would get him to the cliff in one piece.

Seaweed swirled around him, wrapping his leg like a hand trying to pull him under. He removed it with his other foot without breaking rhythm.

A rock appeared in front of him. He rolled left and let the water carry him a safe distance away from it. It was foolish to trust the tide though. He had seen it carry men out to sea and swallow them whole.

When Harlan emerged from the water, legs trembling and blood striping one arm, he bent, tearing mussels off the rocks and shoving them into the pockets of his trousers. Later, he would hand them out to the children who played along the port wall. When he could fit no more, he walked to the vertical cliff face and began the long climb up.

The key to not falling to his death was to test everything before using it to bear his weight.

He was sweating profusely by the time he reached the top, his heart drumming in his chest. As he stood on the narrow ledge between cliff and wall, he looked up, and sure enough, there was his father looking back at him.

No one else had been sent to the flat rock that day.

Taking hold of the rope, Harlan scaled the wall and climbed over the embrasure, dropping to his feet in front of his father. Shapur's eyes lowered to Harlan's bloodied arm.

'Slower than last time,' he said.

Harlan glanced over the wall at the sea. 'It was rougher out there today. Guessing that's why you didn't send anyone else.'

Shapur nodded. 'Good way to clear the head. Get that arm cleaned up. King Oswin and Prince Borin want the bodies hung.'

Harlan's eyes closed. 'The lesson's in their death. Displaying them will only provoke the merchants.'

'King Oswin wants to address them. Make it safe for him to do so.'

'Address them from the wall?'

'In the borough on horseback.'

Harlan cursed inwardly. 'Emotions will be running high in the borough. He'll be safer up on the wall.'

His father turned away. 'I said make it safe, Commander.'

CHAPTER 3

For three days, Blake watched the busy street from the shop window, praying that Kingsley would miraculously appear wearing that lazy smirk of his. He would have dark circles around his eyes from lack of sleep and muddy clothes that Lyndal would manage to get every stain from.

She was the fixer of the family.

Lyndal had spent the previous three days flitting between the shop and the house, finding minor tasks to keep herself busy. 'He's likely stuck in the farming borough,' she would say. 'You're all going to feel pretty ridiculous when he walks through that door.'

A fixer and an optimist.

The youngest of the three sisters was never home. Eda claimed she was hunting, but there was nothing left in the borough to hunt. More likely, she was up a tree somewhere, watching for her brother's return. On the rare occasion Eda was home, she passed time sharpening her knife or adjusting the string of her bow—like she was preparing for war.

'Are you sure she's a girl?' their father used to say. 'The warden will poach her if we're not careful.' He would always wink at Eda when he said that part.

Blake was seated at the table by the wall where Kingsley normally sat, trying to make sense of the notes in the ledger. Dates, orders, payments. She could read just fine, she just could not read Kingsley's handwriting. They were five days from their next delivery, and Kingsley was not there to collect it.

Blake looked over to where her mother was seated in the chair by the open window, sewing like her life depended on it. Candace had barely moved from that spot since Blake had returned from the forest alone. Every few stitches, she glanced out before returning to her work.

'Good news,' Lyndal said, entering the shop from the house. She held up a turnip the size of an egg. 'It's small but oh so beautiful.'

Candace smiled—barely—then turned back to the window.

Lyndal's hand fell a few inches, but she maintained her composure. The girl was pure sunshine, from her golden hair to her glittering laugh that could lift the mood of any room—except that one.

'A successful harvest,' Blake said, trying to make up for their mother's mental absence.

Before Lyndal could declare her plans for the turnip, Eda burst through the shop door, causing the bell to go flying across the room, clattering to a halt against the reams of fabric leaning on the far wall.

Kingsley had promised to fix it the morning he left.

Blake's stomach fell as she took in her sister's pale face and shiny eyes. *Come*, she signed.

Eda had not spoken verbally since their father's death. When her voice had failed to return, she had been forced to figure out another way to communicate with her family. A secret language that came in handy whenever their uncle visited.

There are defenders gathered in the square, Eda signed before fleeing once more.

The turnip fell from Lyndal's hand, and the tablecloth their mother had been embroidering floated down to the floor.

'I'll fetch our cloaks,' Lyndal said before disappearing into the house.

Blake went to help her mother up. 'You don't have to come,' she whispered, taking hold of her trembling hands.

Candace gave her a weak smile. 'He's my only son. Whatever happens, I must bear witness to it.' Her hand fell away when Lyndal returned, wrapping a cloak around each of them.

'Let's not get ahead of ourselves,' Lyndal said. 'Defenders gather in the square for any number of reasons.'

The women raised their hoods as they stepped out into the drizzle, angling their faces against the weather. Their neighbours, Thea and Birtle, were standing on their veranda. Thea cast a sympathetic look at Blake as she passed, while others locked up their shops before joining them on the muddy street. The Suttone family were not the only merchants missing a family member. People spoke in hushed voices as they headed for the village square by the east wall. The wall separated merchants from royalty and military. Merchants rarely entered the royal borough anymore—unless they were headed to the tower.

When they reached the cobblestoned square, the women weaved through the crowd towards the front.

'Where's Eda?' Blake asked, looking over her shoulder.

Lyndal slipped her arm through their mother's. 'How have we lost her already?'

One of Eda's many skills.

They stopped when they saw the cart covered by a canvas sheet. It was surrounded by defenders. Dread filled Blake's stomach. She grabbed hold of her skirt to give her hands something to do. Lyndal glanced in her direction, her smile long gone.

The portcullis rose, drawing everyone's attention. The king rode through, flanked by his two sons and surrounded by a ring of bodyguards. This only confirmed Blake's suspicion about what lay beneath that canvas. The king was there to deliver one of his famous speeches, to express his disappointment. They were designed to make the merchants feel like insubordinate children, but instead of a good spanking, they were forced to watch their loved ones suffer or die.

Blake locked her knees when her legs shook.

The royal men positioned themselves behind the cart, using it as a buffer. King Oswin only ever wore one expression—seriousness. His deep frown lines were evidence of that. His grey eyes were as depressing as the sky framing him. Sharply groomed eyebrows completed the look.

Prince Borin sat tall in the saddle beside him, a mirror image of his father. Despite coming of age, he was still a foot shorter and had yet to sprout facial hair. His hand rested on the hilt of an expensive sword that Blake was quite certain had never left its sheath.

The youngest prince, Becket, now in his sixteenth year, looked like he had been dragged from his bedchamber against his will. He wore no weapon, his hands resting comfortably on the pommel of his saddle.

'I would like to say a few words, Commander,' the king said.

Commander?

Blake searched among the defenders until she spotted Commander Wright standing off to one side. He responded to the king with a nod before his gaze swept over the crowd. Her lungs stilled when his eyes landed on her. She saw the recognition in them and half expected him to step forwards and arrest her given their last encounter. Instead, he looked away.

'It breaks my heart to stand before you today,' King Oswin began, his voice booming across the large space, 'and speak of traitors. These men are your sons, grand-sons, brothers, and fathers. Your neighbours. Your friends. These are people I built walls, sixty feet high, to protect.'

The outer wall had been his first act as king. And he had been building walls ever since.

Candace was trembling now. Blake thought about taking her other arm, but she did not trust herself to move. Lyndal was the best person to care for their mother in a crisis. She had been the one who kept the house running after their father passed, knowing Kingsley had his hands full with the shop and the rest of them were drowning in grief.

Prince Borin spoke up next. 'Imagine our disappointment at discovering that so many of you are stealing from our farmers, Chadorian men who are fighting to meet the needs of this kingdom.'

Blake's gaze drifted back to the commander, who was keeping a close eye on the crowd.

'It falls on me to remind you all, once again, what happens to thieves and traitors.'

Prince Borin signalled to the defenders, and they stepped up to the cart and began untying the ropes holding the canvas sheet in place.

There was a collective intake of breath as they pulled the cover back, revealing twenty corpses stacked in four piles.

A woman close by cried out; another covered her face and turned away. Blake looked from body to body until her vision snagged on a filthy hand draped over another corpse. It was not the hand that stopped her but the simple brass posy ring enclosing the middle finger. She would have recognised it anywhere, because it had once belonged to her father.

She pressed a hand to her chest, willing her lungs to work. The commander glanced in her direction before turning his attention back to the cart. The defenders secured a noose around the neck of each corpse, then carried them one at a time to the wall. They tossed the ropes up to the men waiting atop it and hauled the bodies up the stone, out of reach of their loved ones watching on in horror.

She knew the moment her mother recognised Kingsley, because a hand flew up to hold in her scream. They were all watching as he was dragged from one of the piles, ears filled with dirt and hair painted with clay, and carried to the wall. Blake turned away as they hoisted him up by the neck, searching for Eda.

Where was she?

'This is what comes from your tunnels,' the king said. 'Crushed and suffocated by your own deceitfulness.'

Blake turned to him, wishing she had a rock or something hard to throw.

'From now on, leave construction to our architects,' Prince Borin said. 'Digging holes is not the answer.'

The grief could no longer be contained. People began weeping, her mother among them.

'The meat will come,' the king said. 'The crops will come. The rain cannot fall forever. In the meantime, remember your purpose, *your* contribution. Remember those outside of these walls with nothing left.'

The tears turned into anger. Not surprising. Seeing loved ones strung up for desperate acts was a special kind of torture.

'They deserve a burial!' one man shouted, pushing forwards. He must have crossed an invisible line, because two defenders immediately stepped up to stop him.

'They're not criminals,' another shouted. '*You* are!'

A simple nod from Commander Wright had two more defenders marching into the crowd.

'You need to go,' Blake said, turning to Lyndal. 'Now.' Her eyes returned to Kingsley, trying to reconcile that sight with the person she had raced through the trees just days earlier.

Why did she not make him stay? If she had, he would be standing in the crowd with them.

'We need to find Eda,' Lyndal said. 'The crowd is turning.'

Candace's legs were shaking, her breaths coming in gasps as she stared down at the ground. Their father's death had nearly broken her. The death of her only son would surely finish the job.

'You go,' Blake told Lyndal. 'I'll find her.'

Lyndal gathered their mother close and began pushing her way through the increasingly rowdy crowd.

Blake turned at the sound of the portcullis rising and watched as the king and princes retreated behind the safety of the wall. The defenders had formed a line so straight she wondered how they had found the opportunity to line up their feet. Their weapons were drawn now. They were ready to restore order.

'Eda!' Blake shouted, looking around for her. The man next to her bumped into her, sending her staggering forwards. She remained upright.

Straightening, she spotted Eda on the *other side* of the defenders. Blake froze. Her sister had somehow slipped past the guards and was now standing beneath Kingsley's corpse.

Blake's feet were moving then, eyes fixed on the guards atop the wall whose arrows were pointed at the crowd. She knew it was only a matter of time before they spotted Eda below them. As Blake split from the crowd, she was forced to pull up when she met the tip of a sword. Her gaze travelled along the steel blade and up one heavily muscled arm. Her eyes met Commander Wright's. He retracted his weapon one inch.

'Do you have a death wish?' he hissed. 'Move back.'

She shook her head. 'I need to get my sister.' She looked past him to the wall. 'Please. They'll shoot her.'

The commander glanced over his shoulder to where Eda was now scaling the wall with a blade wedged between her teeth.

'She just wants to cut him down,' Blake said.

He grunted. 'That really your sister?'

She swallowed. 'She's harmless.' Not entirely true. She was a feral cat when cornered. 'She's mute and grieving.' Eda's muteness was irrelevant, but Blake threw it out there in case it helped the cause.

'If I let you pass, they'll shoot *you*.'

'I'm fast.'

'Faster than an arrow?'

The crowd surged forward, almost pushing her into the commander's blade. He cursed as he eased his sword back from her.

'Do not move from this spot. Not one inch. Hear me?'

She nodded.

He sheathed his sword. 'Close the gap,' he instructed the men on either side of him. He stepped back, the defenders instantly filling the space where he had been.

Blake had no choice but to trust him. The fact that he had spared her life a few days earlier helped. She remained where she was, hand in her pocket, wrapped around the handle of her knife. She pushed up on her toes, glimpsing her sister over the men's shoulders.

Commander Wright signalled to the men atop the wall, prompting them to look down. Blake's heart lodged in her throat when one of the defenders pointed an arrow at Eda. He did not fire it though. The commander ran at the wall and, with a few impressive vertical strides, grabbed hold of Eda's ankle and yanked her down. The knife fell from her mouth, and the commander kicked it out of reach as she hit the ground. He could have broken her fall but had chosen not to.

Eda lay clutching her chest, still gasping for air when he grabbed her by the arm and pulled her off the ground, dragging her towards the contained crowd.

Blake did not move one inch—just as he had instructed.

As if sensing his approach, the line of men separated enough for their commander to pass through. He shoved Eda towards Blake. She caught her sister, hugging her close. Eda was alive—still struggling to draw breath, but alive.

'Take her home,' the commander said, drawing his sword and looking away.

'Thank you.' She had to shout because of the noise.

His eyes returned to her.

'Thank you,' she mouthed.

He gave her the smallest nod before his attention was diverted.

A man approached. 'Murdering bastards!' He shoved the girls aside and raised his dagger.

The commander turned his sword and smashed the hilt of it into the man's face.

Blake watched as he crumpled to the ground, blood pouring from his nose and mouth. Her wide eyes returned to Commander Wright.

'Get out of here,' he said, his eyes burning holes through her.

'Hold on to me,' Blake whispered to Eda, drawing her closer and stepping back. 'And don't let go.'

CHAPTER 4

*H*arlan sat on a cot in the infirmary at the barracks. The physician had just finished stitching a knife wound on his forearm and was now bandaging it. Astin sat on the cot opposite, in need of some grown-up company after too much time at Prince Borin's side. One downside of excelling as a defender was that the warden took notice. Shapur had plucked Astin Fletcher from his cohort three years earlier, and the young defender had been stuck guarding the crown prince ever since.

'Never a good sign when the king's speech finishes with more corpses than it began with,' Astin said.

Harlan had predicted the outcome and made sure his cohort was prepared going in. 'You got the prince out just in time.'

'I knew if I left him in there any longer he would try to do something heroic, like leap from his horse and get stabbed through the eye.'

The physician's mouth twitched as he turned away to

"

clean his instruments.

'See?' Astin said. 'He knows I'm right.'

Boots sounded in the corridor outside, and Harlan recognised his father's footsteps. 'God, here we go.'

Shapur appeared in the doorway, gaze landing on Astin.

'That's my cue.' Astin rose and saluted. 'Warden.'

Shapur gave him a hard stare as he passed. He had been glowering at the bodyguard for the past year, ever since he caught Astin with a tavern woman in his bed. Women were not permitted in the barracks—and Shapur Wright was a stickler for the rules.

Harlan thanked the physician as he rose, then walked over to join his father.

'I would have cast him out if Prince Borin was not so attached,' Shapur said.

'You say that every time you see him.'

The pair moved out into the corridor, heading for the exit.

'I'm fine, by the way,' Harlan said. 'I assume that's why you're here.'

Shapur glanced sideways at him. 'If you are walking, you are fine.'

They stepped out into the bleak afternoon light and rounded the corner, looking out at the abandoned training field as they walked.

'I heard you pulled a merchant off the wall and handed her back to her family,' Shapur said, disapproval etched into his weathered face. 'Why was she not disciplined for breaching the defender barrier?'

The problem when your father was warden was that

everything you did got back to him. 'She was just a mute child trying to cut her brother down.'

Shapur frowned at him. 'So she was armed?'

'Her sister was waiting to take her home. Any act of violence towards her would have provoked the crowd.'

'So the sister softened you up?'

It was not too far from the truth. He should have ignored her request and locked up the younger sister, but he had made the mistake of looking over at the family as the brother had been hung on the wall. One look at their faces had confirmed their connection—and triggered guilt for his part in it all.

That was rare for Harlan, who came from a long line of defenders whose loyalty to the role surpassed all else. There had been no question that he would follow in his father's footsteps when he came of age, and Shapur expected his son to put personal feelings aside and uphold the rules like every Wright before him.

He rubbed his forehead. 'It's called compassion.'

'Compassion? Those people showed up armed, shouting abuse at your king. The merchants do not need your compassion. What they need is swift, firm action to bring them into line.'

Harlan drew a breath when the tower came into sight. 'Where are we going?'

'Just keep up, Commander.'

They passed the armoury and stables, arriving at the cliff tower within minutes. Harlan said nothing as he climbed the winding steps behind his father.

When they reached the first cell, Shapur stepped aside so Harlan could see through the small barred window.

There were a dozen people seated on the stone floor with their backs against the wall.

'Every merchant who pulled a weapon on a defender is now dead. That sends a clear message. Any merchant caught inciting violence was arrested and now sits in that cell. What do you think, Commander? Do they deserve to die?'

His father loved to test his moral compass.

'That depends.'

'On what?'

Harlan stepped back from the door and lowered his voice. 'On whether they have family or friends already hanging on the wall.'

'And how is that relevant?'

'A lifetime of grief is a harsher punishment than anything we could inflict.'

Nothing moved on his father's face. 'There is that compassion again.'

Harlan drew a breath. 'What are your orders?' He would remove their fingers or cut out their tongues. Whatever his father instructed him to do, he would do it. That was what it meant to be a defender: following orders without question or conscience.

Shapur took the keys from the wall and held them out to him. 'You will decide the fate of these prisoners, the ones who wished your men injured or dead. It is your responsibility to ensure the merchants never draw a weapon on a defender again.'

Harlan closed his hand around the key and stared at the cell door as his father's footsteps descended behind him.

CHAPTER 5

Blake's father had always been the one to answer the door once the shop was closed for the day. 'Easy now,' he would say when the children leapt to their feet and ran ahead of him into the shop. 'We want to welcome guests, not scare them away.' The children would peer through the window while their father navigated the locks. It was usually Thea and Birtle from next door. Occasionally it was a defender seeking information, and the children would hide in the next room and listen in on the conversation.

After their father passed, Kingsley had answered the door. If it was a defender, he would tell them nothing, because it was more valuable to have a favour owed by the wrongdoer. Plus, the point of a community was to look out for one another. Yes, the defenders were there to protect, but they were also the biggest threat to their survival. They stood between the merchants and the food.

Two weeks after Kingsley's death, the Suttone women were gathered in the main room by the hearth. Another evening of silence. No one really knew how to mourn him. They only knew that being together was better than being alone with one's grief.

Candace sat sewing. Lyndal had her legs tucked up and a book open on her lap—not reading. Eda was stretched out on the floor, poking a stick at the hearth as she studied the flames. Blake watched her, one finger tapping the arm of her chair, wishing she could climb inside her youngest sister's mind.

A loud knock came at the shop door, making the women jump. It was not Thea's soft tap or Birtle's cheery rap. This was the trademark thud of a defender announcing his arrival.

Blake pushed herself up from her chair. 'I'll go.' Yet another reminder that Kingsley was no longer with them.

She smoothed down the skirt of her simple dress as she made her way through the shop and began the tedious task of unlatching the door. It always needed a good tug to get it open after being locked. Blake sent the bell flying as she jerked the door open. She winced as it landed, then turned her attention to the defender standing before her. Her eyes widened as she recognised Commander Wright.

'Merchant,' he said by way of greeting.

It took her a moment to reply. 'Commander...' She looked past him to the horse and cart parked on the street, and nerves fluttered in her stomach. 'What are you doing here?'

The commander gestured to the two men seated in the cart. They jumped down. Blake's hand went into her pocket, grasping her knife; then, realising she stood no chance against the three defenders, she let go.

'We're disposing of the bodies from the wall,' he said, looking back at her. 'I thought you might want to bury your brother. You have my permission to enter the cemetery. Might be better than a mass grave.'

Blake exhaled, hardly believing what she was hearing. 'You brought him here?' She had been avoiding the square ever since the crows arrived. It was the one time birds were safe from being eaten—when they were eating the merchants first.

'I had him put in a body bag.'

That was the moment Blake realised she was witnessing an act of kindness from a defender. Her brain struggled with that. 'Are you delivering all the bodies to the families?'

He shook his head. 'Merchants aren't exactly stepping up to claim the corpses of traitors right now.'

'Kingsley's not a traitor,' she said with conviction. 'He just couldn't watch his family go hungry.'

The commander said nothing as he stepped back from the door to let his men pass. The defenders laid the corpse out on the floor in the middle of the shop, then left.

'Do you have someone to dig the grave?' Commander Wright asked when they were alone.

She tore her gaze away from her brother's remains to look at him. 'I will dig it.'

His eyes moved between hers. 'Make sure it's deep enough or animals will dig it up.'

'Animals? Shallow grave it is. I'll take my bow and hide in the trees. Meat sorted.'

A joke.

A joke as her brother lay dead behind her.

A joke with a man she did not know and who cared nothing for jokes—especially ones told by merchants.

She looked down at the ground between them. 'It's not my first time burying someone. The grave will be deep enough.'

He nodded, handing her a piece of parchment. 'Show this to the defenders at the gate.'

She unfolded it and read aloud. 'Cause of death— drowning.' Her eyes returned to his. 'Drowning?'

'Any hint of disease and your entire household will be quarantined in the lazaretto borough.'

'Kingsley suffocated to death in an illegal tunnel.'

The commander's eyebrows came together in annoyance. 'Again, not going to help your family. I can take him with me now, if you'd prefer.'

She shook her head, realising she was being difficult when she ought to be grateful. 'No. Thank you for bringing him. And for this.' She held up the parchment.

Commander Wright looked past her to where her sisters and mother now stood in the doorway, staring down at the corpse. His eyes returned to Blake. 'Merchant,' he said, nodding once before leaving.

She watched him climb into the cart. Leather slapped rump, and the cart lurched forwards before disappearing into the darkness. Closing the door, Blake secured the locks, then turned to face her family, who all stood with hands over their noses and mouths. The room smelled of death.

Blake swallowed. 'Help me take him out back into the courtyard. We'll bury him in the morning.'

CHAPTER 6

Defenders trained seven days a week—no excuses.

A typical day for Harlan began with a three-mile run followed by sparring with a variety of weapons, such as sword, battle axe, mace, dagger, and lance. The last part was strength training, horsemanship, archery, hand-to-hand combat, or long-distance swimming, depending on the weather and his father's mood.

Harlan was carrying weapons to the armoury when Prince Borin and Astin approached on horseback. The commander exhaled, then placed the weapons on the ground. He turned and bowed before the prince before nodding a greeting at Astin, who gave him an apologetic look in response.

'Commander Wright,' the prince said, pulling up his horse. 'I have business in the merchant borough. Fletcher here thinks I should take extra precautions, given recent events, so you will accompany us.'

Harlan was staring at Borin's new haircut. The straight

fringe made the prince look like a twelve-year-old boy. 'Of course, Your Highness. I'll have a horse saddled and meet you at the gate.' What he actually wanted was a wash and a few hours' sleep before he reported for night duty, but that would have to wait.

Harlan returned the training weapons to the armoury and fetched his sword and daggers. After collecting a horse from the stables, he headed to the gate.

'Sorry to throw you in it,' Astin said when they were out of earshot of the prince. 'He's insisting on going into the merchant borough to ensure his people, and I quote, "do not feel abandoned during these troublesome times".'

Harlan winced.

They walked their horses beneath the archway, the prince adjusting his cloak and brushing his hair forwards. Somehow, he had made that fringe of his even straighter.

'Might have been better off on foot,' Harlan said as they entered the square. 'The merchants haven't seen meat in some time. I wouldn't blame them if they disembowelled our horses before we had a chance to dismount.'

'As long as they don't eat the prince,' Astin whispered. 'Or your father will have *me* disembowelled.'

Harlan bit back a grin.

Men stood talking in groups. Women gathered around the well on the other side of the square, full pails at their feet. The conversation died when the merchants caught sight of the prince.

'Good day to you,' Borin called to one group of men as he passed by. His hand rested on his hip the way his father's always did, but instead of looking powerful, he looked like a pompous fool.

The men said nothing as they lowered into a bow that barely passed as respectful.

They went by a group of children Harlan had given mussels to a few days earlier. Recognising the commander, they made a move towards him but stopped in their tracks when they caught sight of the prince. Harlan nodded at them as he passed.

As they reached the first street, merchants exited the timber-framed shops and congregated on creaky verandas. No one waved. No one spoke. They simply watched. The mud-splattered children playing gameball in their path ran to their beckoning mothers.

As the three men neared the end of the street, Harlan's gaze drifted to the shop where Blake lived. He had watched the merchant carry her brother to the lazaretto borough with the help of her sisters. Their mother had trailed behind with an older couple he did not recognise. He was still not entirely sure why he had taken the corpse to her. Pity was never a good look on a defender. Nor was guilt.

His father had been right. He should never have broken the line to fetch that girl from the wall, should never have handed her over. Grief or no grief, she had broken the rules. Yet as he stood on that wall watching the family dig a grave, he could not bring himself to regret his actions.

Blake had popped into his mind several times since that day. That smart mouth with its ill-timed humour. Those intelligent eyes assessing him, *judging* him. Even in her filthy, dishevelled state that day he had come across her in the forest, with water dripping from her face and lips purple from the cold, she had made him pause in a way he rarely did with women. Perhaps it was the novelty of conversation with a merchant woman who was not afraid of him or trying to sell him sex. There was something honest about her—even when she was lying straight to his face.

He was used to mingling with noblewomen who hid behind their expensive gowns and painted faces. Daughters of lords dumbed down by well-meaning mothers and governesses, highly trained in the art of husband catching. A defender was an adequate choice for any noblewoman, as long as another sibling had already secured someone with a title. The family only needed one advantageous marriage.

Whenever a bit of fun in bed threatened to turn serious, Harlan disappeared into his work. It was easier to find companionship in the port taverns than navigate the games played by nobility.

A woman exited the shop, pulling Harlan from his thoughts. It was one of Blake's sisters, the blonde one.

'Wait,' Blake hissed, stepping out onto the veranda in pursuit of her sister. She stopped when she spotted Harlan.

'This is no time for pride,' the blonde called over her shoulder.

Blake did not move off the veranda, whereas her sister marched straight out into the middle of the road, forcing the horses to pull up.

Astin moved in front of the prince, hand going to the hilt of his sword. 'Move aside, merchant.'

The girl ignored him entirely. 'Your Highness, might I have a word?'

It seemed the entire family was a little crazy.

'I said move aside,' Astin repeated.

'That is quite all right,' the prince said, walking his horse closer. He looked the girl up and down and relaxed in the saddle.

The blonde gave him a wide smile before lowering into a curtsy. 'I told my sister, "Prince Borin is not here for show. He's the people's prince."'

Blake blinked slowly, crossing her arms in front of her.

'You've chosen a glorious day to visit our borough,' the girl continued, looking up at the dense grey clouds above threatening rain.

Harlan moved his horse next to Astin's to better hear the exchange.

'What is it you need?' the prince asked.

The blonde clasped her hands neatly in front of her. 'We're trying to reach my uncle, who resides in the nobility borough, but my sister here'—she gestured to Blake—'keeps getting turned away at the gate. It's my understanding that we're still permitted to communicate with people on the other side of that wall. Am I wrong?'

Merchants were getting turned away at the gate because more and more nobility were cutting ties. Simply put, every merchant needed food, and the moment the shortages began affecting the nobility, they quickly withdrew their charity.

'Your uncle lives in the nobility borough?' the prince asked.

'That's right.'

'Then how is it you came to live this side of the wall?'

Her smile never faltered. 'Love, Your Highness. My mother married the man who sold her cotton. She was blessed with a happy marriage for many years before his passing.'

Harlan found himself watching Blake instead of her sister. She tucked her dark hair behind her ears and shifted her weight from foot to foot, clearly not enjoying her parents' scandalous history being aired on the street for all to hear.

'Our only brother passed recently,' the girl went on. 'My uncle has yet to hear of the tragic news, and I know he would want to pay his respects.'

Borin regarded her for a moment. 'How did your brother die?'

Blake stepped off the veranda onto the street, hands falling to her sides. 'He drowned, Your Highness. A fishing accident.' She glanced at Harlan.

'I hear the rocks in the port borough are very hazardous for novice fisherman,' Borin said.

The blonde nodded. 'Indeed.'

'I am sorry for the loss of the head of your family,' Borin said. 'Of course you must notify your uncle, as the shop is now legally his. He must oversee the running of it.'

Blake spoke up at that. 'My sisters and I are more than capable of managing things here, Your Highness.'

'That is for your uncle to decide,' Borin replied.

Blake bit her lip.

The prince pushed his cloak back. 'I will have Commander Wright here personally deliver the letter to your uncle.' He spoke louder than necessary, ensuring that every spectator watching from the safety of their verandas heard.

All eyes went to Harlan.

So much for sleep. 'Bring me the letter,' he said with a resigned breath.

Blake hesitated before disappearing inside, returning a moment later with it. She stopped at the shoulder of the horse and passed it to him. 'My uncle is Lord Thomas Welche.'

'Of Cardelle Manor?'

She nodded. 'Lady Victoria is my mother's sister.'

He tucked the parchment inside his cloak, feeling Astin's eyes on him. 'I'll bring you his reply.'

'Be sure to tell him I'll happily accept grain in place of patronising words.'

He noted the humour in her eyes. Pretty eyes too. 'Next time ask for me at the gate.'

She looked genuinely confused. 'Why?'

'Because I'll make sure the letter gets through.'

She stared at him a moment. 'And why would you do that?'

An excellent question. 'To prevent you starting an uprising.'

Her eyebrows rose. 'Was that… was that a joke?'

He did not reply, just gathered the reins in preparation for departure.

Blake stepped back from the horse. 'Thank you.'

'Just following orders.' He had not meant that to sound so cold.

She nodded, then turned and walked off. He watched

her all the way to the shop door. When he finally looked away, he found Astin smirking.

Harlan glared. 'What?'

Astin glanced in the prince's direction before replying. 'Is that *the* girl you broke the line for?'

Harlan's mouth flattened into a line. 'Focus on your job, would you? These women carry knives beneath their skirts.'

'I get it now. A pretty thing like that throwing herself at your mercy.'

'She didn't throw herself at anything.'

Astin's grin widened. 'So defensive.'

Blake's sister finally moved aside, and the prince nudged his horse into a walk.

'You're lucky you're on duty,' Harlan whispered to his friend, 'or I'd knock you from the saddle.'

Astin laughed silently.

CHAPTER 7

ord Thomas showed Harlan to the library, then sat across from him to read the letter. Harlan stared at the elaborate collection of books covering one wall while Thomas learned of his nephew's death. The commander wished he had waited outside to give him some privacy.

He need not have worried.

'That is all I need,' Thomas said, dropping the letter on the desk with a loud sigh. 'Another business to manage. More mouths to feed. Do you know if the shop is presently turning a profit?'

Harlan shifted in his chair. 'I'm not acquainted with the family. Prince Borin asked me to deliver the letter.'

That made Thomas sit up. 'The *prince* asked you?' He leaned forwards. 'What does His Highness have to do with all this?'

'One of your nieces spoke directly to him on the matter.'

'That would be Lyndal.' He leaned back again. 'The

prettiest of the sisters, for sure. I shall have no problem finding her a husband. The eldest, on the other hand...' He shook his head. 'Perhaps if I can muzzle her for long enough.'

Harlan was not a fan of Lord Thomas. 'She's been trying to reach you for some time now.'

'I am aware of the fact.'

Harlan's eyebrows rose. 'You are?'

Thomas stood and began pacing. 'Every merchant in the borough is showing up at that gate asking for something.'

The lord appeared to be in his late forties. He still had a good head of hair, which he wore long and combed neatly to one side. His straight back was held in place by an expensive waistcoat.

'The merchants are doing it tough,' Harlan said. 'They're surviving on whatever they can forage or grow right now.'

'Are not we all?'

Harlan looked out the large glass window to where chickens roamed beneath bare fruit trees. Rinderpest had swept through the borough, killing all the oxen, but many families still kept goats. Judging by how taut the buttons of Thomas's waistcoat were, they were getting by just fine.

'Do you know how expensive meat is at the moment?' Thomas went on. 'Pure extortion.'

Harlan looked down at the table. 'At least you have the option to purchase it.' He could not bear to listen to the man complain about the cost.

'You cannot buy live cattle, mind you. It seems they

can only survive on the superior water in the farming borough.' Thomas shook his head at the injustice.

'Water is one way murrain is spread. The farmers have figured out how to contain outbreaks.' Harlan rested his elbows on the table. 'Perhaps you would like me to deliver a hen to the Suttone family on your behalf.'

Thomas stopped walking and looked at him. 'Absolutely not. It will be stolen before it has a chance to lay. I hear the stories coming out of that borough. Rife with crime. Besides, I am responsible for the people residing in this manor foremost.'

'I see.' Harlan rose. 'Would you like me to deliver a response to the family?'

'That will not be necessary. I will travel there in person when my schedule permits.'

When his schedule permits? Harlan barely trusted himself to speak. 'I shall see myself out.'

Thomas took a seat. 'I apologise for your wasted time, Commander.'

Outside, a groom waited with his horse. Harlan took the reins and thanked him, and the boy retreated to the stables. As Harlan prepared to mount, he spotted a flock of chickens scratching at what was once a green lawn but was now a muddy swamp. He glanced in the direction of the house before leading his horse over to them. If Lord Thomas was not prepared to sacrifice one hen to help his family, Harlan would simply take it.

As he reached for the closest hen, a throat clearing stopped him in his tracks. He turned to find a young woman standing on the path that surrounded the house, watching him.

'Afternoon,' he said, taking a step back from the hen.

'Commander Wright,' she said.

Harlan vaguely recognised the face but could not remember her name to save himself.

'Lady Kendra,' she said, helping him out.

'Of course.' He tried not to look like a man who was about to steal a chicken and stuff it into his saddlebag. 'Lovely place you have here.'

'With lovely fat hens,' Kendra said, a smile on her lips. 'You brought my father news of my aunt and cousins, did you not?'

Harlan glanced in the direction of the house. 'That's right.'

'And? How are they faring?'

He moved closer to his horse. 'Perhaps it's best you ask your father.' He suspected the news *would* affect her and did not want to be the one to tell her. If she cried, he would be forced to watch on awkwardly.

'I am asking you, Commander,' Kendra said. 'What say you to an exchange?' She moved closer. 'The information you delivered for one of my healthy birds.'

He really did not want to get messed up in family politics, but he wanted the hen.

'Do not fret, Commander,' she continued. 'My father will not hear a word about it.'

He let out a resigned breath. 'I was delivering news of your cousin's passing.'

Kendra's face collapsed. 'Which cousin?'

'The brother.'

She clasped her hands in front of her and raised her chin. 'How did he die?'

He hesitated for too long.

'The tunnels,' Kendra answered for him. 'Of course it was the tunnels.'

Harlan did not confirm nor deny it.

'My aunt and cousins must be pieces. It has only been two years since my uncle passed.'

Blake's stoic face came to mind. 'The hen, my lady?'

Kendra angled her head. 'Are they not feeding you at the barracks, Commander?'

'They feed us well enough.'

She gestured for him to follow her. Apparently the hen he was getting was not from the flock in front of him.

'I bet livestock fetches a pretty price in the merchant borough,' Kendra said as they walked.

'I couldn't say.'

She gave him a doubtful look as they veered off the path and came to a fenced-off pen containing ducks. She leaned over, snatched one of the ducklings up, and held it out to him. He stared down at the fluffy yellow bird, barely the length of his finger.

'If it is female, it will lay eggs,' Kendra said, helpfully explaining reproduction to him.

'That's a duck.'

She nodded. 'Very good. Perhaps you should have been a farmer.'

'We agreed on a hen.'

'We agreed on a *bird*.'

So they had. He reluctantly took it from her, and the pair returned to the path where they had left the horse.

'Are you close with your aunt and cousins?' Harlan asked.

'As close as one can be with a sixty-foot wall and two classes dividing us.' Kendra smiled at the ground. 'My aunt chose to marry a merchant, and unfortunately it is my cousins who are paying the price for that choice.'

'Why did your father not take them in after your uncle's death?'

She looked up at the window above. 'My father was the one who told my aunt not to go ahead with the marriage. She lived here after my grandparents died. From what my mother tells me, she did not like it much. My father believes people should live with the consequences of their mistakes. He does what he is legally obliged to and not a thing more.'

Harlan sat with that information for a moment. 'Your uncle might not be legally required to provide for the family, but he's morally obliged.' He held up the duckling. 'That's why I'm giving them this.'

Kendra watched him a moment. 'Let me guess, you have taken a shining to my cousin Lyndal.'

He turned and mounted his horse.

'I do not blame you. She is delightful. I only ask that you admire her from a distance, because she will be the one who props up what remains of the Suttone family. If there was ever a girl capable of leaping over class divides, it is her.'

He found it interesting that she was being hailed as saviour of the family because of her looks. She was certainly the smiliest sister. 'Your cousin is quite safe, I assure you. Good day, Lady Kendra.'

～

When Harlan dismounted in front of the Suttones' shop, Blake walked out and leaned against the veranda post, watching him. He reached into his pocket and pulled out the duckling as he wandered over. 'From your cousin,' he said, holding it out for her to take. 'Best not mention it in front of your uncle.'

She took the chirpy little bird and held it up to look at it properly. 'Looks to be a male judging by its darker colouring.'

'You can still eat it.' Harlan gave his horse a pat. 'Your uncle says he'll call on you when his schedule permits.'

Blake looked away. 'No letter, then?'

He shook his head.

'Not too surprising.'

Harlan felt a bit sorry for her, which was far from ideal. 'I'll see what I can do about getting you some food.'

Her cool eyes returned to him. 'You've already spared my sister's life, *my* life, and been forced to endure my uncle's company. I think I can take it from here.'

If she was too proud to accept help, he was not about to beg. 'Fine.' He turned back to his horse, annoyed by her pride but mostly at himself for caring either way. Mounting, he looked at her. 'I won't be so lenient moving forwards.'

She tilted her head. 'Lenient? Right. My sister was winded for about two days thanks to your leniency.'

'She's alive.'

Blake crossed her arms. 'And next time?'

He would not be painted as the bad guy when he had just brought her a duck. 'There shouldn't be a next time. Unless the lesson didn't stick the first time.'

'And what lesson is that?'

He set his jaw. 'When defenders form a line, you stay behind it.'

'She's not even of age.'

'She's old enough to grasp basic laws.'

'Perhaps the laws are the problem.' She bit her lip, gaze falling to the duckling. 'What I meant is—'

'I know what you meant.'

She lifted her eyes to him. 'I don't want you to think I'm ungrateful.'

He swung his horse around. 'Don't worry. Come tomorrow, I shall not think of you at all.'

CHAPTER 8

It was tough work keeping a duckling that age alive.

'Well, it survived another night,' Lyndal announced on day four. 'So far, so good.'

'It slept on my neck,' Blake said, rubbing at her aching muscles. She had been stuck in the one position for most of the night.

'Go fetch the kitchen scraps,' Candace said.

'What sort of privileged life do you think we're living here?' Lyndal asked. 'There are no kitchen scraps. The days of throwing out any part of a vegetable are long over.'

Blake suppressed a smile.

Eda entered the courtyard, looking worried. *Uncle Thomas just pulled up out front,* she signed.

Candace began fumbling with her apron. 'Inside, everybody. Put the duckling in the crate. We cannot have it wandering about the house.'

Blake scooped the duckling up. 'We can't have him thinking we're plebeians, now can we?'

Lyndal poked her in the ribs as she passed by.

It was risky leaving any living animal unattended outside, so Blake covered the crate with a sheet and placed it behind the potted vegetables—which were also prone to disappearing.

'For goodness' sake,' Candace said, finally free of her apron, 'go put a nice dress on.'

Blake straightened. 'Why? Is the queen with them?'

Another disapproving look from her mother. 'How many dresses have I sewn for you? And you choose to wear that.'

Blake looked down at the plain belted dress, a stark contrast to Lyndal's pale green gown tailored perfectly at the waist. 'It's practical.' They were fortunate enough to import fabric and have a clothier in the household. 'I'm not underdressed. Lyndal's overdressed.'

Her mother tutted. Having been raised in a noble household, her standards were higher than the average merchant.

'Why doesn't Eda have to change?'

'Because she's not at marrying age,' Lyndal called out.

'Hush,' Candace said as they walked inside. 'Your uncle will hear you.' She looked at Blake. 'Change. *Now.*'

Blake rolled her eyes but did as she was told.

When she returned, she joined her sisters at the window. Outside, their uncle was securing the horse to the veranda. Her aunt and cousin watched as they held the skirts of their dresses off the ground.

'Behave, all of you,' Candace said before carefully opening the door to prevent the bell from flying off.

'My dear sister,' Victoria said, embracing Candace. 'I am so sorry about Kingsley. I cannot even imagine.'

Candace pressed her eyes shut, then pulled away, focusing on Kendra. 'Look what a lady you have become.'

Kendra kissed her aunt. 'Soon to be eighteen.' Then she turned to her cousins. 'Goodness. Look how thin you all are.' Her own face was round, her cheeks full. 'What a difference a few months can make.'

Blake knew her cousin could not comprehend the hardships facing the merchants. She lived a sheltered, privileged life. It was unfair to hold that against her. 'And you look as breathtaking as ever.'

'It is a good thing we brought a plate of pastries,' Kendra said, slipping her arm through Blake's.

Mentioning pastries was like waving a bone in front of a starved dog. Blake's mouth watered in response.

'How thoughtful,' Lyndal said, looking in Thomas's direction as he joined them. 'You're looking well, Uncle.'

Thomas stepped up onto the veranda, assessing each of them. 'Goodness me. Let us hope there is meat at the market sooner rather than later.'

'Please,' Candace said, gesturing to the door.

The two sisters sat at the table in the main room, and the cousins went out into the courtyard to give them some privacy. Thomas remained in the shop, flipping through the ledger. The lack of financial privacy agitated Blake. She reminded herself that the shop now belonged to him and he was free to do as he pleased with it.

'I hear chirping,' Kendra said, looking over at the covered crate. 'I see Harlan delivered the duckling to you.'

Blake's eyebrows came together. 'Harlan?'

'Forgive me. I meant to say Commander Wright.'

Harlan. His given name was Harlan.

'Now we just need the thing to hurry up and grow,' Lyndal said.

'If I had known he intended to give it to you, I might have offered him a more mature duck,' Kendra replied. 'He was being quite reticent in the beginning.'

'What do you mean?' Blake asked, confused.

Kendra leaned in. 'I gave it to the commander in exchange for information. I thought he intended to sell the bird on the black market.'

Blake blinked. 'You didn't tell him to give it to us?'

Kendra sat back in her chair. 'I might have if I had known how dire the situation was here. There is not a dog to be seen on the street.' She looked between her cousins. 'And now I find myself asking which sister the gallant gesture was for.'

'Blake,' Lyndal said matter-of-factly. 'The commander was accompanying the prince the other day and stared at her through the entire exchange.'

'No he didn't,' Blake said. Sure, their eyes had met a few times, but that was due to their awkward history.

Her eyes went to the crate holding the bird. The man was such a contradiction. All duty and honour one minute and bringing her gifts the next. She was glimpsing a human heart in place of the stone one usually found in defenders. The question was *why*.

'What spell have you cast over the commander?' Kendra asked, her tone playful.

'Look at her,' Lyndal said. 'What sane man wouldn't be attracted to her?'

Attraction seemed improbable. But what did she know? Drunk men whistled after her when she passed the taverns in the port borough—usually while relieving themselves. Though they whistled after most women.

There was Odo, the ship merchant who delivered their supplies. He had offered to marry her the last time she had seen him, but his reasons were of a practical nature. He never mentioned attraction. But maybe that was because Kingsley was at her side.

If she were being completely honest, *she* felt some level of attraction towards Harlan. Her and every other woman in the borough. The man was easy on the eyes.

'Did you hear anything I just said?' Kendra asked, laughing.

Not a single word.

'Perhaps the feelings are mutual,' Lyndal said.

Blake gave her a tired look. 'I have a little more sense than that.'

'I was just saying what a run-down mess the Wright house is,' Kendra said. 'I suspect no one has been out there in years. Probably not since… you know.'

Blake was paying attention now. 'Know what?'

Kendra glanced in the direction of the house, then whispered, 'Since the warden's wife killed herself there.'

Blake's lungs stopped.

'The warden and his son have lived at the barracks ever since,' Kendra finished.

Lyndal tutted. 'A military base is no place to raise a child. How did she... do it?'

'Some say she cut her own wrists and bled out in the tub. Others say she hung herself from the banister.'

Why? Eda signed.

Kendra looked to Blake to translate.

'She's asking *why*.'

Kendra lifted one shoulder. 'She was married to the warden. That is reason enough. He probably had her running laps around the house before breakfast each morning.' She narrowed her eyes on Eda. 'When are you going to start speaking again? You are only a few years from needing a husband.'

'Eda's already married to her bow,' Lyndal joked.

Eda signed profanity at her sister.

'What did she say?' Kendra asked.

Blake jumped in. 'She says Lyndal isn't funny.'

'It looked like something else,' Kendra said, smiling at her youngest cousin. 'We shall make a lady of you yet.'

A string of *verbal* profanity reached them, and they all looked in the direction of the house. Thomas was having a tantrum.

'Stop, you little thieves!' he shouted.

The sound of a bell clanging across the ground followed.

'What on earth?' Lyndal said as the girls rose to their feet and rushed into the shop.

Candace and Victoria were already at the window. Thomas now stood next to a horseless cart, waving an angry fist. 'You will be hanging on the wall by the end of the day.'

'Oh dear,' Victoria said. 'They chose the wrong horse to steal. He will hunt them down.'

Candace headed for the door. 'We still have some time before it's slaughtered.'

Kendra followed her aunt. 'Slaughtered? That is an impeccably bred mare. Only a fool would slaughter such a valuable animal.'

'Hungry people don't care about bloodlines,' Blake said. 'That horse will be stew by the end of the day.'

'Then we must tell the defenders,' Kendra said.

Blake stopped on the veranda. 'I'll find the horse.'

I'm coming with you, Eda signed.

'Fine, but the bow stays here.'

'This is what comes of your kindness.' Thomas ranted at his wife. 'You happy now? The business is broke, just as I suspected. Now the trip in to confirm it has cost me a horse.'

'Hardly any businesses are turning a profit right now,' Candace said. 'We rely on bartering most of the time. That is how a community survives difficult times.'

'Your treasonous son had no idea what he was doing,' Thomas said, stepping closer. 'Yes, I know how he really died.'

'Thomas, please.' Victoria placed a hand on his arm. 'Let us focus on getting your horse back.'

'Give us an hour,' Blake said, stepping down onto the road and passing her uncle. She did not look at him. Every time he spoke to her mother that way, violent thoughts filled her mind.

'I am sending for the commander!' Thomas shouted after them.

Blake pulled her sister along when she slowed. 'Don't make things worse. The sooner we find the horse, the sooner we'll be rid of him.'

Eda adjusted the dagger beneath her skirt.

Blake glanced sideways at her. 'Let's try to settle this like ladies first.'

The girls tracked the thieves through the forest, two boys around the same age as Eda but half her weight. They were arguing about what to do with the animal when the girls found them.

'All right, boys,' Blake said, stepping into sight. 'Hand the horse over and I'll let you walk away.'

The boys exchanged a look.

'This is our horse,' the taller one said, stepping towards them.

Blake crossed her arms. 'No it's not. It belongs to my uncle, who's fetching the commander as we speak. So you can hand it over to me or hand it over to him. Your choice.'

The other boy drew a knife and pointed it in their direction. 'How about you piss off before you get hurt?'

Still want to settle this like ladies? Eda signed.

Blake sighed. 'Not really.'

Eda charged at the armed boy, pinning him face down on the ground as she disarmed him. He spat out leaves and swore at her. Blake walked over to the other one and shoved him hard against the closest tree, her forearm pressed to his neck. She saw his hand go for a weapon and slapped it away. In the next beat, the tip of her own knife was pressed to his stomach.

'We found it wandering the street,' said the boy lying in the mud. He was such a scrawny thing that Blake feared Eda would accidentally snap his spine.

'Lie to me again and I'll cut off your finger and feed it to your friend here.' She would do no such thing, but he did not need to know that.

'Fine,' the boy beneath her arm croaked. 'Take the horse.'

Blake eased the pressure on his throat. 'Now, what have we learned today? Do we take things that don't belong to us?'

The boy gritted his teeth and shook his head.

Grabbing him by the front of his shirt, she shoved him away. 'Off you go, then.' She nodded at her sister, who climbed off the other boy, pushing hair back from her face.

He snatched his weapon off the ground before jogging after his friend.

'You all right?' Blake asked, walking over to the horse.

Eda nodded. *I should have kept his knife.*

Blake smiled. 'Let's get this horse back to Uncle.'

When they turned onto their street, Blake saw her uncle speaking with two defenders. 'Here we go,' she said under her breath.

Thomas fell silent when he saw them approaching, and the defenders turned to see what he was looking at. Blake locked eyes with an exhausted Harlan. His eyes moved over her before he spoke.

'I gather this is the horse.'

'I told you I was going to fetch the commander,' her uncle said, marching towards them. He tore the reins from her hands, making her wince.

For someone who claimed to be a nobleman, the man had no manners. Blake made sure her feelings did not show on her face. 'We found the mare abandoned in the forest.'

Her uncle looked to Eda for confirmation. 'That true?'

Eda nodded.

'Answer,' he growled.

'She cannot speak, Uncle,' Blake said. 'You know this.'

'She *chooses* not to speak, and I will not have it. Kingsley might have let you all do as you please, but you answer to me now. You will do as you are told.'

Blake stepped between Thomas and Eda. 'Grief doesn't work like that. It doesn't care about your demands.'

Thomas reached up and grabbed hold of her face—hard. 'You have enabled her for too long.'

'Lord Thomas,' Harlan said. 'I suggest you thank the girls for returning your horse and let them go inside.'

Something in his tone made her uncle's hand slacken and Blake look in his direction. There was a warning in it.

'And what of the men who stole the horse?' Thomas asked, stepping back from Blake.

'They weren't men,' Blake said. 'They were just boys.'

Harlan wandered closer, eyes narrowing on Blake. 'And how do you know that?'

'We saw them flee.' There were those sharp lying skills again.

Harlan turned to Thomas. 'It seems we're done here.'

'You are still obligated to find them. They might be

criminal boys today, but they will be criminal men in no time.'

Harlan blinked. 'I'll be sure to tell my men to keep a lookout for them.'

Visibly dissatisfied with that response, Thomas led his horse over to the cart and began reattaching it. Harlan gestured to the other defender to help him. When Thomas was out of earshot, Harlan turned his attention to Blake.

'What really happened?'

Blake glanced at Eda. 'Go on inside.'

Eda cast a wary look at Harlan, then signed to her sister, *Stand tall and strong, warrior.*

It was something their father used to say to them.

Blake sighed before turning her attention back to Harlan. 'They were barely Eda's age,' she said when they were alone. 'Impulsive boys who made a terrible choice in the moment.'

'Why are you protecting them?'

She drew a breath. 'Because I've seen what your men do to boys that age.'

'So you what? Politely asked for the horse back?'

'Something like that.'

He rubbed at his forehead. 'I'm going back to the barracks. Do you think you can stay out of trouble for the rest of the day?'

She did not respond immediately. 'Why did you tell me that my cousin sent that duckling?'

'Because that's where it came from.'

'That might be where it came from, but it was given to *you.*'

He sighed as if she were the most exhausting person in the world. 'Well, you're too proud to accept it from me.'

'You could have sold it.'

'I could have.'

She searched his eyes. 'What am I to make of all these acts of kindness?'

'Don't overthink it.'

'I simply wish to know what you expect in return.'

His brow creased. 'I expect you to stay out of trouble.'

'I do… most of the time.'

Amusement flashed in his eyes. 'Let's see if we can get you to *all* the time, boor.'

CHAPTER 9

Lyndal called the duckling Garlic as a joke, and the name stuck.

The bird was becoming far too comfortable in the home, following the women between rooms as they went about their day. And at some point, he had decided that Blake made the best sleeping partner.

On the day the ship was due to arrive, Blake woke early and peeled Garlic off her neck. She placed him on the floor and went to wash. The sun was just peeking over the horizon when she woke Eda. Grabbing their cloaks, they headed for the port borough.

The wall separating the port and merchant boroughs had only been built two-thirds of the way across, allowing merchants to move freely between the two boroughs so they could conduct business and frequent the taverns. The partial wall was mostly to deter sea warriors and limit entry points in case of an attack.

The open access did not stop defenders from asking

questions though, and two girls heading into the port borough without a male escort could be easily misread.

A defender leaning against the wall straightened when he saw them approach. 'What business do you have in the port today?'

If they were male, he would have let them pass without saying a word. Instead, he assumed them to be tavern women. Never mind the fact that many of the defenders who frequented the taverns were customers of those women.

'We're collecting an order,' Blake said, pulling a piece of parchment out of her pocket and handing it to the man.

He ran his eyes over it before handing it back. 'Where's your father?'

Every time that question was asked, it was like having a scab torn off a wound. 'Dead.'

'Husband?'

'Weirdly, I've not been snapped up yet.'

He gave her a tired look. 'Who owns the business, then?'

Blake looked past him to where the merchant ship was being secured to the dock. 'My uncle, but he's not involved in the running of it.'

'And why's that?'

'He lives in the nobility borough.'

'Your uncle a lord, is he?' the defender asked, one side of his mouth lifting in a smirk.

It was all so exhausting. 'Yes, actually.'

One look at his face told her he did not believe her. 'The taverns aren't even open yet.'

Blake blinked slowly. 'Listen, the fabric we're

collecting is our entire business. If you don't let us pass, my family will have no income until the next shipment. We rely on that coin to buy small amounts of exorbitantly priced food on the rare occasions it's available to us. There's no wall here, defender, so please move aside.'

Eda's eyes went the size of plates as she stared up at her sister. Blake could hardly believe the words that had spilled out, but she was so tired of every small thing being a struggle. Was it too much to want an egg for breakfast? To buy a little barley to make bread? To go about your business without being labelled a whore?

Was it too much to ask that the men in her family remain alive?

'What did you say?' the defender said, now looming over her.

Blake's heart was drumming in her chest. 'I…' She did not know how to fix the situation. 'If you don't let us pass, I will take it up with Commander Wright.' Of all the things she could have said…

The man's eyebrows shot up. '*What?*'

Eda looked down at the ground, head shaking.

'He's a close acquaintance of mine.' That made him sound like a customer.

'You're a fucking liar,' the defender said. 'The commander doesn't mix with your sort.'

She did not know whether he was referring to prostitutes or merchants.

The defender pointed to the wall above him. 'Commander Wright's on duty. Shall I have someone fetch him?'

He was calling her bluff.

'That won't be necessary.' The best thing she could do at that point was flee and pray the man did not give chase. Except she did not get the chance, because when she looked up, she found Harlan leaning against the embrasure—looking straight at her. Her lungs squeezed when he straightened, looking from her to the defender.

'That's what I thought,' the defender said.

Before she had a chance to respond, Harlan emerged from the nearby turret, eyebrows drawn together in a disapproving line. He strode towards them.

She felt herself shrinking.

'What's going on here?' Harlan asked, stopping next to the defender.

The man grew taller. 'Commander. I was just telling this young woman, who claims she's a very close acquaintance of yours'—he glanced at Blake when he said that part—'that it's better to return with their uncle if they wish to conduct business in the port.'

Blake cleared her throat. 'I don't think I used the term *close* acquaintance.'

'Those were your exact words,' the defender said, throwing her under the runaway wagon.

Blake pressed her lips together.

'What business do you have in the port today, Suttone?' Harlan asked.

The defender's eyes shot to him. 'So you *are* acquainted?'

Harlan kept his eyes on Blake. 'Miss Suttone and her sister are Lord Thomas Welche's nieces.'

The defender's jaw just about reached the ground.

Blake pushed her own surprise aside. 'I have to pick up

a fabric order from the ship. The borough is open to merchants, is it not?'

'It is,' Harlan said. 'I'm sure my comrade here was just looking out for you. Two women without an escort can invite trouble.'

Blake felt some of her confidence returning. 'How so?'

'Easy prey for drunk patrons and men who've been stuck at sea for weeks on end.'

'Then perhaps your men should focus their attention on the drunks and sea merchants, since that's where the problem lies.'

Harlan's expression darkened. 'Let's go.'

'Where?'

'I'm taking you to the ship so you can conduct your business.' He pinned her with a look. 'That's what close acquaintances do.'

Eda chewed her lip to stop from smiling.

'*Move*,' Harlan said, prompting her to start walking.

Blake stepped past the glaring defender and followed him.

Eda eyed their surroundings as they entered the borough, always alert. The tiny warrior was the only escort Blake needed.

Harlan said nothing until they reached the dock; then he stopped and turned to her. 'You can't bait the defenders like that. I won't always be around to get you out of those situations.'

She took in his angry expression. 'I didn't bait him. And you didn't have to come.'

He looked like he had more to say on the topic, but then he turned to the ship. 'Let's go.'

They stepped around the fishermen scaling fish, fish that would likely go to the royal and nobility boroughs. The smell mixed with the spices being unloaded from the ship.

'He thought we were prostitutes,' Blake said quietly. 'I got mad.'

He glanced sideways at her. 'You could have asked your neighbour to go with you.'

'What for?'

'To make life easier for yourself.'

She rolled her eyes. 'Next time I'll just go along with the suggestion, since the notion of a woman doing business with their skirts down is so confronting.'

Harlan's gaze slid to hers. 'Even the prostitutes have male escorts.'

'I think they're just called customers.'

He looked forwards again. 'Funny.'

His lack of a smile suggested otherwise.

Blake weaved between the merchants negotiating with buyers. She looked over her shoulder to ensure Eda was still following, and her eyes met Harlan's in the process. She felt his stare to the tips of her fingers before looking away.

'Blake?'

Looking around, she spotted Odo standing next to a pile of crates ten feet away. He dumped the one he was holding and turned to her, grinning. His smile faltered when he noticed Harlan beside her.

'In trouble with the law again?' he joked.

Blake made her way over to him. The Irish sea

merchant had taken over after his father lost a foot in a boating accident a year back. 'Good morning.'

Odo looked past her. 'Where's Kingsley?'

Blake felt a sting start in her nose. She swallowed to get rid of it. 'I'm afraid you're stuck with me moving forwards.'

Odo looked from her to Eda to Harlan. 'Clearly I've missed something.'

Blake snuck a glance at Harlan, who was pretending not to listen. 'Kingsley passed away.'

Odo's face fell. 'How?'

So many questions. 'Fishing accident.'

'I'm sorry. Where was he fishing?'

'I'm afraid we're in a bit of a rush today.' She reached inside her cloak and pulled out a coin pouch, holding it out to him. 'It's all there.'

Odo took the pouch and tucked it into his pocket, then disappeared behind the crates. He appeared a moment later carrying six rolls of fabric. 'They're heavy.'

'We'll manage,' Blake said.

Eda took half of them.

'You speaking yet?' Odo asked her.

Eda ignored him. She hated being asked that question.

'Her hearing gone as well?' Odo whispered to Blake.

Blake gave him a tight-lipped smile. 'Thanks for these.'

'Have you thought any more about my offer?'

She had really hoped he would not bring up the subject of marriage in front of Harlan. 'I've been a bit preoccupied.'

He leaned in, voice low. 'Marriage is the best way to help your family right now.'

Harlan was staring directly at her now.

'I'm headstrong, opinionated, and a terrible cook. You can do much better than me.'

'My mother's a superb cook. She'll teach you.'

Odo was an honest and dependable businessman, but that was as far as her feelings for him went. Something in her gut told her it was not enough to sustain a marriage. Perhaps it was because her parents had set an impossible standard.

'Time to go,' Harlan said beside her. 'That everything?'

'It's all there,' Odo said, making himself taller.

'Will you hold the prices for next month?' Blake asked. 'We'll take the same again.'

Odo tilted his head. 'Depends. Are you going to come back to Ireland with me? Leave this kingdom of walls?'

'Let's go,' Harlan said, taking Blake's arm and leading her away. 'He'll hold the prices.'

Odo followed. 'You have no jurisdiction over my business, defender.'

'It's "Commander", and I have jurisdiction over the dock you're standing on and the people you're selling to, so tread carefully, merchant.'

Blake pulled her arm free. 'I can manage my own negotiations.'

Harlan took hold of her arm again. 'This isn't a negotiation, it's extortion. Any offer of marriage should be external to your business arrangements.'

She searched his eyes and found genuine concern in them. 'He's right,' she said, looking back at Odo. 'That's no way to a lady's heart. I suggest you honour our business arrangement and try flowers next time.'

Finally, Harlan stepped back.

'So that's a maybe, then?' Odo said with a lopsided grin.

Blake shook her head as she turned away. 'See you next month.'

CHAPTER 10

*M*arriage?

The sea merchant was kidding himself if he thought a smart girl like Blake was going to settle for a conniving sack of shit like him. Irritation came off Harlan in waves as he stepped off the dock. Seeing the girls struggling under the weight of the fabric did nothing to improve his mood.

'Stop,' he said, tone abrupt. 'Give me those. Both of you.' He took the rolls and tucked all six under one arm.

Eda appeared irritated as she marched off ahead.

Blake sighed. 'We're quite capable of—'

'For the love of Belenus, walk.' He was not entirely sure why he was angry. Perhaps because she let Odo think he stood a chance. Not that it was any of his business who she married.

'Let me at least take one,' Blake said, slowing to walk beside him.

He swung them out of her reach. 'They weigh twice as much as you.'

She was quiet a moment. 'I have no other business contacts besides him. I don't have the luxury of injuring his feelings.'

'You don't owe me any explanations.'

'It's just that you seem annoyed.'

'I was annoyed well before that.' This woman had him behaving like an overprotective guard dog. 'But for the record, you can do better than him.'

She watched him as they walked. 'I barely know what to do with such an enormous compliment. How much better, exactly?'

He had stuck his foot in it now. 'I simply meant that you should find someone local.'

'Have you met the men in my borough?'

'They're not all bad.'

'I guarantee you the man my uncle chooses will be unbearable.'

He glanced at her. 'Surely you'll have a say over the matter.'

'I always have plenty to say over every matter. The problem is Lord Thomas always has the *final* say.'

Harlan opened his mouth wide to relax his jaw. 'Hope he's patient and enjoys saying things twice.'

Blake laughed, and he almost tripped over his own feet at the sound. It was silvery and feminine, her cheeks filling with colour.

'Unkind,' she tutted.

Afraid of what his face might give away, he looked ahead. 'Tell your sister to slow down. It's not safe for her to be wandering off.'

Blake stepped in front of him, forcing him to pull up

quickly to stop from running into her. She was so close he could smell whatever soap she had washed with that morning. It paired perfectly with the salty air in the port.

'Can I show you something before we go back in?' she asked, looking up at him.

She had grown far too comfortable in his presence, yet he did not put her in her place as he ought to have. 'Depends what it is.'

Eda had turned to see what the hold-up was, and Blake gestured for her to wait.

'If I tell you, you'll say no.'

'Then no.'

Blake looked slightly wounded.

'Fine,' he said, unable to see her disappointed. 'You have two minutes.'

Light returned to her eyes. 'Over here, away from everyone.' She turned and signed something to Eda.

'This way,' Blake called to him, stepping off the path.

Harlan sighed before following her.

She came to a stop in the middle of the open space that separated the beach and the wall. Instead of the usual mud, the ground was covered in small rocks.

'What am I looking at?' Harlan asked.

Blake pointed at the lone tree in front of the wall forty yards away. 'See that tree?'

He glanced tiredly in that direction. 'You want to show me a tree?'

She reached inside her pocket and pulled out a knife.

'What are you doing?' He was not worried about his safety but that a defender might see and misread the situation.

Instead of answering him, Blake lifted her skirt past the hem of her wool stocking, revealing another dagger strapped to her leg. He should have been focused on the weapon, but his eyes were on the thigh it was attached to.

He swallowed.

'Don't worry,' Blake said. 'You're quite safe.'

He forced his eyes up. 'I ask *again*. What are you doing?'

'Showing you something.'

His patience was wearing thin. 'You now have one minute.'

A smile spread across her face as she turned to the tree. She positioned her feet, raised the first knife, and threw it with surprising force. He watched it fly through the air and hit the trunk.

And it *stuck*.

'Impressive,' he said, his tone dry.

'Not done,' Blake replied, readying the other weapon. She repeated the process, this time striking an inch to the left of the first knife.

He went to speak, but she cut him off before he got a word out.

'Still not done.'

His gaze fell to her legs. 'Do I want to know where you're hiding the third knife?'

Ignoring him, she nodded at Eda, who was standing six feet away. Her sister drew her own weapon and raised it to shoulder height. Harlan doubted she could make the distance, let alone make it stick. A look of concentration settled on Eda's face. She stilled, then threw the knife.

It hit between Blake's two knives—and stuck.

Harlan blinked, eyes going to the twiggy girl.

Blake stepped into his vision. 'Would you care to see it again?' She sounded rather pleased with herself.

He searched her smug face. 'Who taught you to do that?'

'My father. He told us early on that he wouldn't always be around to protect us, that we needed to take care of ourselves in a world where women were already at a disadvantage.'

'Sound advice.' He moved back. 'Now collect your weapons before I confiscate them.'

'Aren't you curious to see what else I can do?'

He looked back at the path. The memory of her bare thigh was affecting his ability to look her in the eye. 'Get your weapons. We're going.'

Harlan carried the rolls all the way to the house, ignoring the confused look from the defender at the borough's entrance.

Lyndal was in the shop when they arrived. She looked from Harlan to the fabric to Blake. 'Commander.'

He nodded in place of words.

'Ah, come along, Eda,' Lyndal said. 'I need help with something in the house.'

Harlan placed the rolls down on the floor, in the same place he had laid Kingsley's corpse a few weeks earlier. Blake must have had the same thought, because the pain of that memory was there on her face when he looked at her.

The duckling waddled into the shop and flopped down on Blake's foot. It had grown since he had seen it last.

'Still alive,' Harlan said.

Blake bent to pick it up. It nuzzled her hand and whis-tled happily. 'We're keeping it inside to ensure it stays that way.'

He studied her face. 'You're not getting attached, are you?'

'He does make a great neck warmer on those frosty nights.' The faintest of smiles played on her lips. 'My sister named him.'

Harlan pinched the bridge of his nose. 'Of course she did.'

'Garlic.'

His hand fell away. 'At least it's part of the recipe.'

Blake bent to put the duck back down on the ground. 'Well, thank you—again. I'm not sure what I did to get in your good graces, but I'm grateful for it.'

He nodded.

'How these kinds of social exchanges typically work is I say, "Thank you," and you say something nice back, such as "You're welcome".'

He took a step towards the door, ignoring the comment. 'If you need to go to the port again, ask the guards on duty to fetch me. I don't care how well you can throw a knife.'

For a moment, she did not speak, just looked at him. 'I'm beginning to suspect you care whether I live or die.'

'It's my job to protect this borough and the people in it.'

She glanced at the window. 'You're going to be a very busy man when I let all the other women know of your generous offer.'

He grunted. 'I'm only extending the offer to you because you're the type of girl who attracts attention.'

'With my impressive knife skills?'

His eyes moved over her. 'Because of how you look.'

Curiosity piqued on her face. 'And how do I look?'

'You don't come across as the kind of woman who fishes for compliments.'

'You were going to pay a compliment? Do you even know how?'

'Not really.' He released a breath. 'I'm afraid you'll have to source them elsewhere.'

She suppressed a smile. 'Lucky for me, Odo is all sonnets.'

Pure sarcasm.

It surprised Harlan that the man proposing marriage did not think to tell Blake she was beautiful. Blake was not just pretty, she was the kind of girl who made responsible men do irresponsible things—like all the things he had done in the short time he had known her.

The sound of a horse approaching drew him outside. Blake followed, stopping in the doorway.

Astin pulled up out front, looking between them. 'Thought I might find you here. One of your men said you were helping merchant women carry supplies, and I thought to myself, "That is *so* him."'

'What do you want?' Harlan asked, stepping down onto the street.

'Prince Borin wishes to see you.'

Harlan nodded and began walking, ensuring he did not look back at Blake. 'Better not keep His Highness waiting.'

Harlan's father had also been summoned. They entered the throne room together, stopping next to the table where King Oswin, his sons, and the king's advisors were seated. Astin stood by the wall with the other guards and bodyguards. Prince Becket chose not to have a bodyguard, which was fine, because he did not attract the negative attention his older brother did.

'Your Majesty, Your Highnesses,' Shapur and Harlan said, bowing.

Borin turned in his chair to speak. 'We have been discussing the Solar Festival.'

'More of a debate,' the king said, eyes on his eldest son. 'Borin believes it should go ahead, and I do not. Opening the farming borough will only invite trouble.'

'That is what we have an army for,' Borin said. 'I really believe nothing lifts spirits quite like music and a round of gameball.'

Harlan knew the only thing that could truly lift the spirits of the merchants was food.

'It seems my son has forgotten why the wall is there to begin with. Now he wants to open the gate and invite the merchants in.'

Borin's lips tightened in a semi-pout. 'I have not forgotten, and the merchants know well enough by now what happens if they break the law. The Solar Festival is a Chadorian tradition. For many, gameball is the highlight of their year. Nobility versus the beating heart of this kingdom—the merchants.'

It was the crown prince who most looked forward to

the game each year. The more violent, the better, as far as his juvenile mind was concerned. The problem was 'the beating heart of the kingdom' was malnourished, desperate, and angry.

'What say you, Warden?' the king asked.

Shapur cleared his throat. 'I think letting the merchants into the farming borough will not end well for the livestock, Your Majesty.'

'Must it always come back to food with these people?' Borin said, slumping back in his chair. 'The entire kingdom is doing it tough right now.'

Harlan had an urge to shake him—hard. 'The market has not had meat, eggs, or butter in weeks. It's like throwing a carcass before a starved dog and telling it to stay.'

He felt his father's glare. No one had asked for his opinion.

Borin waved a dismissive hand. 'It is a feast. There will be food for all.'

The king looked only at Shapur now. 'Can we do this safely? The merchants outnumber our military twenty to one.'

Borin waited for the warden's response.

'If they are fed, they might play nice,' Shapur said. 'We will need archers along the wall and hundreds on foot. Best not take chances.'

Harlan looked down. It sounded like they were preparing for war instead of a celebration.

The king ran a hand over his beard. 'Very well. Let us pray we do not live to regret this.'

CHAPTER 11

A knock on the shop door drew Blake from the warmth of her bed much earlier than she would have liked. It was barely light outside as she fought the three locks and tugged the door open, sending the bell crashing to the floor.

'I thought you were going to fix that,' Thea said as she entered.

Blake crossed her arms over her nightdress. 'Everything all right?'

Her neighbour leaned closer. 'My cousin just came to tell me she saw eggs come in from the farming borough overnight.'

'Eggs?' That woke her up.

'Birtle's already in line at the market. I suggest you go now and take extra coin. They will not be cheap.'

Blake thanked Thea and went to dress, careful not to disturb her sleeping sisters, then grabbed the coin pouch they kept hidden under a section of wood next to the hearth.

Apparently the entire borough had heard the news of the eggs, because the line was all the way down the street, and the market had not even opened yet. Blake joined the back of the queue.

Defenders strolled up and down the streets, hands resting on their weapons. But there was no fighting among the merchants. No one had the energy for it.

Blake found herself looking out for Harlan. She was doing that more and more lately. Every time the bell at the shop door sounded, she would hold her breath, expecting him to step inside. But he had not been back to the shop since the day he helped her carry the fabric from the port.

That had been six days ago.

'Morning, boor.'

Blake whipped around at the sound of his voice. Warmth spread through her at the sight of him. 'Commander.' She took in his black uniform and broad shoulders. 'Are you queueing for eggs too?'

His mouth twitched. 'I'm preparing for the backlash when merchants learn the price of the eggs.'

Her stomach fell a little. 'How much are they?'

'Four shillings.'

Blake's eyes widened. 'For how many?'

'Per egg.'

'That's… that's criminal. Not one person waiting in this line can afford to pay that much for one egg.' She went to step out of the line, but Harlan stopped her.

'Stay in line,' he instructed.

'There's really no point.'

Harlan's eyes met hers. '*Stay in line.*'

Blake exhaled. 'I don't have enough.'

'But I do.' She tried to step out of the line again, but he caught her by the arm. 'What did I just say?'

'I can't pay you back.'

'I don't need you to pay me back. Quit arguing or I'll arrest you.'

'On what grounds?'

'For being a pain in my arse.'

She relaxed beneath his grip.

They stood together in silence for the next half hour, feet shuffling forwards every time a customer left with either empty hands or empty pockets. Blake was surprised how at ease she felt with him looming over her. Despite his empty threat earlier, she felt safe and somewhat untouchable.

When they finally reached the front of the queue, Blake glanced at Harlan before stepping up to the merchant. 'Four, please.'

The woman did not move. 'Four eggs will cost you three crowns and a shilling.'

'She can do the math,' Harlan said.

The woman looked up at him before turning to fetch the eggs. She placed them carefully in Blake's basket. Harlan inspected each one before handing over the coin.

Blake gave the woman a tight smile. 'Thank you.'

Harlan said nothing as they turned away, eyes sweeping the area is if expecting someone to jump out and snatch the eggs from her hands. It was not an unreasonable thought given the circumstances.

'Must you be so rude?' Blake asked once they had left the market.

He looked down at her. 'Me? She was being conde-
scending.'

'She knew quite well I couldn't afford four eggs. How
was she to know that you were going to pay on my
behalf?' Blake moved her basket to her other hand. 'Thank
you, by the way. I can't tell you how much my family
needs this.' She fell silent when she spotted a defender
approaching. The man looked her up and down before
addressing Harlan.

'Warden wants to see you in the port borough.'

'There a problem?' Harlan asked.

'Ships off the coast. Second time they've passed this
week.'

'Sea warriors?'

The defender glanced at Blake before nodding.

'I'll be right there.' Harlan waited for him to leave
before turning to her. 'Go straight home, and make sure
you eat one of those eggs. Hear me?'

She gave him a mock salute, and he responded with a
disapproving look before striding off.

When Blake arrived home, she found her mother sewing
in the shop. Garlic was beside her, wedged between her
thigh and the arm of the chair.

'Where were you?' Candace asked.

'The market. Where's Eda and Lyndal?'

Garlic rose and dropped off the edge of the chair,
wandering over to greet Blake. She bent to pet him.

'Eda is getting water,' Candace said, sounding tired.

She was sleeping more and more of late. 'Lyndal is inside somewhere.'

'I have eggs.' She held the basket out for her mother to see.

Candace dropped her sewing and stood to inspect them. 'Please tell me we have some coin left.'

'Actually, we have *all* our coin left.' She kissed her mother's cheek. 'Commander Wright paid for the eggs.'

Candace's eyebrows came together. 'Why?'

'He was being kind, I suppose.'

Her mother sighed. 'And what does he expect in return?'

'He's not like that.'

She patted Blake's arm. 'I am too tired and hungry to argue.'

Blake wandered into the house, Garlic in tow, and when she did not find her sister in the main room, she placed the basket on the table and went through to the bedroom.

Lyndal was standing in front of the mirror in one of her best dresses, studying her reflection. She turned when she caught sight of Blake. 'Have you bled this month?'

'Bled?' It took Blake a moment to register the conversation they were having. 'Oh. I haven't exactly been counting the days. Why do you ask?'

Lyndal immediately teared up. 'I *have* been counting the days. This is my second month of... nothing.' She pressed her lips together to stop from crying.

Blake walked over and wrapped her arms around her sister. 'Please don't cry. It'll come back when the food does.' She released her as a thought came to her. 'Don't hate me for asking, but is there another reason it might be late?'

It was the kind of conversation their mother used to be good at. At present, the only thing she was good at was sewing in silence.

Lyndal pushed her away. 'No. My virtue is the only asset I have to offer my future husband. Do you think I'm foolish enough to hand it over to a man without locking him down first?'

A smile spread across Blake's face. 'How foolish of me to think my sensible sister would be swept off course by something as silly as love.'

'Many a merchant have tried.' She adjusted her dress. 'The Solar Festival is approaching. There will be eligible farmers as far as the eye can see.'

'And you and every other merchant woman will be trying to catch one.'

Lyndal looked up. 'Must you rain all over my dreams?'

Blake took her hand. 'Clearly you have an advantage. Look at you.'

'Wasting away and barren.'

Blake tugged her towards the door. 'Not for long. I have eggs.'

Lyndal's face lit up. 'So the rumours were true. Praise Belenus. How many could we afford?'

'None.'

Lyndal stopped walking.

'Commander Wright took care of it,' Blake explained.

Lyndal let out a breath. 'Well, he's playing a very expensive game. Might be cheaper in the long run to simply visit one of the taverns in the port.'

'He was just being kind.'

'He's a defender. I'm quite certain he doesn't know the meaning of the word.'

Blake regarded her sister. 'He's seen the daggers I keep beneath my skirts. I think he knows better than to go poking around under there.'

'Perhaps it's time you left those at home,' Lyndal said, shaking her head.

'Why?'

'Because men prefer their women unarmed.'

'And?'

Lyndal stared hard at her. 'You do realise you'll have to marry eventually or forever be at the mercy of our uncle?'

'Well, defenders don't marry merchants, so it doesn't matter what Harlan thinks.'

Lyndal's brow creased. 'Harlan now, is it? What happened to Commander Wright? And I said nothing of marrying him.'

'Can you imagine what a disaster that would be?' Blake said, looking away.

Lyndal watched her a moment. 'Well, nobility don't marry merchants either, but that didn't stop our parents.'

It was Blake's turn to stare hard at her sister. 'Was that supposed to strengthen your argument?'

There were rare instances of nobility marrying farmers, especially now that farmers had control over the food supply. Noble families with multiple daughters might sacrifice one to a lower class to improve their buying power. Farmers marrying merchants was becoming less common. It was seen as a wasted opportunity. Jumping two class divides, as their parents had done, was unthinkable.

Lyndal threaded her arm through Blake's and resumed walking. 'Let's pray my cycle returns soon, or we might be forced to rely on you to save us.'

Blake feigned offence. 'I can be very charming under the right circumstances.'

'No you can't. You're unapologetically yourself, and I wouldn't want it any other way.'

They stepped into the main room. Eda had returned and was peering into the basket of eggs.

'Go on, then,' Blake said to Lyndal. 'Fry them up with salt and the rest of the onion from last night.' She peered through the doorway at her wasting mother still sewing away. 'I had some nuts at the market, so the eggs are for you three.'

Lyndal looked up from the onion she was slicing. 'You said nothing of nuts. Did the commander buy them for you?'

'Yes,' she lied.

Five minutes later, the smell of fried onions and eggs filled the small room. Blake was salivating so much she could not remain in the house for fear of snatching food from her sisters' plates. 'I'm going to the forest to check for mushrooms,' she announced, rising from the table.

The three women looked up from their food, Lyndal's eyes narrowing.

'The forest will be cleared out by now. You have to go early if you stand a chance of finding any.'

Blake was backing out of the room. 'Can't hurt to check.'

She did not wait around for a reply. Turning, she walked into the shop and snatched Eda's wet cloak off the stand by the door, swinging it over her shoulders as she stepped out into the drizzle. She tugged up the hood and headed for the forest.

When she reached the trees, she moved from trunk to trunk, looking for the wood shavings Harlan had shown her the first day they met. She crouched when she finally found some, trailing a finger up to the hole in the trunk. Pulling out her dagger, she began carving into the wood until she glimpsed a fat white grub. She stared at it for the longest time, hunger wrestling with her mind.

Hunger won.

Blake fetched it out with the tip of her knife and held it in her damp open palm. She watched it writhe for a moment, then, closing her eyes, dropped it into her mouth. She chewed as fast as she could, nauseated by the pop and crunch, then surprised by the slightly sweet taste. She swallowed. It was no replacement for eggs, but it was better than the persistent hunger that had shadowed her for weeks.

With a resigned exhale, she rose and continued her hunt.

CHAPTER 12

Harlan had just returned from the port borough when he spotted Lyndal leaning against the wall ten feet from the entrance. She straightened when she saw him and raised her hand in a small wave. More of a beckoning than a greeting. He made his way over.

'What's wrong?' he asked, stopping in front of her. His first thought was Blake. Maybe someone had stolen her eggs on the walk home. Maybe that someone had hurt her. She probably tried to fight them off instead of just surrendering the eggs, believing her knife-throwing skills would save her somehow. 'Where's Blake?'

Lyndal's eyebrows rose. 'Oh. She went to the forest. Something about mushrooms.'

He relaxed.

'Quick question,' she said, finding a smile. 'This might sound strange, but did you buy Blake nuts at the market this morning?'

His brow pinched. 'What? No. I bought her eggs.' He realised why she had asked that. 'She tell you I did?'

A nod.

'She didn't eat any of the eggs, did she?'

She sighed. 'No, and she ran away before I figured it out.'

Harlan walked off, and Lyndal hurried after him.

'Where are you going?' she asked.

'To strangle your sister.'

Lyndal had to jog to keep up. 'I'm going to assume you're joking.'

'She's like a child in need of constant adult supervision, and somehow that's fallen to me.'

It was clear Blake was trying to step up as the provider of the household now that her brother was gone. And her uncle was as useless as a glass hammer.

Lyndal gave up her chase, stopping in the middle of the road. 'I saved her some of my egg. Tell her that—if you find her.'

He would find her. He did not have a choice. Left to her own devices, she would likely starve to death.

Harlan headed straight for the forest. It was a sizeable area, but his tracking skills were sharp enough to pick up her movements. He followed them, soundless, until he spotted Blake crouched in front of a tree, carving into the trunk. He remained hidden for a moment, watching as she pulled an aureate grub out with her knife and tossed it into her mouth. She closed her eyes and chewed, swallowing quickly, then turned, back sliding down the tree. Her facade was down. She looked exhausted, depleted—

and still beautiful. Her eyes closed as she leaned her head back.

Harlan stepped out from his hiding place and walked over to her. He was about to speak when Blake sprang to her feet with surprising agility, a knife pointed at his face. He caught her wrist. Normally, anyone who pointed a weapon at him would be disarmed and lying face down in the mud a beat later, but he let her go the second she relaxed her arm.

'You scared me,' she said, lowering the knife. 'What are you doing out here?'

'Why didn't you eat the egg?'

She shifted her weight. 'How do you know I didn't?'

'I saw your sister.'

She swallowed. 'I gather from your expression it was the one who talks.'

'You told her I bought you *nuts*?'

Blake closed her eyes. 'She needed them more than I do. They all do.'

He brushed his nose, his temper rising. 'You getting food from somewhere I don't know about?'

Her eyes opened. 'No.'

'Then you *all* need it.'

She stared at him a moment. 'Why are you angry?'

It was a fair question. Now to come up with a logical answer. 'Because you're out here eating grubs.'

'You told me to eat them. You said they were safe, that they were as good as meat—'

'They are, but you don't eat them while your sisters gorge themselves on eggs.' He needed to stop, to calm down.

He needed to care less.

Blake did not respond straight away, just watched him. 'I'm sorry.'

Now he felt like a complete bastard. 'Don't.' He rubbed his brow. 'Don't say that.' His eyes went to the hole in the trunk behind her. 'How many did you find?'

'Six.' She scrunched her nose up. 'How you eat them with a straight face I'll never understand.'

She moved to sheathe her dagger, but he reached out and caught her hand.

'Before you do that, I want to show you something.' He pointed the dagger at his face. 'Keep your hand there.'

Her eyebrows came together in confusion, but she did as she was told. His hands hovered on either side of hers.

'Watch,' he said, smacking the back of her hand and inside of her wrist. The dagger flew from her grasp, landing on the ground four feet away. 'Fingers can't grasp a weapon when your hand bends at that angle.' He went to pick up the knife and gave it to her again. 'Now point it at my stomach.'

Her hand dropped. 'Like this?'

He nodded, then repeated the action, this time from above. The dagger went flying once more. Again, he fetched it for her. Their eyes met as he lifted her arm so the weapon was pointed at his chest. He ignored the foreign sensation in his gut that came with being close to her.

'If you point it straight at me, at my chest, I can't disarm you so easily,' he said. 'Not without potentially cutting myself.'

The weapon remained where it was. 'So what will you do?'

Something in her tone made the small hairs on the back of his neck stand to attention. His eyes moved between hers as he slowly took hold of her wrist. He tugged her forwards, pinning her dagger hand to his hip. Her other hand landed on his chest.

'First, I make sure you can't stab me.' He ran his hand along her arm, shoulder, neck. She sucked in a breath when he gripped her hair. 'Then I bring your pretty face to my knee and break your nose.'

Her lips parted. 'Rather aggressive.'

'They don't train us to be gentle. They train us to be efficient.' He was watching those lips now.

'You're forgetting one thing.'

'What's that?' Their faces were so close he could almost feel her breath despite the misty rain.

Her own knee went up, stopping an inch from his groin. He did not so much as flinch. 'You're forgetting I have knees too.'

He released her dagger hand but kept hold of her hair. 'A defender forgets nothing. Your nose would be broken and the knife stuck in your ribs before you had a chance to gather your thoughts.' He let go of her hair, fingers slipping through the damp, silky strands before falling to his side.

Neither of them stepped back.

'Why did you teach me that?' she asked.

'So you know for next time.'

'Next time I point a knife at a defender's face?'

His mouth flattened into a line. 'Point a knife at a defender and you'll find yourself displayed on the wall.'

'I just pointed a knife at you.'

'That's different.'

She tilted her head. 'Why is it different?'

He felt like he was walking into some kind of female trap. 'Because you're not trying to hurt me.'

She took a step back, releasing some of the tension that had built between them. 'I once thought about stabbing you beneath these very trees.'

'You were just upset.'

She took another step and leaned her back against the trunk. 'You took pity on me that day.'

'I did.'

She looked disappointed. 'And still you take pity on me.'

He did not like what she was implying. 'I don't pity you.'

'Then why the gallant gesture today?'

'Gallant gesture? It was a few eggs. Don't get excited.' He noted her wounded expression. 'What are you fishing for? Some kind of confession?'

'What could Commander Wright possibly have to confess?'

'I don't know.' He stared at her. 'Maybe you want to hear that I'm attracted to you.'

She swallowed. 'How ridiculous. No defender could be attracted to a merchant woman at a time like this. We're all wasting limbs and depressed faces. We reek of grief and desperation.'

Blake always smelled like fresh air and the cotton sold in her shop. 'You don't blend in—trust me on that.'

She looked up, studying the branches above her. His gaze fell to her slender neck, then away.

'You don't blend in either,' she said. 'Despite your matching uniforms, haircuts, and'—her eyes returned to him—'warrior physique.'

He felt her eyes on him like it was a hand. 'What makes me different?'

'You bring me corpses and buy me eggs.' She smiled, but it faded.

He wished she was in front of him again, his fingers wound in her stringy mess of wet hair, the other holding her hand—preferably without the weapon in it.

He took a large step back. 'I'll have some food delivered to you tonight.'

She pushed off the tree. 'Why?'

'You know why.'

'No I don't.'

She was killing him. He was not one for words—especially with women. His interactions with them tended to be a lot more... primal. No need to speak of feelings. 'Because the thought of you eating grubs doesn't sit well with me.'

'You mean the grubs you told me to eat when I got hungry enough?'

'That was before.'

'Before *what*?'

Before he had seen her claw at the mud, trying to save her brother. Before he had witnessed her broken expression as they hung him on the wall. Before he had met her uncle and seen what she was up against, watched her steal a horse back from thieves, seen her throw a knife, pet a duck, and hustle in the port borough like she had been doing it her whole life.

Before he realised how much he wanted her to survive this eternal famine.

'I have to go,' he said, straightening. 'And so do you.'

She drew a breath. 'Why? Is there a curfew now?'

'There will be if you don't go home and eat some proper food.'

They watched each other a moment.

'Will you be at the Solar Festival tomorrow?' she asked, shoulders dropping a few inches.

'I'll be on duty, as will most defenders.'

She crossed her arms in front of her. 'When do the defenders get to celebrate, then?'

'We don't. We make it safe for everyone else to celebrate.'

Pity passed over her face. 'Perhaps defenders should have another day off and let the merchants defend our walls for a few hours.'

'That's a truly terrifying thought.'

She shrugged. 'I'm fairly skilled with a bow, you know.'

'I don't doubt that.'

'Well, I'm going tomorrow, in case you were wondering. Lyndal wants to find a farmer husband.' Some light returned to her eyes.

'What about you? Do you want a farmer husband?'

She scrunched up her nose. 'Someone has to stay here to keep Eda out of trouble.'

He nodded. 'Well, be smart tomorrow. There'll be a lot of ale-infused men wandering around the place.'

'The drunker the better. It gives us women a better chance of getting the ball.'

He blinked. 'What?'

'Eda's insisting on joining the game.'

He shifted his weight. 'I assume you told her no.'

'I told her I would play too.'

'*Play?*' Harlan straightened. 'I'm to remain in the farming borough for the event.'

She blinked. 'And?'

'And it'll probably move into the merchant borough at some point.' He felt his patience slipping as she stared back with a blank expression. 'It's a violent game, and the players won't care if their opponents are men or women.'

She closed the gap between them, and he tensed.

'You're worried about the violence?' She looked around. 'We live violence every day in this borough. It's the reason the square in our village is stained with blood and bodies decorate our walls.'

His eyes fell to her mouth, and an overwhelming desire to taste her had him leaning forwards. Her head tipped back slightly, as if inviting him closer. She had spoken of attraction, but what he felt could not be reduced to something so ordinary.

He stepped back and drew a breath.

Blake's lips came together, and she looked past him in the direction of the village. 'I guess I shall see you at the festival.' She bowed her head. 'Good day, Commander.'

He stepped aside. 'Merchant.'

CHAPTER 13

$\mathscr{B}$lake rarely gave much thought to her appearance. She chose clothing based on comfort and practicality, considering whether a dress would restrict her movement in an archery contest, or if the weight of a skirt would prevent her from running if the need arose. Sometimes she even selected a dress based on whether food spills would show on that colour.

But on the morning of the Solar Festival, she found herself standing in front of the cupboard where the girls' dresses hung, wondering which one would *flatter* her slim frame. She took them out one at a time and held them against her, studying her reflection in the mirror. This was the first time she had given thought to what colours went well with her complexion.

The Solar Festival was a celebration of Belenus, the god of sun and fire, and it called for reds, oranges, and yellows. While the nobility covered themselves head to toe with gold and rubies, the merchants found more creative ways to join in: headpieces with dyed feathers, painted faces, and bold dresses with interesting features.

Blake pulled out the orange two-piece gown Lyndal had worn to the festival the year prior. In theory, it should not have fit, but Blake had lost weight over the course of the year, so she was able to squeeze into it. The cut of the dress was designed to push her breasts high and hold her waist in. There were not huge amounts of her to push and pull, but the gown helped. The skirt ballooned from the hips, giving them a fuller appearance. Ruffles of red fabric had been sewn along the bottom, so it looked as though flames licked the hem of the skirt. She would need to wear a lighter skirt beneath it for gameball. There was no way she could kick and run otherwise.

Lyndal walked into the room and stopped dead in her tracks. 'Who are you, and what have you done with my bad-dressing sister?'

Blake looked down. 'Do I look ridiculous?'

'You look amazing.' Lyndal went over and began tugging at the neck of the dress. 'I think we can get those breasts even higher.'

Blake slapped her sister's hand away. 'I don't need a chin rest.'

Lyndal circled her. 'Oh, I have some good ideas.'

'For what?'

'Hair, face. Do we still have that beeswax leftover from last year?' She walked over to the small dresser against the wall and began rummaging through the top drawer. She held up a tiny pot and turned to Blake with a triumphant expression. 'I'll mix a little with some turmeric for your eyes and the flower dye for your lips.'

She returned to Blake and started fiddling with her hair. 'Yes, up for this dress. You could borrow Mother's gold earrings.'

'You mean the ones we sold a few months back?'

Lyndal sighed. 'Well, you don't need them anyway. Just look at you. Last year I had to drag you along to the festival, and this year you look ready to steal the heart of every man in attendance.'

'Hardly.' If she were being honest, the dress was for Harlan. She wanted him to look at her the way she saw men look at Lyndal. What did that say about her?

'Sit,' Lyndal said. 'I'll start with your hair.'

'What about you? Don't you need to get ready?'

Lyndal waved a hand. 'Yes, yes. In a minute.' She brushed Blake's hair back with her fingers, braided it loosely with a few extra turns here and there, then twisted it into a bun at the nape of her neck. 'Look at that gorgeous neck—and not one man in the borough has seen it.'

Blake rolled her eyes. 'There's a good reason for that. Hair keeps the neck warm.'

Lyndal disappeared from the room and returned a few minutes later with two bowls containing coloured pastes. She sat on the bed facing her sister. 'Is this for him?'

'Who?'

Lyndal shook her head. 'You know exactly who. Commander Harlan Wright.'

Garlic had joined them on the bed, and Blake reached out to pet him. 'Such an effort would be a complete waste. The most a merchant like me can expect from a man of his rank is an unwanted pregnancy.' Though, after her conversation with Lyndal, Blake had done the math and figured out that her courses had stopped also.

'Close your eyes,' Lyndal said, using her finger to brush the paste along Blake's eyelids all the way to her hairline. 'Do you think that's what he wants from you?'

Blake opened her eyes. 'What?'

'Do you think he's the kind of man who ruins and discards women?'

'I barely know him.' Perhaps he was that man, though her gut told her otherwise. He was more protective of her than Kingsley had been when he was alive.

'Lips together,' Lyndal said.

Blake pressed her lips together to smooth out the red paste.

'I have some tea leaves for your lashes,' Lyndal said. 'Just remember not to rub your eyes.'

Blake watched her as she walked over to the drawer to fetch it. 'What about during gameball? Is all this going to be a mess of colour on my face.'

'Probably. That's the price you pay for getting involved in men's sports.'

'Blame Eda.'

Lyndal sat back down on the bed. 'Oh, shush. You're the older sister here. You could have told her no.'

Blake sighed. 'Except that I've lost the ability to deny her anything.'

'And it shows. She's like a little outlaw, terrorising the borough. You better keep a close eye on her today, because Mother has completely lost control of her. She listens to you—occasionally.' She rose from the bed, pulling Blake up with her. 'If the sun doesn't pour through the clouds when you step into that borough, I will be very surprised.'

Blake turned to look in the mirror. 'I'll settle for the rain stopping for a few hours.' She barely recognised the woman looking back at her. There was something mature about her, something… alluring. 'I'm going to freeze.'

'You can wear my red cloak to and from.' She rested her chin on Blake's shoulder. 'I know I'm not supposed to say this, but I think it's nice he likes you—even if nothing can ever come of it.'

'You're only saying that because he sent oil and a cabbage to the house last night.'

Lyndal pinched her arm. 'No. I just think any man who makes you see yourself as the rest of us do is a hero.'

Blake turned to face her. 'What did I do to deserve such a sister?'

'I honestly can't think of one thing.'

It was Blake's turn to pinch her. 'It will be a lucky man who wins you.'

Lyndal laughed the comment off. 'I really just want to have some fun today. Constantly looking ahead to the next disaster is exhausting. I'll say yes to every man who asks me to dance and laugh so much it sustains me for the rest of this miserable year.'

'If you say yes to every man who asks you to dance today, you'll be unable to walk home. I won't be carrying you on my back like Kingsley did last year.'

His name hung in the air between them. Their smiles faded.

'I miss him,' Lyndal said. 'Every day. Sometimes I put

five spoons out for dinner instead of four, and when I remember, it feels like he's died all over again.'

Blake took her hand and pressed it to her heart. 'I miss him too.'

They were silent a moment. Then Lyndal's eyes fell to the hand Blake was holding.

'Dear God. Your breasts are a pillow of flesh propping up my hand.'

Blake let go and turned away. 'Changing now.'

'Don't you dare,' Lyndal called to her back. 'They'll make the perfect headrest for the walk home.'

Her laughter followed Blake out the door.

CHAPTER 14

*D*efenders lined the road on either side of the wall, supervising the merchants' arrival. It was the job of the farming commander to watch the livestock and Harlan's job to ensure every merchant in attendance was on their best behaviour.

The feast was being held in the borough's square. They had roped a section off for royalty, nobility, and clergy. The food on that side of the rope was of a significantly higher quality—and mass.

It had been five years since that wall was built, and the Solar Festival was now the only time merchants got to enter. It was also the only time they saw live animals—from a safe distance.

Harlan wandered beneath the red banners erected around the perimeter of the square, eyes moving over the new arrivals, committing each face to memory. He had a knack for spotting concealed weapons. While it was not a crime for a merchant to carry a weapon into the event, drawing it at the wrong time and in the wrong company could easily turn into one.

There was no sign of Blake yet. Unless he had missed her arrival. Doubtful, as he kept wandering back to the gate to check. But once the streets and square were full, he was forced to remain where the majority of merchants were. He positioned himself against a wall, watching the musicians set up. Lutes, wind instruments, tambourines, drums. Past them were food stalls with queues stretching along the main road. Farmers were selling black bread, soup, and onions fried with mushrooms. The smell of oil, salt, and garlic mixed with the fruity scent of blackberry wine in the air.

It was an hour later when he spotted Lyndal dancing. She wore a red dress with yellow feathers threaded through her hair. Every man with working sight was looking in her direction, but Harlan's focus was elsewhere. He was looking for Blake. When he could not find her, he ambled around the edge of the square, searching. He came across Eda and her mother seated with a plate of food between them, but no Blake.

Boisterous laughter made him turn to the men gathered around the barrels of ale. Some were already on their way to drunk, which meant they would either be useless for gameball later or trouble for the game. Harlan's gaze drifted back to the dancers as the musicians struck up a new song, and his gaze snagged on a woman in an orange dress.

It was Blake.

He stilled, a frozen figure in a sea of chaos. It barely looked like her, yet it was unmistakably her. She looked like she belonged on the other side of the rope. Her hair was braided and tucked, her dress figure-hugging, her lips painted the colour of fire. It was not simply the dress and the paint that made him stare—though the dress gave many reasons to—it was the brilliant smile lighting up her face as she danced with a merchant man completely unworthy of her. He did not have to meet the man to know that.

They circled one another, Blake's head tipping back with laughter every time the tempo of the music changed. It was the sight of her happy that made him stare. It was the sight of her away from *him*. He stood completely transfixed until the song finally ended. Even then, he could not look away as she clapped and caught her breath. The man she had danced with leaned in to say something. Grinning, harmless. So why did Harlan want to drag him off to the tower?

Blake laughed—*laughed*—said something back, then curtsied before stepping away. Her eyes swept the crowd like she was looking for someone, and an irresponsible part of him wanted to be that someone. He felt the moment her eyes landed on him, like warm water splashed over his face on a frosty morning. The hairs on his arms stood up as Blake's eyes creased at the corners in place of a smile. Then she was walking towards him, one hand holding her skirt off the ground.

'I was beginning to think you weren't coming,' Blake said, stopping next to him. She looked out at the other dancers. 'I should have known I would find you lurking in the shadows.'

'Wouldn't have picked you for a dancer.' Those were

his first words, despite the compliments piled up in his throat.

She eyed him. 'Everyone enjoys dancing—even defenders who might pretend otherwise.'

He snuck a glance at her. 'I prefer to watch.'

'Anyone in particular?'

'People concealing weapons, mostly.'

'Oh, fun.' She pressed her lips together to stop from smiling. 'Sometimes I forget you aren't human like the rest of us.'

His eyebrows came together. 'Someone has to maintain order at these events.'

'Because self-regulation for a merchant is *unthinkable* nowadays. Someone must tell us when we've had enough dancing, enough fun, enough to drink.' She paused. 'Enough to eat.'

Apparently looking like a goddess was going to her head. 'Something you want to say?'

'Nothing that won't get me into trouble.'

More laughter came from the men gathered around the ale, pulling their attention.

'Look at those men over there and tell me what you see,' Harlan said.

Blake angled her head, observing the men for a full minute before replying. 'I see they're nearing drunk. They'll probably brawl at some point, over something insignificant, like a comment made about another man's wife or daughter. At least one will grab the backside of some poor girl while dancing and finish with a bloody nose.' She paused. 'I also see men exhausted by the effort of providing for their families, in desperate need to forget the hardships that await them tomorrow.' She looked up at Harlan. 'For the record, I think the heavy presence of defenders is both demoralising and unnecessary.'

Harlan regarded her. 'Want to know what I see?'

'I'm sure you'll tell me regardless.'

'The man on the far right is married to the woman serving the ale. He's not looking at his wife though. He's watching the redhead dancing three couples in.'

Blake sighed. 'So? A married man isn't blind to the beauty of other women, despite what their wives might want to believe.'

'She's watching him as well.'

'Mutual attraction is not a crime, though you defenders are always changing the rules.'

Harlan pointed at another man standing in the group. '*That's* the woman's husband. He's been looking between the pair the entire time I've been standing here. He knows about the affair.'

'Presumptuous.'

'What do you notice about him?' he went on.

Blake studied the man a moment. 'He has a kind face. I can see by his clothes that his wife takes good care of him. He's a little older than her judging by his hairline.' She looked up at Harlan. 'Is that what you see?'

He shook his head. 'I see long-held jealousy. He's constantly checking his surroundings and not drinking as much as his friends because he's readying for something. He has a dagger concealed at his right hip, and I can tell by the way his hand keeps returning to it that he'll use it at some point.' He met her gaze. 'And he's just one man in an enormous crowd.'

Blake's expression softened. 'I actually feel sorry for you. Your occupation has taught you to look for the worst in people. That can't be an easy thing to switch off.'

He faced forwards. The last thing he wanted was her pity.

'So, no dancing for you, then?' she asked.

'No.'

She nodded. 'I guess I'll have to find another partner.'

'Guess so.'

She remained where she was. 'Can I ask you something?'

He looked at her, waiting.

'Will it bother you to see me dancing with other people?' Her voice was quieter now.

The correct answer was no. He had no right to be bothered, no claim on her. His hands twitched at his sides. 'You're here to have fun, so go have fun.'

Blake looked away. 'I will.'

It was better this way, better to lie to her face than lead her on. They would never dance together. That was not the world they lived in.

'Thank you for the cabbage and oil, by the way,' she said, clearing her throat. 'While I'm very appreciative, please don't feel obligated to do that again.'

'I didn't feel obligated the first time.'

That wariness had returned to Blake's eyes. He had chased away the laughter.

'Go,' he said, tearing his eyes from hers.

She nodded and walked back to the crowd. He watched her the entire time, and then he watched her for the rest of the day.

CHAPTER 15

Blake tried to block Harlan out, but whenever she glanced in his direction, which was often, she found him watching her. She danced. She sat with the single women from her borough as they discussed the eligible farmers and laughed whenever one of them looked in their direction. She even took a walk with Lyndal to get a better view of certain farmers who had piqued her sister's interest, then listened to detailed recounts of the dances they shared.

'I'm boring you,' Lyndal said when Blake stifled a yawn.

'Not at all. Tell me again which one is the youngest of four brothers.' She gave her sister a mischievous smile.

Lyndal sighed. 'Point taken. Come on. Let's go get some blackberry wine.'

'We don't have any coin.'

'It's fine. Trust me.' She tugged on Blake's arm, leading her over to the younger boy working at the stall. She put on her most brilliant smile as she pulled out her empty coin pouch. 'Two, please.'

Blake prepared herself for humiliation.

'You from the merchant borough?' the boy asked as he placed the cups in front of her. He was no older than sixteen.

Lyndal's smile grew. 'I am. Importers of fine cotton. You must be from another borough, because I would definitely remember that face.'

The boy's cheeks coloured. 'No, merchant borough, same as you.' He held out his hand. 'Importer of wine—when we can get it.'

Lyndal took his hand for a second before asking, 'How much do I owe you?' She reached into the empty pouch as she awaited his answer.

The boy glanced sideways at the man serving at the other end of the table, likely his father, then leaned closer to her. 'These are on me.'

Lyndal picked up the cups. 'What a gentleman you are. Be sure to come find me later for a dance.' She flashed him a final smile before turning and walking off, Blake following at her heel.

'I guarantee you if I tried something like that, it would end with me being arrested,' Blake said.

Lyndal handed her one of the cups. 'That's because holding a knife to someone's throat doesn't have quite the same effect.' She bumped her cup against Blake's. 'Cheers.'

They found a bench to sit on and watched the dancing for a while. Blake found herself looking over to where Harlan had been earlier, but he was no longer there. Disappointment swelled in her. She liked having him in sight. He looked ridiculously good in that black uniform of his. It fit him like a second skin, highlighting every curve of his muscular frame. Not that she had anything to compare it to because she had only ever seen him that way.

'What I like about farming men is that they have a good covering of muscle,' Lyndal said.

Blake rolled her eyes. 'Because they have food.'

Her mind went to Harlan again, a wall of solid muscle. Her neck heated at the memory of the day prior. Her hand pinned to his hip, the feel of his breath on her face and hair. He had held her in place with such ease, and instead of fighting it, she had leaned into his masculine scent. She knew the kind of strength he was capable of but had not been afraid in the slightest. Perhaps there was gentleness to be discovered in the commander.

'Well, look who's back,' Lyndal said, lifting her drink to her lips.

Blake glanced over and found Harlan standing in the spot he had been earlier. As if sensing her eyes on him, he looked straight at her.

'He hasn't taken his eyes off you all evening,' Lyndal whispered. 'If there's any doubt left in your mind as to his feelings, dismiss them this instant.'

'It doesn't matter. What he feels, what I feel. None of it matters.'

'What do you mean, how *you* feel? How do you feel?'

'It doesn't matter.'

'Why do you have to be so private? It's very annoying.'

Blake smiled into her drink.

A young man approached, fair shaggy hair reaching

down to his eyes. Lyndal sat up a little straighter when he stopped in front of them, but he extended a hand to Blake.

'Care to dance?'

Lyndal gave Blake a push in his direction. 'She'd love to.'

Blake snuck a glance at Harlan as she rose. He shifted his weight as her hand was swallowed by another's. The man led her into the centre of the square, and she could feel Harlan's eyes on her the entire time.

'Name's Col,' the merchant shouted over the music, pulling Blake to him.

It was a little closer than the song required.

'Blake.'

'I know who you are. I knew your brother.'

She tripped at the mention of him, but Col righted her. 'Oh. He never mentioned you.' Not really surprising. Kingsley had been private like her.

'They won't get away with it,' Col said. 'We might be hungry, but we're not stupid.'

Blake seemed to have forgotten all the steps of the dance. 'They?'

'The defenders. They can only bend us so far.'

Her feet stilled, and she stared up at him, feeling trapped within his grip. 'Us the merchants?'

He nodded. 'Every person they've hung on that wall is noted up here.' He tapped his head.

She took the opportunity to increase the space between them, but his hand returned to her back, drawing her close once more. 'I've seen you talking to the commander. You learn anything we should know about?'

'We?'

'There's plenty of people like us hurting right now.'

There was the 'us' again.

'He doesn't talk about his work.' Was that what people thought she was doing with Harlan? Getting information? A smarter idea than stupidly falling for the man who had helped hang Kingsley on the wall. 'I'm afraid I'm proving to be a terrible dance partner. Blame the wine.'

She had barely had half a cup.

'Just tell me what you know. Has he said anything about the port wall?'

So that was why he had asked Blake to dance and not Lyndal—information. 'I don't know anything.'

'There are rumours they're going to close it.'

'It's part of a supply chain. They can't close it.'

'They can do whatever they want.' She was done. She tried to pull her hand free, and when he did not let go, instincts took over and she shoved him away with her spare hand. He released her and stepped back with a look of surprise. 'When a lady says she wants to sit down, you don't keep hold of her, you show her to her seat. Do you think you can remember that for next time?'

Col's face reddened. 'Kingsley always said you were a pain in his arse.'

His words cut, but before she had a chance to retaliate, a defender stepped up to them and took Col by the arm.

'Let's go.'

Col's eyes widened. 'What did I do?'

'Harassing this woman. *Move.*'

'Harassing?' Col looked at Blake as the defender began dragging him away.

While he had proven to be a bit of an arse, he did not

deserve to be locked up for it. 'We were just dancing,' she said, following them with a sigh. 'You can let him go.'

'My orders come from Commander Wright. Take it up with him.'

Harlan.

Blake turned, searching for him. She saw him disappear behind a group of women. Jaw set, she followed. Couples swirled in her vision, strangers stopped in front of her, people shouted things when she clipped their shoulders passing by. She dodged, pivoted, and rose up on her toes when she lost sight of him. Head shaking and hands curled into fists, she stopped and turned in a circle. He did not get to thrust himself into her life, interfere whenever it pleased him, and then just stroll off without any explanation.

A black cloak caught her eye, the end of it disappearing behind a nearby house. If he thought he could hide from her, he was wrong. She strode after him, mind racing with all the things she would say. She slipped between the two houses, the noise dulling as she stepped into the shadows. Hands caught her waist, and she inhaled as she was spun around. Harlan's face came into view, mere inches from hers. Her lungs stilled, and her angry words dissolved on her tongue.

They stared at one another. His expression was relaxed while her own was tense. It was almost as if he had expected her to follow him. He took hold of her hand, raising it to shoulder height. His other hand drew her so close her stomach brushed the front of his uniform. His eyes never left hers.

'One dance,' he said, his voice vibrating over her skin.

She should have stepped out of his grasp, told him no. There were few moments when a merchant had that kind of power; it seemed a shame to waste one. But the warmth of his calloused hands through the fabric of her gown held her in place. 'One dance,' she breathed.

He led her in a small, slow circle, keeping time with the music drifting in from the square. It was not a dance she had ever performed before, but her feet followed his. Not one misstep between them.

The commander could dance.

'Did your mother teach you to dance?' Blake asked, suppressing a shiver as his hand moved a few inches up her spine.

'Why do you ask?'

She shrugged. 'I'm having difficulty picturing the warden doing so.'

He exhaled though his nose in place of laughter. 'Yes, my mother taught me. Though it's been a while.'

Her mind was mud, and she struggled to collect words. 'Did you know I would follow you here?'

'I hoped you would.'

She pressed her lips together when his fingers moved once more. 'Is this the kind of dance where you kiss me at the end?'

His eyes searched hers. 'Do you want me to kiss you at the end?'

Once again she was the merchant with her hand out, always in need of something. 'Since when does a defender ask a merchant what they want?'

He drew her even closer, their feet still moving in sync. 'Don't do that.'

'Speak the truth?'

'Reduce this to a defender-merchant moment. I haven't danced with a woman since I was ten.'

She swallowed and her feet stopped. Harlan took one extra step before stopping also.

'Yesterday in the forest,' she said, wishing she could bring more volume to her voice, 'did you want to kiss me?'

He nodded. 'Yes.'

She had no idea how to respond to the confession. Her inexperience was drowning her. 'You could kiss me now if you wanted to.'

A moment stretched out between them before he stepped closer, his knee pushing hers, forcing her to step back. He kept going, as though it were part of the dance, guiding her backwards until her shoulders met the wall of the house. She sucked in a breath. Harlan stretched her arm higher still, pinning her hand to the wall. His chest was pressed against her pounding heart. His fingers trailed up her side, shoulder, and neck, settling along the curve of her jaw.

She waited, heart beating at twice the speed of his. He wet his lips and lowered his mouth to hers. It was hard and soft all at once. The scent of sage and salt enclosed her, and the taste of—

Harlan broke the kiss as the sound of laughter reached them. They both turned their heads as another couple rounded the corner of the house. The pair fell silent when they spotted Blake and the commander and retreated a beat later. Harlan pressed his forehead to Blake's for a moment, his breaths coming faster than before the kiss. She did not know if that was a good thing or a bad thing.

'Return to the festival,' he said. 'I'll follow shortly.'

She blinked. 'Now?'

'Yes, now.' He released her and stepped back. 'We can't be seen leaving together.'

Blake was instantly cold with all that space now between them. Slowly, she straightened and smoothed down her dress, brought a finger to her lips where his had been moments earlier, wiping the edges where the paint might have strayed.

'I'm on duty,' he said as she stepped past.

She shook her head, eyes on the ground. 'It's all right. You… you don't have to say anything else.' Out of the corner of her eye, she saw him run a hand down his face.

'I'm sorry,' he said, just as she stepped into the light.

Blake's eyes closed as the words landed. She did not reply, just continued walking.

CHAPTER 16

They built the fires fifteen feet apart, the flames reaching ten feet high while the smoke painted the sky an eerie shade of grey. The cattle and sheep were brought in from the paddocks and driven between the two fires. The smoke was supposed to protect livestock from disease and promote fertility.

If only it were that simple.

People stood in their social or family groups, clutching cups of ale, watching the chaos of frightened animals as they were herded towards flames by farmers and working dogs. The merchants' bleak expressions spoke volumes as all the meat they could ever imagine was paraded in front of them. Harlan moved between them, ready for trouble, but there was no trouble, only longing. Seeing the livestock all together like that made it look like there was plenty of food to provide for the entire kingdom, but Harlan knew breeding had once again declined year on year.

The commander allowed himself a glance at Blake. She

had an arm around Eda as they stood watching the animals disappear into the smoke. She was angry with him. He could feel it. It was in the set of her mouth and her refusal to look at him.

He *had* kissed her.

Well, he had started to kiss her. Then he had sent her walking. She was probably wondering what she did wrong, when it was him who was in the wrong by starting something they were in no position to finish. Now all he could taste was the blackberry wine from her lips.

He faced forwards as the last sheep ran between the fires, a dog snapping at its back hooves. The crowd grew restless. The reason for that was simple: next up was gameball.

Two teams.

Two chapels.

One inflated pig's bladder.

First team to kick the ball through the chapel door of the other team's borough would be this year's winner.

Men were already stretching and running on the spot as they eyed their competition. The women gravitated to one another, their excitement growing. A handful were preparing to join the game. Unfortunately, Blake and Eda were among them.

Harlan was instantly agitated. How was he supposed to do his job and play bodyguard at the same time?

He made his way over to her, making no effort to hide his annoyance. She was removing her skirt when he stopped in front of her, revealing a more practical one beneath it. He cleared his throat, but she made a point of not looking up.

'Blake,' he said.

She straightened, crossing her arms. 'Yes?'

She was angry all right, but if she thought that gave her licence to play in a game that always ended with at least one death and many more injured, she was insane.

'Yes, *Commander*,' he corrected, matching her level of childishness.

Her eyes narrowed into slits. 'How can I help you, *Commander?*'

'What are you doing?' He kept his voice low so as to not attract attention.

'It's tradition for at least one member of each household to participate.'

'Yes, one *male*.'

She leaned in. 'Well, our family is fresh out of those.'

He drew a calming breath. 'Most of these men are twice your weight.'

'Then perhaps you should have them all arrested and locked up.'

His jaw was working now. She had no fear of him—and it was entirely his fault. 'Now you bring that up? It was obvious you wanted out of that conversation. I took care of it. You should be thanking me.'

'*I* was already taking care of it.'

He rubbed his forehead. 'There will be bloodied noses, broken bones. If you get hurt, they'll just leave you on the side of the road.'

'Have a little faith, defender.'

Harlan looked past to her to her family, who were pretending not to listen. 'Don't say I didn't warn you.'

Prince Borin stepped up onto one of the tables, and

everyone fell silent. He perched a fist on his hip like he was posing for a portrait. Astin waited next to the table, hand on his weapon as he watched the crowd.

'The coming together of Chadorians at this yearly festival is indeed a highlight for all of us. It is an opportunity to open the gates and celebrate as one. It is a time to acknowledge all that we have in common.'

Blake looked down at that.

'Like gameball,' Borin added.

Not one merchant laughed.

Borin clapped his hands, and the man holding the ball threw it to him. He held it up triumphantly. 'Chadora's cherished farmers against our hard-working merchants.'

Cheering broke out among the merchants and farmers, drowning out the polite claps of the nobility across the rope.

'Apparently we're not cherished,' Lyndal whispered to Blake.

'The rules are simple,' Borin continued, 'in that there are no rules. May the best borough win.'

Harlan looked at Blake, opened his mouth to speak, then changed his mind and walked away.

Did he think her a complete fool? She had attended enough gameball events to know how they worked. She knew the risks—and she knew the rewards. Prince Borin was obsessed with the game and would favour the winning borough. King Oswin, on the other hand, was content watching the young noble ladies who always found ways to position themselves in front of him. It was rumoured that the king's wandering eye was one reason his wife, Queen Fayre, remained at Dunnottar Castle in the newly formed kingdom of Toryn. A rumoured Toryn lover was the second reason.

'The game will commence at the wall to ensure the match is a fair one,' the prince said.

Was it fair that the merchants were walking skeletons in comparison to the farmers? Blake thought not. Still, she followed Prince Borin's horse all the way to the gate and got herself into position.

'In honour of Belenus,' Borin said, throwing the ball up high.

The players surged forwards while the spectators stood a sensible distance away. Blake's eyes were on Eda more than the ball, worried she would get trampled in the rush. But her sister slipped expertly between the men, her feet sticking every time she was knocked.

Blake held back and waited to see which way the ball would go. A merchant reached it first, booting it away from the gate. Another was ready, scooping it up and tucking it to his chest as he sprinted back in the direction they had come. A farmer stepped into his path, throwing his shoulder into the man.

Blake heard the snap of bone, and the merchant slammed into the ground, his head splitting open on impact. There was a collective gasp from spectators as they edged forwards for a better view. Nothing like a bit of blood to pique interest.

The farmer tore the ball from the merchant's limp arms and tossed it long to someone waiting by the gate. It never made it though, because Blake was ready. Leaping up, she snatched the ball from the air and landed with soft knees. She had to hurry, because she was no match for the men coming at her.

'Run!' she called to a merchant nearby, tossing it to him as he took off.

He made it about six steps before being tackled. Everyone cheered. The farmer who had taken him down grabbed the ball and ran back in the direction of the gate.

Slam.

A body hit Blake, knocking her sideways. She rolled as she landed so the man who had followed her to the ground could not do any more damage. When she got to her feet, her eyes met Harlan's. He gave her the slightest shake of his head.

Don't go in there, he was saying. He could not follow her.

Of course she had to go in there. Eda would not bow out now.

Eda.

Blake turned just in time to see her sister disappear beneath the archway. 'Eda!'

So much for staying together.

Blake took off at a run after her, but by the time she reached the gate, Eda was already bringing the ball back through.

The crowd cheered her.

'Keep going,' Blake said. 'I'll clear a path.'

The rest of the team were still behind them. Not surprising, given how fast Eda was. With her arms pumping and eyes fixed on the chapel in the distance, she ran her heart out. Blake hitched up her skirt in order to match her speed, cutting off any farmer who neared her sister.

They were halfway to the chapel when some of the other merchants finally caught up.

'Pass it,' Blake called over her shoulder. She had seen men three times her size be mowed down a few yards from the chapel door.

Eda did not pass the ball.

The players opened their hands, calling for it.

'Give it to them!' Blake said.

Eda picked up speed instead, and Blake cursed. The girl always had something to prove.

Blake saw a farmer approach from the side. She slowed to block him, barely remaining on her feet when he hit her.

'Pass it!' she shouted at her sister, partly winded. Her voice barely carried.

Up ahead, farmers stood blocking the chapel door.

'Give me the fucking ball!' one merchant shouted, moving closer to Eda.

With a look of defeat, Eda finally threw the ball to him. The man caught it and positioned himself between the merchants flanking him. Blake and Eda slowed. It was best to remain back in case they lost the ball again.

And they did.

Blake looked over her shoulder to where merchants, including one brave woman, stood ready. The farmers arrived in packs then, creating safe pockets for the ball to pass through.

Sweat beaded on Blake's forehead. It was about to get bloody, and Eda was standing in the middle of it all.

'Move out of the way,' Blake said.

Her sister ignored her.

Blake found herself looking around for Harlan, but neither the spectators nor defenders had caught up to the game yet.

'Eda,' Blake said, turning back to her sister.

Her sister was no longer there. She was now running straight for the man with the ball.

'Eda!' Blake took off after her, deciding that when she finally caught hold of her sister, she was going to tie her to the closest tree.

Slam.

A large man slammed into Blake. The bones in her neck ground together as her head snapped sideways. Her teeth hit so hard she expected them to shatter like glass in her mouth. Her body landed as if someone had dropped her from atop the wall, bones creaking with the force.

Someone shouted her name.

Then darkness swallowed her.

CHAPTER 17

*B*lake woke to a cool hand on her brow. She blinked her eyes open and looked around the room, trying to figure out where she was.

Home.

Home in her bed.

She rolled her head to focus on her mother's worried face. It was not the relief she was expecting to see.

'I'm all right,' Blake croaked, looking past her to where Lyndal stood doing her best impersonation of a smile. There was something strange about it, like if you were to cover the lower half of her face, the top half would tell a completely different story.

She looked around for Eda as the memories from the game returned. Her sister had ignored her warning and gone for the ball. Blake remembered going after her and then… Had she fallen?

'Where's Eda?'

The least her youngest sister could do was sit at her bedside and pretend to be worried.

Blake looked between them, waiting, but her mother looked down and her sister turned away. 'Where is she?' When she tried to sit up, Candace's hand landed on her shoulder.

'You hit your head very hard. The physician said you're to remain in bed.'

She could not remember that part. 'Where's Eda?'

Lyndal brushed invisible lint off her dress. 'She… ah, hasn't returned home yet.'

Blake narrowed her eyes on her sister. 'What does that mean?'

'I mean in the panic of tending to you, we sort of lost track of her.'

'Lost track of her?' Blake propped herself up onto her elbows, shooing away her mother's hands this time. 'She's more than capable of making her way home.'

Lyndal pressed her lips together before replying. 'They've closed the gate, and we think she might still be inside the farming borough.'

Blake shot up at that, regretting it when her head pounded, causing her eyes to close.

'Harlan's looking for her,' Lyndal added.

Blake glanced to the door, trying to gauge the time. 'It's still light out, so that's something.'

Lyndal and Candace exchanged a look.

'What?' Blake asked, not trusting her eyes suddenly.

'It isn't still light,' her mother said. 'It just got light.'

It was the next day.

'It's morning?' Blake asked, panic rising. She looked down at the large graze on her elbow. 'What happened to me?'

'You collided with a farmer the size of a bull,' Lyndal said. 'You're honestly lucky to be alive. You've woken a few times since, but you were never really with us.'

Her mother wrung her hands in her lap. 'Commander Wright carried you here, then stood out in that room until dark.'

'Oh.'

'He just about wore through the floor with his pacing,' Lyndal said.

Blake closed her eyes. 'He was probably waiting around to say, "I told you so."'

'He was the first one to reach you,' Candace said. 'Then the things he did to that poor man.'

'What man?'

'The man who hit you,' Lyndal said. 'Commander Wright beat him until his face was no longer recognisable.'

Blake blinked away the image, then pushed herself to a stand, taking a moment to steady herself and ensure her legs would hold.

'Did you hear what I said?' Candace asked, rising as well. 'The physician especially said—'

'Yes, I heard what he said. Where are my shoes?' She reached for the cloak draped across the end of her bed.

Head shaking, Lyndal left the room. She returned a moment later and helped Blake into them. 'I'm coming with you.'

Blake did not argue.

'I shall wait here in case Eda comes home,' Candace said.

The girls stepped out into the crisp morning air,

Blake's arm through Lyndal's. The streets were quiet as people slept off the festivities. Only a handful of children played gameball as they waited for their parents to rise.

'So what's the plan?' Lyndal asked.

'We go to the royal gate and ask to speak with Commander Wright.'

Lyndal slowed. 'But he's in the farming borough looking for Eda.'

Blake shook her head. 'He would have found her by now.'

'Meaning?'

Blake looked at her sister. 'Meaning something is wrong.'

Two defenders stood leaning against the portcullis when they arrived. They straightened as the girls approached.

'I need to speak with Commander Wright,' Blake said when they were within hearing range. 'It's urgent.'

The taller guard looked her up and down. 'And you are?'

'Blake Suttone. The commander has been looking for my sister, Eda.'

The men exchanged a look.

'You mean the little chicken thief?' the taller one asked.

Blake gave him a confused look. 'Chicken thief?'

He wandered closer, hand resting casually on his weapon. 'Young girl. Same eyes and hair as you. Caught with a chicken stuffed in her dress.'

Blake felt like someone had thrown icy water over her. She gripped Lyndal's arm with her spare hand as she swayed. 'You must be mistaken. Our sister is no thief. Please, just let me speak with Commander Wright.'

'He's busy. Now off you go before we lock you up as well.'

'As well?' Lyndal said.

'Your sister's in the tower with the rest of the trouble-makers from the festival.'

Blake's knees threatened to give way. 'No she's not.' She could not have been arrested.

Lyndal began pulling Blake away from the gate. 'Come. He'll come to the house.'

Blake anchored her feet. 'Is he in there? If you tell him I'm here—'

'Move along, both of you,' the other defender said, taking a few steps in their direction.

Blake felt the sting of tears. 'Please—'

'I said move along!'

'Stand down, defender' came a voice from the other side of the portcullis.

Blake's eyes shot to the gate where Harlan now stood. They watched each other through the latticed wood as the portcullis went up. The expression on his face spoke volumes. She knew whatever came out of his mouth next was really going to test the strength of her legs.

Harlan ducked beneath the rising portcullis. 'I thought the physician said you were to remain in bed,' he said when he reached her.

Blake did not want to waste time talking about the physician. 'Do you know where she is?'

He exhaled and gestured away from the guards. When

Blake did not move, he took her arm. 'I've got her,' he told Lyndal.

Only then did she trust herself to walk, knowing he would not let her fall. Lyndal followed, her footsteps controlled and even.

'She's in the tower,' Harlan said when they were out of earshot of the other defenders.

Blake's foot rolled, but he kept a firm hold of her.

'She was caught trying to smuggle a hen into the borough,' he added.

Blake glanced at Lyndal, whose face had turned a ghostly white.

'Will they let her go?' Lyndal asked.

'She'll stay there until she's sentenced.'

Blake tried to breathe in, but it was as if her lungs had forgotten their one job. She pulled out of Harlan's grip to see if that would help. It did not. When she tried to walk back to the gate, her legs folded, and her knees hit the stone.

'Leave her,' Lyndal said when Harlan went to move. 'Just give her a second.'

Blake pressed her fingers into the icy stone as she waited for the body tingles to stop. She tried not to be sick. Harlan rested his hands on his hips and stared at the road.

No one moved or spoke for the longest time.

Once Blake had a handle on her queasiness, she sat back on her heels. 'The sentence for livestock theft is hanging.' She closed her eyes as nausea rolled over her once more.

'She's still a child,' Lyndal said. The words came out on a laugh. 'They won't hang a fifteen-year-old girl over a chicken.'

Blake swallowed against the tightness in her throat. 'Can we get her out?'

Harlan stepped up and lifted Blake to her feet. She could feel the warmth of his hands through her cloak. Tears prickled her eyes as she looked up at him, but she did not let them escape.

'I'm working on it,' he said, 'but the crime happened in another borough. I have no jurisdiction there.'

She was not one to beg, but her eyes pleaded with him. 'Your father is warden.'

'It doesn't matter. His loyalty is to the crown. His attachment is to the law, not me. That's why he's warden.'

A sob tore through Blake, one she had been holding in since her brother's death judging by the force of it. The thought of Eda locked up in that tower with no way to communicate with the guards was too much.

Harlan pulled her to him, pressing her head to his chest. She had not thought him capable of comfort, but he continued to prove her wrong.

'Lyndal,' he said, 'I need you to take your sister home.'

Blake did not want to go home. She wanted to stay where she was, with his heartbeat drowning out her thoughts. 'Please.' She did not even know what she was asking for.

'Go with Lyndal,' he said, firmer that time.

Blake knew Lyndal's despair ran as deep as her own. That was what made her stand and go with her sister. She saw her own misery reflected when she finally turned to Lyndal.

'Let's go.' Her sister's voice barely carried the two feet between them. The rock of their family was cracking down the middle.

Blake took the hand extended to her and walked away.

CHAPTER 18

Harlan went by the tower to make sure Eda had received food and water before going to see his father. Shapur had just finished training and was standing over a basin of steaming water with a towel wrapped around his hips.

'I can always tell when you want something. You have this wounded puppy look,' Shapur said. 'Out with it, then.'

Harlan stepped into the room, hating asking his father for anything. 'I spent the night in the farming borough trying to locate a young merchant girl.'

Shapur snatched up his shirt and began dressing. 'How old?'

'Fifteen.'

Shapur continued dressing. 'A young woman. Did she get locked in by accident?'

Harlan drew a breath before proceeding. 'Locked in the tower, actually. Only found that out this morning. Tried to steal a chicken, I believe.'

'Serious crime in these times.' Shapur eyed him. 'What is your interest in the matter?'

'I know her.'

'So?'

'So, I would like to see her released to her family.'

Shapur turned to face him properly. 'This another one of your good deeds? I thought you wanted the respect of your men.'

'I do.'

'Yet you show up at my private quarters, with that bleeding heart of yours, asking for favours.'

The towel dropped, and Harlan looked away while his father tugged on his trousers. 'You left your post yesterday.'

He had expected that to come up. 'A merchant woman was hurt. I helped the family get her home.'

'Yes, I heard you gallantly carried her the entire way in your arms. This girl in the tower connected to that woman by any chance?'

His father knew everything that happened within Chadora's walls.

'They're sisters.'

'Ah.' Shapur belted his trousers. 'The crime happened in the farming borough. You have no jurisdiction there.'

'Which is why I'm here. I never ask for favours. I never really ask for anything.'

'But now you are asking me to overstep.'

Harlan did not reply.

'These the same sisters you helped in the square? The same girl you pulled from the wall and let walk free?'

Harlan exhaled. His father really did miss nothing. 'Yes.'

'I see.' Shapur took a few steps towards him. 'I cannot help you, and you should not be asking me to.' When Harlan went to speak, the warden raised a hand. 'However, Lord Thomas Welche of Cardelle Manor is the girls' uncle, is he not?'

Harlan should not have been surprised that he knew that. 'Yes, but they're not exactly close.'

Shapur crossed his arms. 'Even so, I am certain Lord Thomas will be eager to preserve his family's reputation.'

He was right. Thomas would never speak up for them, but he might speak up to keep his own family name out of the mud. 'I'm supposed to be on duty soon.'

Shapur turned away. 'You have two hours, Commander. I suggest you get a fast horse.'

'Back so soon,' Lord Thomas said, leaning back in his chair and staring hard at the commander. 'Is this about my niece Eda?'

So he had heard. 'Yes.'

Thomas nodded thoughtfully. 'You know, I always thought Blake would be the one to drag my family down —even lower than her mother did. The girls' father was a decent sort of man for a merchant, but he had no proper control over his children. Do not even get me started on Candace. She has had her head in the clouds for as long as I can remember. It is the children who have run that household since their father's passing. The only one with any hope is Lyndal.'

Harlan was forced to listen to him go on and on about the inadequacies of the family. He only let him continue in the small hope it would build rapport between them. Eventually he intervened.

'I believe if you sit down with the farmer and the commander of the borough, you might prevent this going any further.' Harlan cleared his throat. 'Perhaps Eda's inability to communicate—'

'She is a common thief with no respect for anyone,' Thomas said, cutting him off. 'She knew exactly what she was doing. Even her lack of speech is a choice, one I am certain she continues because it angers me.'

Harlan's eyebrows lifted slightly. 'I'm sure that's not the case.'

'I would not put it past her. I see the way she looks at me. Loyal to her mother with no regard for her future. A spinster in the making.'

Harlan had barely spoken yet was already losing his audience. 'Unfortunately, your family connection is well known throughout Chadora, which makes it difficult to ignore.'

Lord Thomas tapped a finger on the arm of his chair. 'Which is why I will step in and see about getting her sentence reduced. Her death would be memorable, whereas a little discipline will be forgotten in a week.'

Now he was getting somewhere. 'Why not sweep the entire ordeal under the rug and save yourself any embarrassment at all?'

Thomas leaned forwards. 'Because we cannot have a young girl of thirteen —'

'Fifteen.'

Thomas waved the correction away as though it were unimportant. 'A child on the brink of womanhood *thieving*. It always seems to fall on me to teach those children life lessons. That is what comes from poor mothering, I suppose.'

'I think time spent in the tower is lesson enough for a young woman,' Harlan said.

'My own daughter perhaps, but not that one. She has a rather thick skin.'

Harlan shifted his weight to his other foot. 'No one wants to see a young lady harmed over a chicken.'

'My wife and daughter would be most upset if she were hung. They have an enormous amount of empathy for those less fortunate than us. The Suttone family serve as a constant reminder to my daughter that things could be far worse. Every young woman needs reminding sometimes of how bad things can get if one veers off course.' He leaned back again. 'Leave it with me. I think a public apology and a healthy display of remorse should satisfy. She might think twice next time before taking what does not belong to her.' Thomas picked up his quill and dipped it into the pot of ink, preparing to begin a letter.

Harlan did not move. 'Eda is mute, my lord. Won't that make an apology rather difficult?'

Thomas looked up from his letter. 'As I said earlier, the girl is selectively mute. She spoke just fine as a child. In fact, before the wall was built, I used to have a headache every time the family left our manor. Eda used to talk incessantly. She will speak if given no choice on the matter.' He returned to his letter. 'I appreciate you coming by, Commander. I assume you can see yourself to the door?'

Harlan nodded. 'Yes, I can see myself out.'

'It's not something she can just turn on and off,' Blake said, pacing the length of the veranda.

Harlan had expected her to say that. He remained on the street, watching her in the dark. He had just come off duty.

'It'll come back when the grief eases its grip on her,' she continued. 'I know it will.'

He looked off down the street. 'How's your head?'

She stopped walking. 'My head? My head is fine.' She stepped down onto the street. 'When was the last time you slept?'

His eyes met hers. 'Why do you ask?'

'You were looking for my sister last night, were with my uncle this morning, then on duty this afternoon.'

'And I will sleep tonight.'

She held his gaze. 'You look exhausted.'

For a man who did not have a tender bone in his body, he had the strangest impulse to reach up and touch her hair.

'What's going on in that mind of yours?' Blake asked, leaning her back against the veranda post. The lantern light seeping through the edges of the shuttered window gave the illusion of colour in her face.

His thoughts were not for her ears. 'Your sister will be brought to the square in the morning. Father Garsea will hear her confession and apology.'

'Father Garsea?'

'You know him?'

She nodded. 'Friend of my uncle.' There was disappointment in her voice. 'And if she doesn't speak?'

'Your uncle seemed confident she would.'

'Oh, and he's never wrong about anything.' She tried to smile but failed. 'Will you tell her how much we need this from her?'

The duck had wandered out and was loitering at Blake's feet. He watched it preen non-existent feathers.

'Yes. I'll tell her.' His gaze travelled up from the duck. 'I need a favour from you as well.'

'Anything.' The word came out as a whisper.

It made him look up. 'Leave your weapons at home tomorrow. No matter what happens, know that nothing you say or do in the moment will alter what takes place. Interference only puts you and the rest of your family at risk. Trust me on that.'

She searched his eyes. 'You're making me very nervous, Commander.'

'No weapons. No emotional outbursts or heroic displays. You swallow down your feelings and you let them out later. Understand?'

'I understand.'

'I'm not messing around here. This isn't like gameball,

where you just do as you please with no thought as to the consequences.'

'I understand,' she said again. 'No weapons. No emotional displays. No heroics.'

Satisfied, he stepped back. 'Make sure the rest of your family gets the message too.'

'I will.' When he turned to leave, she said, 'I heard you carried me home.' She swallowed. 'And that you waited while the physician tended me.'

He said nothing.

'I hope to repay you the same kindness one day,' she said.

There was that impulse again. 'You plan on carrying me five miles?'

'Five?' She scrunched up her nose. 'Farther than I thought. Perhaps I'll send for a horse, or just supervise your men doing the heavy lifting.'

'I'm sure they would love that.'

She suppressed a smile.

'No weapons. No emotional displays. No heroics,' he said.

'I'll be on my best behaviour.'

He pointed a finger in her direction. 'No matter what.'

She held up her hands. 'No matter what.'

CHAPTER 19

The following morning, Harlan waited by the enclosed cart filled with the men and women being sentenced that day. He straightened when Eda stepped out into daylight, her face stained with tears. Dark circles enclosed her eyes.

'You all right?' he asked as she took a seat inside the cart.

Eda stared at him from the bench seat, the same wary expression on her face that Blake usually wore.

He moved closer. 'They want to see your remorse. They'll pardon you, but you're going to have to use that voice of yours. You hear me?'

Eda's eyes welled up in response. She opened her mouth as if to speak, but nothing came out. Her chin dropped, and her eyes closed.

A whip cracked, and the cart lurched forward.

'Do it for your sisters,' Harlan said, walking alongside the cart. 'A few words—for them.'

She looked up at him, signed something with her hands.

'I don't understand,' he said.

Her hands fell to her lap.

'Blake needs this.' He stopped walking and watched the cart pull away, dread coiling around his spine. When he turned back, he spotted his father standing out front of the mess hall, watching him. Shapur nodded once before striding off.

With a heavy breath, Harlan headed for the gate.

They positioned themselves towards the front of the crowded square, Blake's arm linked through her mother's as she watched the gate. She wanted to be close enough to see her sister properly but not so close as to draw attention.

'For goodness' sake,' her mother said, pulling her arm free. 'You are holding so tightly I can no longer feel my hand.'

'Sorry.'

'It'll be all right,' Lyndal assured everyone. 'Eda will do it. She has to.'

Blake wished she had Lyndal's optimism in that moment.

The sound of the portcullis rising made them all look in that direction. They watched as six defenders walked through ahead of the cart, carrying those to be sentenced. The crowd fell silent as they approached.

'She's in the cart, towards the back,' Lyndal said.

Blake swallowed when her eyes met Eda's. All confidence left her. She forced a smile, a nod of encouragement.

Please.

Prince Borin was next to ride through, surrounded by defenders as though he were riding into battle instead of a crowd of peasants. The warden followed closely behind. Harlan's father. All sharp lines and a scowl so deep she questioned whether the man ever wore any other expression. She wondered whether Harlan would be just like him in a few years. There were times she could sense a smile bubbling below the surface. She was desperate to see it, to discover those things that made him forget his own seriousness.

Harlan was last to enter the borough, his eyes snapping straight to Blake as though he had known where she would be all along. He did not acknowledge her, just let his gaze linger a moment before facing forwards again.

They lowered the gate.

No long speech from the king, then. First piece of good news in some time. Of course, Prince Borin stepped up in his absence, saying a few token words before they brought the prisoners in front of the crowd.

Blake could not have torn her eyes from Eda if she had tried.

One at a time, the prisoners' crimes and sentences were read aloud. Their guilt had already been decided. This was not a trial—it was a reminder for everyone watching.

This was what happened when you did not follow the rules.

They sentenced three thieves and a rapist before Eda. Within minutes, three men were hanging from the wall, and a woman had lost her hand.

Blood sprayed the ground a few feet in front of Eda, who was shaking despite her best efforts not to. Her age would work in her favour, and it would be the only time in her life her gender would be an advantage. Plus, she had Harlan onside.

Commander of merchants.

Defender of walls.

Protector of little sisters.

'It'll be all right,' Blake said to her mother, who was trembling between them.

Lyndal rubbed Candace's hand, practically blue from the icy temperature. 'Of course it will.'

The crowd fell silent as the defender reading the sentences stepped in front of Eda.

'Eda Suttone is charged with theft of livestock,' he began. 'Father Garsea has travelled here from the nobility borough to hear her confession.'

They made it sound like he had travelled from lands afar instead of through one gate.

Everyone turned to watch the man dressed in orange robes make his way over to Eda. The priest was in his late fifties and had one of those faces that gravitated down.

'I love how they call it "theft of livestock",' Lyndal whispered to Blake. 'Like she rounded up a herd and drove it through the gate. It was one chicken.'

Blake could not look away from Eda as the priest turned to face the crowd.

'God is merciful,' he began.

Another speech.

'A young woman prepared to throw herself at the mercy of Belenus is a child worthy of his forgiveness. Let us hear what this young woman has to say.'

A tight breath came from Candace. Blake took her hand again and squeezed, daring a look at Harlan, who stood to one side. He did not look back at her.

'What say you to Father Garsea?' the defender holding the scroll prompted.

The Suttone women held their breath, and Blake's pleading eyes burned at her sister.

Eda's mouth opened, then closed. Her eyes went to the crowd, looking between the three of them. Blake gave her a nod of encouragement.

Speak.

Eda looked back at Father Garsea, eyes welling up.

'Oh God,' Candace breathed out, covering her mouth.

Eda could not do it.

'You must forgive the girl's silence, Father,' Harlan said, stepping forwards. 'She's mute.'

Father Garsea stared long and hard at Eda. 'I was told there is nothing physically wrong with her.' He paused. 'It seems the devil has hold of her tongue—and now she does his work.'

Blake stepped forwards, but one look from Harlan pinned her in place. She had made him a promise. Her breathing sped up as her mother cried behind her.

'Perhaps she could write her apology,' Harlan suggested.

'I doubt very much a note will release her from the devil's clutch,' the priest replied, turning to face the warden. 'I suggest ten lashes to relieve her poor soul.'

Lashes.

'No weapons. No emotional displays. No heroics.'

Blake's shoulders fell a few inches, her mother's crying growing louder.

'Get it done,' Shapur said to the defenders nearby.

Harlan ran a hand down his face. 'Her inability to speak has nothing to do with the devil.'

Father Garsea waved him off. 'We wish her freed from the hand of Satan.' He turned back to the crowd. 'Let us pray for this young woman.'

Blake thought she was going to be sick.

'No,' Candace cried behind her.

Blake turned. 'Keep her quiet.'

Lyndal nodded and pulled her mother to her before squeezing her eyes closed.

It was Blake who watched as her sister's hands were tied to a post near the wall, Blake who flinched as Eda's dress was torn open at the back.

'I'll do it,' Harlan said, walking up to the defender holding the whip and snatching it from his hands.

Blake flinched again. *What is he doing?*

'Let the man do his job,' Shapur said, glaring at Harlan.

Harlan stared at the defender still standing in his way and looking confused. *'Move.'*

He was supposed to intervene, to protect, not join in the torture. As he turned his back to the crowd, to Blake, she told herself he had a plan. But then he was standing behind Eda, flicking the whip.

Blake's hand shook violently as adrenaline coursed

through her. Her eyes met Eda's for a moment, and she wanted to scream, run to her, cut the throat of anyone who dared stand between them.

'Interference only puts you and the rest of your family at risk.'

Harlan's words from the night before stopped her.

'Trust me.'

Did she trust him?

Eda continued to watch Blake with a broken expression. Swallowing, Blake raised her hands and signed, *Stand tall and strong, warrior.*

Eda's tears stopped, and she gritted her teeth.

'God, be merciful,' the priest said, addressing the crowd. 'Because of your constant love. Because of your great mercy. Strip away her sins.'

Eda closed her eyes, and when she opened them again, she stared straight ahead with a stoic expression. Harlan looked down at Eda's delicate back, skin, and ribs, like every other merchant. No meat or fat to protect her from the harsh leather. He would not dare lift a whip to her sister. Blake was sure of it. He had asked her to trust him, to leave her weapon at home, to remain silent.

And she had obeyed.

Up went the whip. There was a slight pause before it came down on Eda's back.

Blake flinched as if the leather had hit her own skin. Her eyes widened in disbelief. The betrayal she felt threatened to drown her. When Harlan raised the whip again, she could barely believe it.

'Stop,' she said, maybe out loud or maybe in her head.

Lyndal was crying behind her now.

'May she recognise the devil in her,' the priest said. 'May she cast him out and be conscious of her sins.'

Harlan lifted the whip and struck Eda again.

'Stop!' Blake shouted, stepping forwards.

Someone grabbed her arm, and she turned to see Birtle.

'You'll only make it worse,' he whispered.

How much worse could it get?

Birtle pulled her to him, the way a father did, shielding her view. She could still hear the whip though. Harlan seemed to have found a rhythm. Or perhaps he was trying to block out the priest's voice.

'She has sinned against you!' Father Garsea went on. 'You are right in judging her!'

The people of Chadora may have been driven by desperation to worship Belenus, but their Catholic roots were ever present.

Blake covered her ears, and they roared in protest.

'Fill her mind with wisdom.' The priest's voice was a distant hum. 'Let her be free once more.'

Silence.

Blake's hands fell away from her ears. She looked up just as Harlan threw the whip *at* the defender he had taken it from. He went to untie Eda, who was shivering but dry-eyed.

'Is she not supposed to remain tied up there until the setting of the sun?' Prince Borin asked from atop his horse, looking to the warden for confirmation.

'His Highness is right,' Shapur said, moving forward.

Harlan whirled around. 'It's done. Now you want her left here to freeze?'

All the muscles in Shapur's face tightened.

Harlan drew a slow breath. 'I'd like permission to release her to her family.'

Shapur nodded once before stepping back.

'Move!' Blake shouted at the people standing in her way.

She met Harlan's eyes as she stepped up to Eda. His were full of remorse, and hers were pure fire.

'I've got you,' Blake said, tugging the torn dress up and covering Eda's icy shoulders. She pulled the now loosened piece of rope off her sister's wrists just as Eda's legs gave out. Blake caught her. When Harlan stepped forwards to help, she pulled Eda away from him.

'You've done enough.' Then, leaning in so only he would hear, Blake added, 'Come near my sister with a whip again and I will wrap it around your neck and watch the life drain from your eyes. Your father can hang me from any wall he chooses.' She gathered Eda closer. 'I won't stand silent next time, *Commander*.'

CHAPTER 20

The physician squinted down at the red lines striping Eda's back. He said nothing for the longest time as he poked and prodded. Blake's stomach was twisted into knots as she waited for him to speak.

Harlan had done that.

She still could not quite believe it. Her mood kept swinging between gutted and blind rage.

Adjusting Eda's dress, the physician rose from the bed and turned to Candace. 'Never seen anything like it. The skin is completely intact. I doubt there will be a scar to show for it.'

'What?' Blake said, opening her sister's dress and looking for herself. While the ten marks were confronting at a glance, the physician was right. They were welts, not wounds.

'The defender who did this clearly was not trying to leave a lasting impression.' The physician chuckled lightly to himself. 'That is a lashing for show if I have ever seen one.' He picked up his bag. 'Not suggesting it did not hurt.' He patted Eda's head. 'But it could have been far worse.' He stepped past Candace towards the door. 'A bowl of soup and a good night's sleep should do the trick.'

Candace brought a hand to her chest as she followed him to the door, her relief palpable. 'I appreciate you coming.'

Lyndal was staring at Blake from where she sat on the bed opposite. Blake knew exactly what she was thinking.

'Don't say it. It doesn't change anything. He still whipped her.'

Lyndal raised her hands in innocence. 'I didn't say a word.' There was a pause. 'However—'

'Here we go,' Blake mumbled, straightening Eda's dress.

'He volunteered in order to protect her from any actual harm, and he risked a lot doing that—including your feelings for him.'

'If by feelings you mean a relentless urge to break his nose…' Blake crouched beside her sister, stroking her hair back from her face. 'What the hell were you thinking taking that chicken?'

Lyndal laughed. 'Now you're angry at *her*?'

'Well, this is all her fault.'

Eda brought a hand up to sign. *I'm sorry. I saw an opportunity—*

'While I was unconscious? We were supposed to stay together. Not only do you refuse to talk, but you refuse to listen.'

Lyndal rose. 'How about we let her rest?'

'She's lucky she's already hurt, or I might have been

tempted to belt her myself,' Blake said as Lyndal dragged her from the room.

Once outside, Lyndal turned to Blake. 'You're angry. I get it. But I think Eda deserves some reprieve, don't you?'

Blake closed her eyes. 'I shouldn't have said that.' When she went to re-enter the bedroom, Lyndal caught her arm.

'Give yourself some time to calm down and her some time to reflect. You know I love that girl, but she's out of control at times. You're right, but that doesn't mean you have to point it out when she's already feeling miserable.' She walked over to stir the soup. 'Perhaps it's time you stopped indulging her wild side.'

'I don't indulge her.'

Lyndal cast a knowing glance in her direction as she ladled watery soup into a bowl. 'I'm not arguing with you today, not after hearing the things you said to Commander Wright.'

Blake swallowed. 'You heard that?'

'I'd be surprised if the warden himself didn't hear it.' She stepped past Blake, heading for the bedroom. 'The last thing I'll say about all this is that you have a very small window of opportunity to make things right with the commander before you lose the respect of the only man brave enough to care for you.'

Blake crossed her arms. 'If he's that easily deterred, then he's not that brave.'

'Easily deterred? You threatened to strangle him.'

Blake followed her into the bedroom. 'He *whipped* her. Now I'm supposed to thank him?'

'You're supposed to show some understanding,' Lyndal

replied. She turned and handed the bowl to Blake. 'Feed your sister. I need to check on Mother.'

Blake looked down at Eda, who was now sitting up, watching her.

You wouldn't wake up, Eda signed. *And it was my fault.* She brushed a tear away. *I thought if I could make you some real soup...* Her hands fell to her lap.

With a resigned sigh, Blake sat on the bed and fed her sister the soup.

～

'What the hell was that?' Shapur growled as he burst into the room Harlan shared with Astin.

Thankfully, Astin was still on duty.

Harlan had been waiting for his father to show up and reprimand him. He rose from his cot. Whatever his father was about to say and do, he deserved all of it.

'Did that whip even touch her?' Shapur asked, stepping up to him. 'Because from where I was standing, your efforts looked half-arsed. Then you just send her home to relax for the afternoon?'

'She was supposed to be pardoned.'

'She was supposed to beg for forgiveness.'

Harlan rubbed one eye. 'She's mute.'

'And all that to impress some merchant girl you have no future with.'

There was some truth in that. Not the trying to impress Blake part but the no future with her bit. He knew only too well what happened to men of noble birth who married below them. It tore families apart and destroyed lives.

It killed people.

'And the disrespect you showed Prince Borin did not go unnoticed,' Shapur went on. 'What the hell were you thinking addressing him with that tone?'

He had not been thinking. He had been reacting. He had been failing.

'You behaved like a fucking child out there. Weak. And in front of your own men and every merchant watching on. I thought I had trained it out of you. I blame your mother for this.'

That was the end of Harlan's patience. 'What?'

'She always indulged that part of you. It is the reason we ended up with a three-legged hunting dog of no use instead of putting the animal out of its misery.'

Harlan felt his blood rise. 'That dog was her only companion until her death. Would you have stripped her of that too if I had not intervened?'

Shapur pointed a finger in his face. 'Do not speak of things you do not understand!'

'It's almost as if you *wanted* her to die alone.'

It was too far.

Shapur grabbed him by the shirt, his other hand raised and balled into a tight fist. Harlan's hands remained at his sides while his father played at the edges of restraint. If the man wanted to punch him to feel better, Harlan would not stop him.

Shapur released him with a shove, and the two men stared at one another.

'Your insubordination has consequences,' Shapur said,

reining in his temper. 'You will remain at the barracks and oversee training of new recruits until I can trust you to command that borough. Am I understood?'

Harlan felt only relief. 'Yes.' At least he could avoid Blake's deathly glare for a while. Not that he could hold it against her. He had volunteered to whip her sister. No man who raised his hand and said, 'Let me do it instead,' was ever going to come off looking good. The distance would give him a chance to get his head together and his feelings for Blake under control. But it also meant there would be no one around to protect her from herself—and despite common sense, he wanted to be that someone.

'I suggest you train early tomorrow,' Shapur said, heading for the door. 'It is going to be a long day for you.'

CHAPTER 21

Harlan walked the line of recruits, looking each one hard in the eye as they readied for their first excursion outside the walls. Or rather *over* the walls. None of them looked at their feet, so that was progress.

He stopped in front of Roul Thornton, a well-muscled lad Shapur had caught fighting for money in the port. For whatever reason, the warden had taken a shining to him, suggesting he do something useful with those bruised fists of his.

'Ready to go over the wall, defender?' Harlan asked him.

'Yes, Commander.'

Roul claimed to be twenty, but Harlan guessed he was closer to eighteen. 'Good.' He continued walking. 'Over the wall, down the cliff face, then you must navigate your way to the port borough, where you'll exit the water via the beach.'

'Isn't that quite far?' asked one of the younger boys.

Harlan turned to look at him. 'That a problem?'

He had been in the training role for less than two weeks, and every man before him had been a defender for around the same amount of time. They were as fresh as they came.

The defender who had asked the question shook his head. 'No, Commander.'

'I'll be there to hold your hand if you need it,' Harlan said. The other men snickered. 'I have extra training for the final two out of the water, so make sure that's not you.' He jogged off in the direction of the wall. 'Let's move out!'

The young defenders sprinted after him, some overtaking him in their eagerness to be first over the wall. They would be spent by the time they reached the water—assuming they made it that far. Harlan said nothing because it was the best way for them to learn.

Set a pace. Stick to it.

They reached the ropes along the wall and climbed. Skin and muscle burned. It was the kind of pain that quickly became addictive.

One recruit beat Harlan to the top, his face set with determination. He was halfway down the rope on the other side when he prepared to jump the rest of the way. Harlan thought about warning him, but he was not the young man's father. There was a cry of pain as feet hit the uneven ground below. The recruit grabbed his ankle as he rolled onto his back, cursing.

Harlan shook his head and looked up at the defender guarding the wall. 'We're going to need the medic down here.'

The defender gave him a knowing grin before walking off to fetch him.

Harlan clapped the injured recruit on the shoulder as he passed. 'Just sit tight.'

The cloud was low and thick, completely covering the water below. Waves slammed into the rocks. The recruits hesitated—except Roul, who lowered himself over the edge without speaking a word.

Harlan followed.

Some of the men would freeze with fear halfway down. Some would change their minds and try to climb back up. Some would tire and slow.

At least one would fall.

Harlan took his usual route, a path he had perfected over the years. It was not the most direct way down, but it was the safest—and ultimately the quickest. His feet were first to hit the rocks at the bottom. Roul's were second.

Harlan took a moment to study the water patterns. 'The safest way through will be to swim farther out away from the rocks.' He knew many would struggle to navigate their way through them.

Yet another lesson to take away.

Harlan dove beneath the waves coming at him, eyes open and one arm extended in case of rocks. When he was out past the white water, he rolled onto his back for a moment to rest, floating until his heart slowed enough to begin the long swim. The recruits popped up around him, waiting to see what he would do next.

He began to swim, and the others followed closely.

They were about halfway to the port beach when something snagged Harlan's vision. He stopped to tread water, peering through the mist. It was likely one recruit trying to be clever and overtake him out of sight.

'That a fishing boat?' Roul asked behind him. 'Should we warn them we're in the water so they don't accidentally hit us?'

Harlan narrowed his eyes. 'Chadorian fisherman know better than to venture this close to the rocks.' All it took was one rogue wave and the vessel would be smashed to pieces.

Harlan glimpsed the stem post of a boat through the fog and stilled. It was not a fishing boat. He turned to the men, signalling for them to be quiet. He pointed to his eyes, then behind him.

'Sea warriors?' Roul whispered.

Harlan nodded and indicated for everyone to be alert and listening.

The other men were looking between themselves with slightly panicked expressions when a boat cut through the fog nearby.

Shit.

Harlan signalled to his men to go underwater and prayed they would do it without splashing about the place. He slipped below the surface and watched the boat pass overhead. Warriors stood at the front of the boat, bows in hand, looking down their arrows at the surrounding water. Harlan knew those defending the walls would not see them through the fog, and he was acutely aware that the men in the water with him were unarmed and stood no chance of surviving if they were spotted.

When he could hold his breath no longer, he broke

the surface, quiet and careful. The recruits were not so quiet, gasping in greedy lungfuls of air as they stared after the boat. Harlan silenced them with a glance. Sensing something behind him, he looked over his shoulder and spotted another boat heading towards them.

Down, he signalled.

The men drew a large breath before slipping under the surface once more. It was not just one boat passing this time but four, heading to the cliff face, where Harlan had planned to send the recruits. He gestured for everyone to remain calm as a fifth boat passed overhead. They all desperately needed air, but if they swam up prematurely, a boat or an arrow would hit them.

When no more boats followed, they swam up, silent this time.

'You think there's more of them?' one recruit asked, wide-eyed.

Harlan suspected they were all along the coastline. They had been scoping out the place for months.

The sea lifted them high before plunging them down again. Some of the less fit men were struggling. Harlan checked his surroundings before speaking.

'Thornton, you're with me. The rest of you will swim fifty yards west, then make your way inland. Stay as close to the rocks as possible without killing yourselves. I want eyes in all directions.'

'What are you going to do?' asked one defender.

Harlan glanced at Roul. 'We're going to the port. It's the easiest entry point, so that's where most of their boats will be.' He waited for Roul to object to the suicide mission, but the recruit just listened. 'Stay together,' he told the others.

He watched the men until they were out of sight.

'What's the plan, Commander?' Roul asked, sounding surprisingly confident as he surveyed their surroundings.

Harlan wiped water from his face. 'Stay invisible and don't drown.'

Harlan and Roul treaded water, watching the long boats lined up fifty yards from the shore. The warriors did a final check of their weapons before slipping into the sea. It was not that the two defenders were too late to stop them, but they had no means to do so. They were sitting ducks with one dagger between them, while the warriors had swords, daggers, shields, bows, and arrows slung over their backs. They moved like wolves, stealthy and silent.

Harlan tried to come up with a viable plan. Yes, he could do plenty of harm with one knife, but not from that distance and not with those odds.

One warrior remained in each boat, keeping guard. They were younger and likely less experienced than the men going ashore. That would work in his favour.

'They after food?' Roul whispered.

'Everyone's after food.' Harlan signalled for Roul to follow him, pointing to the closest boat where the young warrior was standing at the front of the vessel, looking towards the shore.

Roul nodded.

Slipping below the surface, the men swam slowly over

to it, deep enough to not be visible from above. They tucked themselves against the hull of the boat as they surfaced, taking a moment to catch their breath.

Carefully, Harlan lifted his shirt and drew his dagger, listening for movement above. All was silent—and time was running out. Clamping the knife between his teeth, he reached for the side of the boat and nodded to Roul. The defender sank down and took hold of his foot, hoisting him into the air. Harlan burst from the water and fell into the boat. The startled warrior turned, eyes widening when he saw the defender. He reached for his sword, but much too late. Harlan's mouth opened, and the blade dropped into his hand. A beat later, the knife flew through the air, lodging itself in the warrior's chest. Harlan was on his feet a moment later, stealing the man's sword before kicking him overboard. He knew he had only a few seconds before the warriors in the other boats realised what was happening.

Roul hauled himself into the vessel just as they released the first arrow.

'Stay down,' Harlan said as another arrow whistled overhead. He crawled to the back of the boat where he had seen a bow, thanking God for the supply of weapons at his disposal.

The sea warriors had come prepared for war.

Harlan tossed another bow to Roul, along with a quiver of arrows.

'I've seen you shoot,' Harlan said. 'You're a decent shot. But let's see how you go under pressure.'

A nod was his only response.

Harlan readied himself. The only way they were

getting out of there alive was with steady minds and hands.

He held two fingers up to Roul, and then they both shot up. Roul hit the warrior manning the second boat while Harlan took out the man in the third. They ducked when arrows were returned, flattening themselves against the bottom of the boat. Roul looked to Harlan for further orders. The commander held four fingers up, then got to his feet, shooting at the fifth boat. He reloaded his bow and took out the warrior in the last boat who was shooting at them. As quickly as he could load the arrows, Harlan released them at any man still moving.

'Eyes on the vessels,' he told Roul, bringing his fingers to his mouth and whistling as loudly as he could. The whistle was one used to alert defenders to intruders in the absence of a horn, but it was drowned out by the screams of women from the port.

'Safe to say they've made it ashore,' Roul said.

Harlan cursed. 'Grab whatever weapons you can swim with. We need to alert the warden to the boats along the east wall. This could be a diversion.'

He tried not to think about Blake, trapped in the merchant borough with nowhere to run or hide. He had been trying not to think about her for the past two weeks, but the tenacious little merchant had well and truly lodged herself under his skin.

'How do you plan to get ashore with at least a hundred warriors standing in our way?' Roul asked.

Harlan had another look around the boat, and some cage fire arrows tucked away at the stern of the ship caught his eye. He could tell what they were because the arrowheads were packed tightly with tow. He picked one up and sniffed it. They had soaked it in mutton fat. 'We need to make sure their attention is diverted elsewhere.' He picked up the nearby flint, handed an arrow to the recruit, then pulled his knife out, striking it with the dagger.

'Isn't fire wasted on wet enemies?' Roul asked.

'We're not shooting them at the warriors,' Harlan replied. 'We're going to make sure the bastards can't leave.'

Finally, a spark turned to a flame, lighting up the tip of the arrow. Harlan used it to set fire to the other arrows, then loaded it into his bow, aiming at the boat farthest from them. 'You'll need to compensate for the extra weight.'

With a nod, Roul loaded his own bow and started shooting. They kept firing until there was just one arrow left. Some went out and others smouldered, eventually growing to flames.

'Let's go,' Harlan said once all the other vessels were burning. He swung his legs over the edge and dropped the last arrow into the boat behind him.

The weapons made it a bit more difficult to swim, but Harlan knew by Roul's determined face that he had chosen his accomplice well.

'Wait,' Harlan said when their feet finally hit the sandy bottom. He looked up and down the beach, where men fought all the way from the rocks to the dock. Some warriors had made it to the wall. If they made it into the merchant borough, the defenders would be in trouble.

Hiss.

'Shit,' Roul said as an arrow whistled overhead.

Hiss, hiss, hiss.

They turned to see new boats pulling into the bay, replacing the ones now burning.

'This isn't good,' Harlan said.

Hiss.

An arrow sliced through the water so close to Harlan he felt it brush his leg.

'Head for the rocks at the end of the beach,' he said as he loaded his bow. He had to raise his voice to compete with the sound of battle. 'I'll cover you.'

Roul shook his head. 'Shouldn't I stay with you?'

Hiss.

Pain exploded in Harlan's shoulder, sending fire sensation along his arm. He cursed and dropped his bow.

Roul's eyes widened. 'Oh shit.'

Hiss.

An arrow struck Harlan's arm. 'Fuck,' he grunted, the sea turning red around him.

'We need to get you out of the water,' Roul said, grabbing hold of him.

Harlan pulled free of his grip. 'You need to find the warden and tell him about the boats along the east wall.'

'I will—'

'Now. Leave me here. Go.'

Roul flinched when an arrow hit the water beside them.

'You've got a sword and two working arms,' Harlan said. 'If you make yourself known to our men, they'll get you into the merchant borough.' When Roul hesitated, he added, 'That's an order, Thornton.'

'I can't leave you here to bleed out.'

'You can if I order you to.' When Roul still did not move, Harlan said, 'I will kill you myself if you don't start following orders.'

Roul hesitated, then turned towards the beach.

'And for the love of God, draw your sword,' Harlan said. 'You're going to need it.'

Pounding on the shop door made Blake jump in her chair. She looked over at her mother just as a defender flew past the window.

'Lock all doors and remain inside,' he shouted.

Lyndal rushed into the room. 'What on earth is going on?'

The three women met at the window and looked down the street. They could hear fighting.

'Who's brawling?' Lyndal asked, sticking her head out of the window to see better.

Blake walked over to the door and tugged it open, ignoring the defender's instructions. Eda caught the bell as she entered the room. Blake gave her an impressed look before stepping outside.

'He told us to stay inside and lock the door,' Candace called after her.

Blake stilled and listened. It was not the sound of a few men fighting but hundreds.

'Who are they fighting?' Lyndal asked from the safety of the doorway.

Before Blake could respond, Thea emerged from her house, clutching her husband's sword. Her eyes met Blake's. 'Sea warriors,' she said with a resigned breath before stepping off the veranda.

'Where are you going?' Blake called out.

'Birtle's in the tavern,' Thea said over her shoulder. 'He'll be first to die if I don't do something.'

The sight of a middle-aged woman strolling off to face sea warriors was a reminder that merchant women did what they needed to in order to survive and protect the people they love. They did not have the luxury of hiding. They were soldiers in their own way. Not out of choice but necessity.

Eda exited the shop, bow in hand and quiver on her back, and stepped down onto the street.

Blake walked to the end of the veranda. 'Where on earth do you think you're going?'

'Eda!' Candace called from the door. 'Get back here at once.'

Eda slung her bow over her shoulder and walked backwards, signing, *Better to stop them at the gate than wait for them to reach us.*

'That is what the defenders are doing,' Candace replied.

'I'm locking the door,' Lyndal said, throwing her hands up. 'With or without you inside.'

Blake closed her eyes. 'Sea warriors don't care about locks.' Eda was right. If they reached the shops, it would be too late. 'Wait. I'm coming with you.'

Her mother's mouth fell open. '*What?*'

Blake went inside and fetched her knife and Kingsley's bow. Her mother and Lyndal followed her from room to room.

'What exactly is your plan?' Lyndal asked, picking up Garlic before the duck could run out the front door.

'The defenders will fight out in the open,' Blake said. 'If we hide in the trees, we can pick off the strays that slip past them.'

'Have you lost your mind?' Candace said. 'They will shoot you from the trees.'

'They'll assume the arrows are coming from atop the wall.' Blake stepped outside. 'Lock the door behind me.'

'You said sea warriors don't care about locks,' Lyndal yelled, crossing her arms.

She had said that.

When Blake did not reply, Lyndal added, 'If you return here with an arrow through your eye, don't expect me to help you.'

Blake rolled her eyes. 'Love you too.'

Eda was waiting in the middle of the road, her bow already loaded.

'Don't look so pleased with yourself,' Blake said, reaching back for an arrow. 'We still have to return alive.' She looked up at the frenzy of seagulls overhead. The port must have been a war zone if the birds were braving the merchant borough. It was such a rare occurrence she actually thought about shooting one from the sky to collect on the way home for dinner, but the fighting up ahead drew her attention. A small group of defenders was trying to contain the influx of warriors forcing their way into the borough.

The women slowed, watching the combat for a moment. What sea warriors lacked in discipline, they made up for in strength and brutality. Her father had once described them as efficient fighters. She had not really understood what that meant until now.

Blake lifted her bow and took aim at the closest warrior, hitting him between the ribs. It was not enough to kill him but enough to enable the defender fighting him to finish the job.

'Behind the shops,' Blake said, gesturing towards the shadows. 'We can reach the trees from there without being seen.'

As they walked, they heard the gate that separated the royal borough from the port going up. Reinforcements had arrived. There were shouts as defenders spilled out onto the beach.

The girls stopped at the edge of the shadows, watching as the defenders struggled to maintain the line along the gap in the wall.

The sound of a horse approaching made the girls shrink back. It was Harlan's father.

'Hold that line,' the warden shouted. 'Reinforcements are on their way.'

When a warrior broke through, Shapur rode forwards to deal with the man himself, slicing his throat open.

'Warden!' came a voice from the other side of the line.

Shapur swung his horse around to look. 'Let him through! He's one of ours!'

Another warrior burst through the line, axe swinging

at one defender and a shield at another. Blake took aim and released, hitting him through the neck. Defenders ascended on the man like wolves. The warden glanced in Blake's direction, then turned his attention back to the dripping man standing in front of him.

'What is it?' Shapur asked.

The sand-covered defender stood to attention, trying to catch his breath. 'Commander Wright's still in the water.'

'What?' Shapur looked past him to the port.

'Training drill, sir. He was shot trying to come ashore. He told me to deliver the message that there are boats along the east wall. We have more men out there as well.'

'Alive?'

'They were when we parted ways. There are six boats burning offshore, but more arrived.'

Blake's lungs froze in place.

Injured?

Harlan could not be injured. He was… impenetrable.

Shapur turned to the defender standing next to his horse. 'Send more archers to the east wall and tell them to look out for defenders.'

Another warrior broke through the line and charged towards the horse. Eda took aim and shot him. Shapur looked in their direction again.

'Show yourself,' he shouted.

Blake gestured for Eda to remain where she was, then drew a breath before stepping into view.

Shapur walked his horse towards her, stopping ten feet away. 'Merchants should be inside. What are you doing out here?'

She gave the only answer she could think of. 'Helping, sir.'

His eyes fell to her bow. 'You want to help?'

She nodded.

'Then go home and lock your door as instructed.' He turned his horse, swinging his bloodied sword as he trotted away.

Blake returned to Eda and slumped against the wall. Her chest was heavy and her mind racing. She looked over as more defenders arrived, forming a line behind the fighting men as they prepared to enter the port.

Blake pushed off the wall.

Don't go, Eda signed, reading her.

'I need you to stay here,' Blake said. 'Do you under-stand? I can't be worried about you.'

Eda shook her head.

'He's in the water, injured.'

He's likely dead already, Eda signed, her eyebrows drawn together in a hard line.

Blake blinked away the image. That was not a thought she would entertain. Harlan had given of himself far more than a man in his position should. And all she had given him in return were headaches.

Of course she had to find him. 'I'm sorry.'

Eda sighed and looked away. Then she reached behind her and pulled a handful of arrows from her quiver, handing them to Blake. *Don't fight*, she signed. *Run. No one can catch you when you run.*

Blake brought her forehead to her sister's, eyes closing for a second. 'Thank you.'

I'll make sure you get to the wall. After that, you're on your own.

Blake kissed her sister's head and turned away before she could change her mind. She checked her knife, stretched out her neck, and loaded her bow.

Eda adjusted her feet, raised her bow, then nodded to signal she was ready.

Drawing a breath, Blake took off at a sprint, mapping out a path as she neared the wall. As the new arrivals marched through the gaps created for them, she slipped seamlessly into the steady stream of men, ignoring the shouts that followed her.

'Merchants are to remain inside!' Shapur shouted.

Blake looked back at him and saw his eyes narrowed at her. She faced forwards again, heart pounding as she was carried into the port.

The men dispersed and joined in the fighting, and Blake's feet froze. She took in the sight before her. Blood and chaos. That was all she could see. Men fighting, men screaming on the ground. Men with missing arms and faces painted with blood. The noise shook the ground beneath her. And the smell. Metallic and overpowering, filling her nose and throat. Her stomach lurched involuntarily. She had seen death up close before, but not like this.

Her eyes went to the taverns, where women were being dragged outside, screaming, and thrown to the ground. That was the moment she realised she was in as much danger as any defender around her.

She needed to move.

She needed to *run*.

Off she went, though slower than normal because of the bow. Warriors glanced in her direction as she flew past. Then one stepped into her path, forcing her to pull up. Panicked, she lifted her bow and aimed it at his face. The man raised his shield, smacking the arrow aside before continuing towards her. Reaching back, she loaded her bow and tried again. The warrior hit it away with his axe this time.

Her hands slackened around the bow.

Turning back was no longer an option, and even if it was, she was not sure she would choose it. Not when Harlan was in the water.

She reloaded her bow and aimed it at the warrior's face. When he raised his shield this time, she dropped her aim and shot him in the leg.

The man roared.

It was enough to get past him. She was off running again, arms pumping and eyes focused on the sea. She feared what she would see if she turned her head in either direction.

Her feet finally hit the water, but she did not slow down. Slinging her bow over her head, she dove into the frigid sea, emerging twenty feet from shore with a gasp. Her lungs closed in protest as she breathed in thick smoke. Boats burned in the distance. She coughed and looked around.

'Harlan.'

The beach was long, the ocean big, and her voice was carried away by the smoke blowing in from the west. She swam away from it as Harlan would have done if he were alive. She turned in the water, glancing back at the beach where defenders now outnumbered the warriors. And yet they were no better off for it.

'Harlan,' she called.

Her mind raced, and her heart pounded in her ears. She stilled when she saw something floating in the distance. A body with multiple arrows protruding from it. A wave rolled the man towards the rocks at the end of the beach. She swam towards him, fighting the current the entire way.

'Harlan!'

She could tell by the fletching that the arrows belonged to the sea warriors. The closer she got, the faster she swam. When she reached him, she caught him by the arm and rolled him over, taking in bloody water as she did so.

At first she did not think it was Harlan. Her eyes searched the pale face and blue lips that did not resemble the powerful defender she knew. But the longer she stared at him, the more familiar he became.

'Harlan,' she breathed. She resisted the urge to shake him and checked for a pulse instead. Her hands were shaking too much, her fingers too frozen to tell if he were alive or dead. Dead, surely. There were five arrows in him.

Five.

He coughed, and hope soared in Blake. She pulled his icy body closer to her, breathing against his cheek. 'You're all right. I've got you.'

His eyes opened for a moment, and he coughed again, this time bringing up water.

'Good,' she said. 'Get it out. You're alive, and you're going to stay alive. You hear me?'

She knew she needed to get him out of the water if he stood any chance of surviving his injuries.

Get him warm.

Stop the bleeding.

She wrapped an arm around him and positioned herself beneath him, careful to avoid the arrow in his shoulder. How many arrow wounds could a person survive? She had no idea. There were another two in his arm, one in his side, and one in his back. That one scared her the most.

She studied his face as she began swimming towards the rocks at the end of the beach. His eyes were shut, his mouth slack. 'Open your eyes. You need to stay awake.'

His eyes fluttered open, looking straight up at the sky. He coughed again, more seawater exiting his body.

'Good,' she said. 'That's good. Almost there.'

The weight of him kept pushing her head under the water. She was not the strongest swimmer, which did not help matters. She kicked her legs as hard as she could until finally her feet touched the bottom.

Relief pulsed through her.

She stopped to catch her breath, coughing up water of her own. The rocks would provide some cover if she could make it there without being spotted. Thankfully, the warriors were being kept occupied by the defenders. She gripped Harlan under the arms and guided him towards the shore, taking advantage of any small wave that propelled him closer to the beach. 'Still awake?'

No reply. His eyes were closed again.

'Eyes open, Commander. That's an order.'

They opened, meeting hers this time. 'You're crazy.' His voice was barely recognisable.

She attempted to drag him from the water. 'That's hardly news.' At least he was talking. That had to be a good sign. 'You've always known I'm crazy,' she panted.

His head rolled to one side. 'I'm too heavy.'

Her eyes closed for a moment. 'Let me worry about that.'

He was lodged in the sand with water washing over his face. He continued to cough it up. When Blake lost her grip and fell backwards, he said, 'Stop.'

She got straight back up on her feet and took hold of him again. 'I need to get you out of the water.' She saw him wince as the arrow lodged in his back snagged on the sand. She rolled him onto his good side, heaving with the effort. A sob sat in her throat alongside defeat and exhaustion that threatened to spill over at any moment.

Anchoring her feet, she used all her remaining strength to drag him onto the sand. When only his feet remained in the water, she collapsed beside him, panting and dripping. Then she was kneeling next to him with no idea what to do next. There were no blankets to warm him with, no physician to remove the arrows. She knew better than to touch them.

Her eyes travelled up to his face. His eyes were closed again. She shook him. 'I didn't do all that for nothing. Open your eyes. Look at me.'

He did, but gone was the light from them. The golden rim had faded to a dull brown.

'The fighting will stop soon,' she said. 'Then you'll get the help you need.'

He blinked. 'Are we winning?'

Blake looked out at the beach. They were still fighting, and she could not tell.

A shadow passed over them, and she drew Harlan's sword as she shot to her feet. A warrior with braided hair came to a stop in front of them. He held a longsword in one hand and a round wooden shield in the other. His shoulders were three times the width of Blake. It seemed the widespread famine had skipped this particular tribe.

'What do we have here?' the man said, looking from Blake to Harlan.

Blake stepped over Harlan so she stood between them, sword pointed at the man's chest. Her hand was not as steady as she would have liked. 'If you leave now, I'll let you live.'

Amusement filled his eyes as he stared down at the sword. 'I don't think that belongs to you.'

It was the first time Blake noticed that the sword was not Harlan's. She tried not to let the surprise show on her face. She was not particularly good with any sword, but if she had pulled her knife out, the man would have laughed at her.

'I don't think it belongs to you either,' she said, lifting her chin. 'This is an English sword used by cavalrymen in the ninth century. Double-edged blade. Decorated pommel. Valuable—and likely stolen.'

She might not have been a strong swordsman, but she knew a lot about them. Her father had taught her all about weapons—just not how to kill a warrior with one.

A low chuckle came from the man. 'I think I'm going to quite enjoy taking it from you.'

'Blake,' Harlan said behind her, sounding worse by the second. 'Run.'

She dared a glance behind her and saw his eyes were closed, and he was shivering. She could tell by his colour they did not have long.

Lunging forwards, she went for the warrior, hoping to catch him off guard. He lifted his shield and blocked the blow with minimal effort. She tried again, then again, only to be met with laughter.

He was literally laughing at her.

'I was really hoping you might have *some* skill.' He stepped up to her so quickly she tripped over Harlan in her effort to get away from him. Harlan did not even open his eyes as she landed. One positive was that the warrior was focused only on her. He stepped over Harlan as she scurried back.

A mistake.

Harlan's hand shot up, grabbing him by the ankle. His eyes blinked open as he twisted the warrior's leg, causing the man to lose balance and fall.

That was Blake's opportunity—probably her only one.

She leapt up and drove the sword into the man's leg. He arched his back and roared through gritted teeth before swinging his shield and smashing it into Blake's head.

The sword fell from her hand.

Her ear rang, the pitch like claws on her brain. She held her ear as she staggered sideways, determined not to fall. She watched the warrior get to his feet, despite his injury. Lifting his good leg, he lined his foot up with Harlan's head, his face tight with pain and anger.

Blake reached into her soggy pocket and pulled her knife from its sheath. She threw it as fast and hard as she could, striking the man in the neck. His hands flew up to his throat, his foot returning to the ground.

During the exchange, Harlan had also drawn a knife. He reached one trembling hand up and sliced the back of the warrior's knee. Blood poured freely down the leg, pooling on the sand.

Even in the throes of death, he managed to protect her.

The sea warrior's eyes went as wide as plates. The sword and shield dropped onto the sand, and his knees gave out. Seeing that he was about to fall forwards onto Harlan, Blake ran at him, kicking the man in the chest so he tipped backwards. He slammed into the sand before going still.

Blake dropped down next to Harlan and pressed her forehead to his. 'Stay with me. Please.'

Harlan had stopped shivering, and she had no idea if that was a good or bad sign. She wanted to scream for someone to help him, but she knew he did not have it in him to fight off any more warriors. She just hoped the number of defenders now pouring onto the beach meant it would soon be over.

'Hide,' Harlan whispered, turning his head closer to hers.

'I'm not leaving you.'

'I can't protect you.' His voice was barely audible.

She pressed her eyes shut. 'I don't need you to protect me. I just need you to live.'

The sound of boots pounding on the sand made her

reach for the sword. Determination filled her. She would keep him alive, no matter the cost.

With a huge inhale, she rose to her feet again, gripping the weapon with both hands as she turned. There stood Harlan's father and four defenders. Two of the men held a wicker stretcher. Shapur looked down at the sword in her hands.

'I suggest you lower that weapon, merchant.'

It took her a moment to realise this was the help she had been waiting for. Exhaling, she stepped back from Harlan and dropped the sword on the ground. They laid the stretcher down and, counting to three, carefully lifted Harlan onto it.

'Watch the one in his back,' Blake said.

Shapur frowned in place of a response. 'Take him straight to the infirmary,' he instructed the men.

They carried him off up the beach. Blake ran after the stretcher, relieved to see the defenders had created a safe path all the way to the royal borough gate. As they walked, she watched him struggling to breathe and prayed they were not too late. Shapur's eyes were on her the entire time—she could feel them—but he never told her to leave.

Her boots squelched as she jogged to keep up, stepping over dead bodies and injured men. The air was rank. Not even the ocean could disguise the smell of death. She glanced over her shoulder and saw the entire beach was painted with blood. The water lapping the sand was a vibrant shade of red.

Her head snapped forwards, and she found Harlan looking at her. His fingers twitched. She no longer cared what Shapur thought. She took his icy hand in her warm one and squeezed as much life into it as she could manage.

'You're so cold,' she said.

'You're bleeding,' he croaked.

Blake reached up and touched the side of her face, fingering the sticky blood that ran from her hairline to her neck. She had not even realised. At least the ringing in her ear had eased.

'This is as far as you go,' Shapur said when they reached the gate. 'A defender will see you back to the borough.'

Blake nodded and looked down at Harlan, whose eyes were closed again. Bending, she said into his ear, 'I need you to survive.'

He did not move.

She stepped back from the stretcher when they carried him off. The sooner they got him to the infirmary, the sooner they would treat him. Shapur glanced at Blake as he passed her but did not say a word.

'Let's go,' the defender said to Blake.

Blake watched Harlan through the portcullis as it was lowered. When he was out of sight, she turned away and followed the defender back through the battleground.

CHAPTER 23

They were not so much dreams as hallucinations.

Harlan was face down in the water, too weak to swim, to roll over. Too weak to draw breath. He could not feel his arms or legs. Then he felt too much all at once. Water roared in his ears, and blood stained his vision.

Open sea in all directions.

Waves with no pattern.

The first time he was able to anchor himself in reality might have been hours later or months. He had no sense of time. He was not sure what had actually occurred and what his mind had conjured up. The first thing he did was check that he had both arms and legs.

His arms were bandaged but still attached. The effort of wriggling his toes was enormous, but it confirmed both legs were still there.

'Is he actually awake this time?' Astin said from somewhere in the room. 'Because we've had a few false starts.'

Harlan turned his head, searching for his friend through blurry vision.

'Give him a moment' came the familiar voice of the physician. He swirled into Harlan's view and picked up his hand, pressing two fingers to his wrist. 'Much better. Happy with the colour of those wounds too.'

Harlan wanted to speak, but it felt like someone had glued his tongue to the roof of his mouth while he slept.

Astin stepped into view. 'Blink if your brain is still working.'

Harlan could not have laughed if he wanted to.

'Fletcher has visited you every day for the past two weeks,' the physician said, tutting. 'He is all bravado now that you are awake.'

Harlan dislodged his tongue and swallowed. 'Did he weep?' His voice was scratchy and raw.

'I wept from laughter when you pissed the bed,' Astin said. 'Does that count?'

The physician moved between them, head shaking. 'Let us get you sitting up, shall we? We need to get some water and broth into you. See if we cannot have you walking by the end of the week.'

Astin stepped up to fluff his pillow for comedic value while the physician helped Harlan up. It took a moment for the dizziness to settle.

'I shall be back shortly,' the physician said before leaving the room.

Astin filled a cup with water and brought it to Harlan's mouth without making a joke.

'Has it really been weeks?' Harlan asked, leaning his head back.

Astin nodded and dragged a chair next to the bed. 'No one thought you would live. The blood loss alone should have killed you. Then there were the injuries, including damage to one of your lungs. And the physician couldn't get your temperature back up for the longest time.' He leaned his elbows on his knees. 'Your father's been dropping in too, in case you're wondering. Hasn't said much, but he keeps showing up.'

Harlan let his eyes close. 'Did the recruits make it?'

'They hid like frightened dogs, so they may wish they hadn't when you're back on your feet.'

'And Thornton?'

'Who?'

Harlan's eyes opened. 'He was with me in the water. I sent him ashore.'

'Ah.' Astin nodded. 'Yes. Quite the hero. Though a true hero would have carried you up the beach on his back while fighting.'

Harlan started to laugh, but the pain stopped him. He wanted to ask about Blake but did not know how to bring her up.

'And then there was the other hero of the moment,' Astin said, saving him the trouble. 'The young merchant woman who ran into battle armed with a longbow and a handful of arrows. She fought off warriors three times her size and searched an ocean on the slight chance you were still alive.' He waited for Harlan to react.

Harlan could not make jokes or dismiss it like he normally would. 'Is she all right?'

'Who?'

Harlan gave him a tired look.

'She's fine. She keeps coming to the gate.'

Blake's bloodied and tear-stained face flashed in his mind. 'What does she want?'

'What do you think? To know if you're alive.' Astin leaned back in his chair. 'The men guarding that gate are sick of the sight of her.'

Harlan imagined her showing up every day, determined as always, only to be sent away each time. 'Have you seen her?'

'Once. She was a bit banged up. Blended in with the defenders though. Wish I'd been there on the beach. Not that it wasn't fun seeing Borin shit his pants atop the wall.' He was quiet for a moment. 'I'm surprised by Blake's apparent devotion to you, given everything that happened with the tunnels and her brother.'

Harlan picked up the cup of water and tried to drink it without help. It spilled down his chest. 'We've never really spoken about it.'

Astin's eyebrows rose. 'But she knows?'

Harlan brought the cup to his lips again and took a large gulp, welcoming the cool sensation on his throat. 'She knows who I am.'

'But does she know what you did?'

Harlan stared hard at the drink. 'I met her for the first time that day. She was standing next to one of the shafts when the tunnels collapsed.'

'"Collapsed" makes it sound like an accident.'

'I should go see her.'

Astin rose from the chair and placed a hand on Harlan's good shoulder. 'While I acknowledge you're doing much better with the cup, you should take things one drink at a time. I'll update her. Do you have a message you want me to pass along?'

There were a hundred things he wanted to say. He took a moment to think about what she may need to hear from him. 'Tell her I survived.'

Astin waited for more. 'That's it? No promise of unbridled passion beneath the stars?'

'When was the last time you saw stars?'

'Fair point. I'll tell her you survived, recite a quick sonnet, then be on my way.'

'You don't know any sonnets.'

Astin ran into the physician carrying a steaming bowl of broth at the door. 'He'll need you to feed it to him. He didn't do so great with the water.'

Blake had just collected money from a customer when she spotted Fletcher walking down the street towards the shop. Their eyes met through the open window, and Blake's hands instantly went clammy. She knew he was Harlan's closest friend. If there were bad news, he would be the one to deliver it. If Harlan had recovered, he would have come in person—she was sure of it.

'Is that Prince Borin's bodyguard?' Lyndal asked, walking up beside her.

'Yes.'

They watched as he stepped up onto the veranda, but he did not enter the shop.

'What's he doing?' Lyndal whispered.

Blake swallowed. 'Waiting to speak to me, I think.'

'Oh.' Lyndal placed a hand on her sister's back. 'Want me to come with you?'

Blake shook her head and went out front, closing the door behind her. 'Defender.'

Astin gave a small bow of the head. 'You're looking better than the last time I saw you.'

The right side of Blake's face had been twice its normal size and every colour of the rainbow. She had also had stitches along her hairline.

'Don't look so worried,' Astin said, reading her face. 'It's good news. I have a message from Commander Wright.'

Her heart sped up. 'Is he awake? Talking?'

'Both, actually.'

Blake let out a breath and held her stomach. 'Thank Belenus.'

Astin studied her for a moment. 'I just came from his bedside, where he's sitting up for the first time in weeks.'

Blake was hanging off his every word, not caring that the defender could see her heart beating through her dress. 'So much time had passed, I thought…' She could not finish that sentence. 'You said you had a message for me.'

Astin nodded. 'Yes. He said to tell you he survived. I suspect you have something to do with that.' He glanced in the direction of the window where Lyndal stood with her arms crossed and a wary expression. 'There was some pretty poetry he wanted me to recite on his behalf also, but I'm afraid I wouldn't do it justice.'

Blake breathed out a laugh, releasing some of the tension she was holding.

Astin's eyebrows rose. 'Why are you laughing?'

'Because Commander Wright is a man of action, not words. I'm pleased at least one of you has a sense of humour though.'

A smile flickered on Astin's face. 'I guess you do know him. I'm sure he'll be by when he's back on his feet.'

Blake bit her lip as she looked out to the road. 'Are the defenders getting meat in the barracks at the moment?'

His brow creased. 'Some. Why do you ask?'

Her eyes returned to him. 'Because he'll need good healing foods for a while.'

The door creaked behind Blake, and Garlic waddled out, stopping at her feet and eyeing the defender.

'Our guard duck, Garlic,' Blake said by way of explanation. She bent to pick him up, stroking the new feathers that had finally come through.

'Should I avoid eye contact with it?' Astin asked.

'Probably best.' Blake placed him on the ground and shooed him back inside.

'Would you like me to pass a message along to the patient? Is there anything you need?'

She already had what she needed—he was awake. What to say to the man who had consumed her every thought since that day on the beach? 'Tell him to focus on getting better.' She hesitated. 'Also, tell him I looked well, strong. Maybe tell him I got eggs from the market and whatever else he needs to hear.'

Astin stared at her for the longest time. 'And are any of those things true?'

There had been eggs at the market, but none they could afford. The few vegetables they had, Blake was secretly putting in her sisters' bowls before going out into the forest to eat insects. She glanced away. 'Can you just tell him anyway?'

Astin nodded slowly. 'Good day, merchant.'

'Defender.'

CHAPTER 24

It was another two weeks before Harlan was walking. His wounds had closed, and his strength had returned, though he tired quickly.

'At least another two weeks before you can resume training,' the physician told him. 'I suggest you take up reading.'

Harlan spent the next week trying to gain back some of the weight he had lost and taking walks outdoors to get some colour back in his face. While he was desperate to lay eyes on Blake, he was determined not to show up looking sickly.

During the second week, he grew restless and told his father he had to get out of the barracks for a few days.

'And go where?' Shapur asked.

Harlan brushed a finger down his nose. 'I thought I might go to the house, see what kind of condition it's in.'

Shapur squinted and looked away. 'Suit yourself.'

The house had sat abandoned for years. Occasionally his father would call in to ensure there were no squatters living there, but he never lingered. Harlan had avoided the place completely. It held too many memories.

His mother humming in the garden.

His father lifting him onto his horse.

His parents dancing outside together when they thought he was asleep.

His father smiling when his mother entered the room.

His father *smiling*.

When had he stopped? When had she?

Nothing like a near-death experience to bring childhood memories to the surface. Usually he would just shove them back down again, but he had another idea this time.

'I want you back training in seven days,' Shapur said before walking off.

Harlan requested a horse and filled a saddlebag with supplies. He rode out into the merchant borough, stopping his horse in the square and looking off down the street where Blake lived. Drawing a breath, he nudged his horse forwards.

People moved off the road as he approached, watching him pass by. He was halfway down the street when he spotted Blake playing gameball with a group of boys half her age. She looked thinner than he remembered but no less beautiful. She kicked the ball to another boy and shoved her opponent lightly, laughing when he shoved her back.

Blake truly was a sight when she laughed.

Her hair was out, a dark mess going in all directions as she ran and played. She kept tucking it behind her ears, and it kept springing free every time she moved.

It seemed a shame to ruin the moment, so he just stood there watching, drinking in every visual of her. He thought about turning away and leaving her be, but a part of him knew there was no turning away from her anymore. He was greedy for more, wanting to feel her eyes on him.

A few breathless steps and a kick of the ball later, he got his wish. Blake's arms went up as the ball sailed through a target marked out in charred wood. Some of the boys groaned and kicked the ground while others roared with excitement and ran circles around Blake. She reached out to ruffle their hair and caught sight of Harlan. The smile froze on her face.

'Let's play again,' one boy said.

She looked back at him. 'Maybe later.'

Harlan pushed his horse into a walk, meeting her half-way. His eyes fell to the hem of her skirt, which was covered in mud. 'Merchant,' he said by way of greeting.

Blake looked him over. 'Commander.' She reached out to pet his horse. 'Good to see you up and about.'

He looked past her to where Candace Suttone was now chasing the duck down the street. 'I thought you would have eaten that thing by now.'

Blake turned to see what he was talking about, then, spotting the rogue duck, ran into its path. She snatched it up off the ground and pressed it to her chest. 'We need to fatten him up first.'

'You're attached,' he said matter-of-factly.

She frowned up at him before turning to her out-of-breath mother.

'He just took off after you,' Candace said, taking the

bird from her daughter. She straightened when she recognised Harlan. 'Commander Wright. I was not aware you were back on duty here in the borough.'

'I'm not,' he said. 'I still have another week of leave.'

Blake glanced at the bag attached to the back of the saddle. 'Are you going somewhere?'

'Yes, actually. I'm going home.'

'To the nobility borough?' Candace asked, confused.

He nodded and watched the boys play for a moment before saying, 'I was wondering if you could spare your daughter for the day?'

Light filled Blake's eyes. 'I've been little use to them so far today. You don't mind, do you, Mother?'

Candace stared wide-eyed at her. 'Well…'

Harlan removed his foot from the stirrup and took hold of Blake's arm, pulling her up behind him. 'She's safe with me, I assure you.'

Lyndal and Eda had wandered out onto the veranda and stood watching them.

'I was under the impression that your family home is currently unoccupied,' Candace said.

Harlan nodded. 'That's right.'

'It's just for the day, Mother,' Blake said.

Harlan had the right to remove any merchant he pleased from the borough without explanation, yet he waited for permission from this woman.

'You really will take care of her?' Candace said, looking him straight in the eye.

'I really will.'

~

Blake had jumped on the back of that horse with no hesitation, and now they were going to his family home in the nobility borough. Too bad she was dressed like a beggar. She tried not to think too much about the details and simply enjoy the rare prospect of adventure—and a very much alive commander seated in the saddle in front of her.

'Hold on to me,' he had said as they moved down the street, away from her fretting mother.

There were many layers of fabric separating her hands from his body, but the contact still made her stomach dance. She grew nervous as they approached the portcullis. It was the first time in years she had been near the gate and not had soldiers firing questions at her or shoving her back. She gripped Harlan a little tighter as they passed the guards.

Harlan must have noticed because he looked over his shoulder at her. 'You all right?'

'Yes.'

He faced forwards again. 'You're safe with me.'

She knew that in theory, but years of conditioning was not a simple thing to switch off.

They rode in silence beneath tall trees alive with birds.

Birds.

The large houses they passed had stables and well-kept gardens with roaming chickens. When they reached the first hill, they turned off the main road, and Harlan pointed to a modest house enclosed by a crumbling stone wall.

'That's it.'

The gate sat ajar. One hinge had come away, which

meant it leaned at an angle. The horse slipped easily through the gap with no need to dismount. Harlan did not bother closing it.

The green lawn was mostly weeds, which now covered the path that surrounded the charming two-storey house. To the right was a collection of bare trees that had likely once been an orchard. It had been years since trees produced fruit in Chadora. The bees had disappeared like the food.

The air smelled of rosemary and mint, which had taken over the small garden under the window. Blake made a mental note to take some home with her.

Despite the obvious neglect, there was so much beauty. She could picture leaves on the vines that climbed the west wall, blossoms on the fruit trees, and flowers in the bare garden down the side.

'Not quite as I remember it,' Harlan said, pulling up the horse.

Blake's gaze travelled up the wall to the moss-covered roof. 'How long since you've been here?'

'Too long.' He nudged the horse into a walk and navigated the overgrown path to the stables out back.

She dismounted first, looking around at what was once the mounting yard. She rubbed the ground with the toe of her boot and found stone beneath the dirt and debris.

Harlan led the horse to one of the stalls, and while he was unsaddling it, Blake followed the sound of running water. The ground behind the stables sloped down to a creek that widened farther down. Returning to the stable for a pail, she went to fetch water for the horse. As she was coming back up the hill, she found him watching her.

'I didn't bring you here to work,' he said.

She smiled at the ground. 'I don't mind, really.'

He took the pail from her when she reached him.

'Are you allowed to carry heavy things?' she asked, looking up at him.

He nodded and kept watching her. 'I haven't thanked you yet.'

'For what?'

'For saving my life.'

She was having difficulty forming coherent thoughts with him standing that close, but she did not move away. 'I hope you didn't bring me all the way here just to thank me?'

His expression turned serious. 'I suppose I missed you.'

Blake pressed her hands to her sides. 'I really didn't think you were going to survive. I felt so sick when they carried you off.'

His eyes searched hers. 'You told me to survive, so I survived.' He stepped back. 'Let me give this to the horse. Then we'll brave a look inside.'

He placed the water in the horse's stall and fetched the saddlebag he had brought with him. Everything she was feeling as she watched him seemed to be lodged in her throat.

His eyes narrowed on her when he returned. 'What's wrong?'

Everything. 'Nothing.' She forced a smile.

The light bleeding in around the curtains cast eerie patterns over the furnishings in the main room. Some were covered with linen, the rest covered in dust. There was a fireplace built into the wall at the far end, to their left a small library, and to their right a kitchen.

'Upstairs are the bedchambers,' Harlan said, placing the bag down and going to open the curtains. Dust swirled around him. He moved to the fireplace and began stacking it with wood.

Blake walked around the room pulling linen off the furniture. She sank down into one of the fat cushioned chairs and looked around. 'These are comfortable enough to sleep in.'

He turned to face her, sitting back on his heels. 'Well, don't fall asleep for too long. I don't think your mother will appreciate me returning you home late.'

She studied him a moment. 'Tell me why you brought me here.'

Picking up a dusty flint, he struck it until he got a flame. 'I already told you.'

'You wanted to thank me?'

'Yes.'

'And you missed me?'

A nod. 'Yes.'

She watched him work for a moment. 'You know, it's too late to shut me out now. I'm already here.'

He turned his head, the now lit fire reflecting in his liquid eyes. She felt the intensity of his stare in her stomach.

'You ran through a battlefield and fought off a warrior you could never beat alone,' he said. 'All for the small chance that I would survive my injuries. That's why you're here.'

She let his words settle. 'So it's gratitude.'

'It's more than gratitude.'

She swallowed. 'How much more?'

He ran a hand down his face. 'You could have died that day.'

'You would never let that happen.'

His eyebrows pinched. 'You shouldn't have that kind of faith in me. You should be smarter than that.' He looked around the room. 'I want you to promise me you'll never be that reckless again.'

'I can't promise that.'

He made his way over to her on his knees and took hold of her face. 'You're infuriating.'

Her legs opened as though luring him closer of their own accord. 'Are you going to kiss me again?'

'Do you want me to kiss you again?'

'Yes.' *More than anything.* She slid to the edge of the chair, but still he hesitated. 'What's the matter?'

He pushed her hair back, studying the small red scar along her hairline. 'I can see your heart thudding through your dress. Are you scared?'

She shook her head. 'That's not fear.'

He lifted her from the chair and sank back on his heels, lowering her to his lap. 'We need to be safe.'

She swallowed. 'Haven't you noticed the distinct lack of babies in the borough? Pregnancy is the least of our concerns right now.'

His brow was creased with concern. 'Have you done this before?'

She shook her head. 'But lucky for you, I'm a fast learner.'

A chuckle rose in his throat, and Blake was treated to a rare smile that turned her insides to water. She felt an urgency she had no idea how to articulate. 'Are you going to kiss me now?'

Harlan brushed his thumb across her bottom lip. 'Always so impatient.'

He brought his mouth to hers, and the sensation spread through her like warm honey. She wound her arms around his neck as heat travelled along her spine. She deepened the kiss, needing more of him. When she pressed her fingers into his skin, he pulled away and looked at her, his lips wet and breaths coming faster.

'You tell me what you like, and you tell me when to stop,' he said. 'Understand?'

She saluted. 'Yes, Commander.' She took hold of his face and kissed him, hips tipping forwards, seeking warmth and sensation.

He brought a hand to her hip and ground her against him. She sucked in a breath, the fire inside her burning brighter.

'I like that,' she whispered into his mouth.

His other hand went to her other hip, and he did it again. She tipped her head back that time. Impatient for more, she sought the sensation for herself, rocking against him.

His mouth went to her neck. 'Shit.' He whispered the word against her skin.

She straightened and looked at him. 'Can you take your shirt off?'

He kissed her once, then reached back, tugging his

shirt over his head. She traced the arrow scars with her fingers.

'Do you still have pain?' she asked.

'No.'

She doubted he would admit it if he did. Sliding off his lap until her knees hit the floor, she bent to kiss each scar. 'I'm so happy you survived.'

'Me too.' His words were breathy.

Straightening, she unbuttoned the front of her dress and pulled it down to her waist, watching his face the entire time. His eyes followed her every movement. When she went to remove her breast band, he reached up to help her. Then she was kneeling in front of him, naked from the waist up.

Harlan's eyes travelled up to hers, lust and something else swirling in them. 'You sure about this?'

She nodded, reminding herself to breathe.

Getting to his feet, he picked her up like she weighed nothing and wrapped her legs around him. 'Hold on to me.'

They were skin to skin for the first time.

'Where are we going?' she asked when he started walking away from the fire.

'Upstairs. We're going to need a bed for the things I want to do to you.'

She buried her face in his neck and smiled against his warm skin.

CHAPTER 25

*H*arlan had always thought himself incapable of gentleness. Historically, his encounters with women had been rushed, a pounding of flesh, chasing one mutual goal. He did not do intimacy. Sex had always been a means to an end. Not that he was a selfish lover but a practical one. Methodical in his approach.

He was not gentle with people. And others were not gentle with him. Why would they be? He was six feet two inches of brick.

His mother had been gentle though, but at some point he had forgotten the fact. Or her. Or simply repressed both out of necessity. He recalled the way she spoke to him as a child, the way she brushed his long hair back from his face every time his father said it was time he had a cut.

Gentle.

Warm.

And with the softest hazel eyes.

He had felt the need to warn Blake about this missing part of him. 'I don't want to hurt you.'

She had gripped his face, forcing him to look at her. 'Then you won't hurt me.'

She had far too much faith in him. She was right though. Even when driven mad by desire, he had handled her like a porcelain doll.

When they lay together afterwards, Blake tucked against him, two things hit him: that had been the best sex of his life, and he was in *deep*.

'Hungry?' he asked, pushing hair off her face.

She blinked up at him, cheeks still flushed and lips swollen. All he wanted to do was kiss her again. That was new. Normally when he was done, he was *done*.

'Merchants are always hungry' was her reply.

She meant it as a joke, but his chest tightened. 'I'm going to need to keep you better fed.'

She stretched to kiss him, and his entire body paid attention.

'We're going to have to work on your sense of humour,' she said.

His mother had always had a sense of humour. Being in the house again was making him remember those things.

Sitting up, he swung his legs over the side of the bed and handed Blake her dress before slipping on his trousers. He stood to belt them, watching her as he did so. She was skin and bones compared to the noblewomen he had been with. 'I have cheese, black bread, and salted fish.'

She climbed off the bed to adjust her dress. 'I'm going to have a quick wash in the creek first.' She glanced at the window, trying to gauge the time. It was passing too quickly.

'The water will be freezing.'

'Not as cold as the ocean I dragged you from.' Her eyes returned to him. 'I can fetch some water to heat over the fire if your sensibilities can't cope.'

He reached up and ran his thumb over her lips. He was quickly becoming obsessed with touching them—especially when they were wet. There his body went, getting ahead of itself again. 'Let's go.'

The creek was fast running but clean. Harlan stripped off first and stepped in. The rocks along the bottom were smooth but not exactly stable. He reached back for Blake. 'Take my hand. I don't want you to fall.' He was overprotective to the point of insane, he knew that, but he could not seem to help it.

Blake let her dress fall all the way down and covered herself with her other hand, as if he had not just seen every inch of her body up close. He guided her over the rocks until they were at the deepest point, and then they both sank down into the water. She seemed to look everywhere but at him.

'Why won't you look at me?' he asked.

Her eyes returned to him briefly. 'I'm looking at you.'

'Not really.'

She drew a breath and focused on him—hard. 'Better?'

'Yes.'

She shook her head. 'Can I ask you something?'

He nodded.

'What age were you when your father moved you to the barracks?' She swam closer.

'Eleven. After my mother died.'

Blake sank lower in the water, watching him. 'Do you remember her well?'

A nod. 'She was a lot like you, actually.'

'Funny and good with knives?'

He splashed her, then wiped her face. 'She put everyone else first—until she couldn't.'

Blake reached up to touch the angry scar on his shoulder. 'How did she die?'

Lonely. Isolated. Rejected. Humiliated. He would never know exactly what pushed her over the edge in those final days. 'She hung herself from the stairwell.'

Her fingers stilled. 'I'm sorry.'

He moved the conversation on. 'Your turn. How did your father die?'

She went to withdraw her hand, but he caught it and brought it to his neck. He wanted her to keep touching him.

'His heart just gave up one day.' Blake moved her other hand to his shoulder, and he pulled her closer so she was straddling him. 'Mother always said he would die on his feet. He was doing work outside the business, always looking for ways to earn a little extra.'

'Did the shop not provide enough income?'

Her fingers drew circles on his skin, making his eyes want to close.

'The business made as much as any other during that time. "When will it be enough?" my mother used to ask him.'

'And what was his reply?'

'Silence.'

Harlan dragged her closer by the hips, enjoying the way her breath changed. 'Was it because she was born in the nobility borough?'

Blake nodded and glanced towards the stables. 'I think so. He was trying to give her a life he was in no position to offer.'

He pushed her hair back and kissed the soft skin beneath her ear. 'I'm sure she knew what she was giving up when she married him.'

'She knew it was the end of grand feasts and fine dresses, but I don't think anything could have prepared her for the sudden loss of family and so-called friends.'

He knew something of that.

Her eyes returned to him. 'Do you think the class divides would be the same if they had never built the walls?'

Harlan rubbed her cheek with his stubbly face. 'The divide between rich and poor has always been there—and it's not going away with the removal of a few stone bricks.'

She thought on that for a moment. 'I think the walls deepen the divide considerably. The poor have fewer options, leading them to resent those with a clear advantage. Look at the farmers. They were no better than us, and now they're treated like royalty.'

'Hardly. They have their own struggles and pressures, trust me.'

'They have control of the food, the food every merchant is prepared to die for, that my brother died for.'

He blinked, guilt eating at his insides. He should have told her everything about that day. She deserved to know the truth. But he knew the second he told her, she would push him away. Her eyes would fill with hate instead of desire. 'You must know by now I won't let you go hungry.'

Her gaze travelled down his face to his lips. 'Of course you say that as I sit naked in your lap.'

'I would say the same thing to you if you were fully clothed.'

She breathed out. 'I know what this is. I'm not a fool. When we return to the merchant borough, it'll be as if today didn't happen.'

'That right?'

'And noble fathers with too many daughters will continue to throw them in your direction until one sticks.'

'None have stuck so far.' Blake had though.

'Well, you still have plenty of years ahead of you.'

He did not want to think ahead to a future she was not part of, but she was right. He had witnessed first-hand what happened when a man of noble birth took a merchant from her family and thrust her into this environment. The consequences were unthinkable. Plus, even if he were selfish enough to try, he knew Blake would never leave her family.

'What's going on in that mind of yours?' she asked.

'Just thoughts.'

She touched his jaw. 'Tempting, isn't it? To waste the precious time we have together wallowing?'

He drew her closer. 'What do you suggest instead?'

She pressed herself against him. 'Even *you* must be hungry by now.'

'Starving.'

His mouth found hers.

It was Blake's idea to eat outdoors. It reminded her of childhood picnics before mud overtook everything. The drizzle had stopped, and the weeds were long enough to serve as a barrier between blanket and mud.

'Why aren't you eating?' she asked when she noticed Harlan lying back watching her.

'I've had enough.'

She tilted her head. 'Liar. You should be eating more than me to get your strength back.'

He tucked his hands under his head. 'I don't want you to go.'

Dread pooled in her stomach. They had an hour at best before they had to leave. 'Well, it'll be much quieter here without me, and you've made it perfectly clear in the past that you prefer your own company.'

He sat up, watching her with a serious expression. 'That was true once. Now I find myself seeking out your incessant talking and strong opinions about the world.'

'Incessant talking?' She flicked his leg. 'If you prefer your women without opinions, then you chose from the wrong borough. We merchants hold very strong opinions about everything.'

He smirked. 'I don't think it was much of a choice. One meeting and you were under my skin.'

Her brow creased with disapproval. 'You make me sound like a parasite.'

'A welcomed parasite.'

She laughed. 'Oh, the poetry from your mouth.'

He was smiling too, and she would have done anything to make that smile last a little longer.

'If it's poems you want,' he said, 'then you definitely chose from the right borough. You just chose the wrong man.'

'Well, who would you recommend instead?'

'For sonnets?'

She nodded.

'Prince Borin,' he said without hesitation. 'I'll put in a good word for you.'

She scrunched her nose up and looked over at the grazing horse. 'What if I were to stay here with you?'

Harlan's smile faded. 'What?'

'There's a shipment arriving in four days. That would give us three whole days together.'

He rested his arms on his knees. 'Your mother would never allow it.'

'The lectures upon my return *would* be relentless, but it's difficult for her to tell me no from the other side of the wall.'

'And what of your reputation?'

She drew a breath. 'My reputation isn't that great anyway. Rumour has it I'm an incessant talker with strong opinions.'

He worked hard to suppress a grin. 'Three days of you. Three days *inside* you. I might struggle to let you leave at the end.'

'You're being very presumptuous about how we'll spend the time.' She looked down at her lap. 'We're both sensible people capable of enjoying time together and parting amicably. We get whatever this is out of our systems and move on with our lives.' That last part stuck in her throat.

He watched her intently. 'Is that what you want?'

'What we want and what we get are two very different things.'

He thought on that for a moment. 'Logic suggests that the more time we spend together, the higher the chance of forming an attachment.'

Too late. Though she would sooner die than admit it aloud. 'All I know is this opportunity won't come again.'

He exhaled. 'Explain your plan to me.'

She cleared her throat. 'I'll simply write to Mother and tell her the invitation has been extended a few days. I assume if we take the note to the gate, someone will deliver it on your behalf?'

He continued to watch her. 'Your mother doesn't strike me as stupid.'

Blake exhaled. 'If you would rather me leave—'

'I'd rather you stay. I'll take whatever time you give me.'

She swallowed. 'Good. I'm going to need some parchment and ink.'

Harlan woke to the sound of scrubbing coming from downstairs. He shot upright, looking around for Blake and finding the bed empty. Reaching for his trousers, he found them gone from the floor. A clean pair sat folded on the nearby chair. He snatched them up and tugged them on before heading downstairs, where he found Blake wrapped in a sheet on her knees, with a scrubbing brush in her hand and a pail of soapy water beside her. Her hair was swept up, but strands had come loose. She paused and tucked them behind her ears before resuming. He stood on the stairs, marvelling at her ability to look like a goddess while doing something so mundane.

'What the hell are you doing?' he asked, looking around at the dusted furniture and swept floors. 'How long have you been up?'

She sat back on her heels, keeping a hold of the brush. 'Just a few hours. Look at this floor. The wood is beautiful. Once I realised what lay beneath all that sticky dirt, there was no stopping me.'

His eyes went to the clothes drying in front of the fire. She had even done laundry. 'I really don't want you doing chores.'

'This place is a lot of work for one person. You should welcome the help.'

'I'd prefer to welcome you back to bed.' He liked the way her cheeks coloured at his words.

'Work now, fun later,' she said, resuming scrubbing.

Harlan made his way into the kitchen to prepare some food and found it had also been cleaned. The pots had been rinsed and now sat lined up above the swept hearth. Guilt hit him once more. He did not deserve her, even for a few days. He had planned to fill her in on some things during their ride back to the merchant borough, but now it would have to wait, because he was not about to ruin the time they had carved out—time that would never come again.

'I won't lie,' Blake said, entering the kitchen. 'I snooped through your food.'

Of course *she* would not lie. He was the only liar between them.

'How are you at frying eggs?' she asked, pushing up onto her toes and kissing him.

He just wanted to pull her to him and devour that mouth of hers for the rest of the morning, but his desire to fatten her up won—just. 'I'll light a fire.'

They ate together at the table like a regular couple would in their home. Afterwards, she took the dishes down to the creek while he tended the horse. When she did not return straight away, he wandered down to the creek and found her floating naked, her arms sweeping the water's surface as she stared at the trees above.

Harlan knew he would never visit that creek without seeing that image ever again.

He thought about joining her, but then she started to hum. It was the sound of her content, and he could not bring himself to intrude. He went to chop wood instead.

Harlan was almost finished when Blake finally climbed the creek bank. He stopped to watch her walk towards him, the dishes perched on one hip and her dripping hair swept to one side.

Another mental image to store away.

'You need some goats,' she called to him. 'They would get these weeds down in no time.'

He smiled to himself. 'Everyone needs goats right now.'

'But yours might survive longer than five minutes. A goat in the merchant borough is another matter entirely.'

'You've kept that duck alive.'

'His name is Garlic. Why you refuse to address him as such, I have no idea.'

A low chuckle rose in him. 'Really? You have no idea?'

She scrunched her nose up. 'Can you do something for me?'

Anything. He would do anything for her. 'What's that?'

'When you get your goats, can you name them Clove and Ginger?'

'Absolutely not.'

'You won't be able to forget me then.'

There was no chance in hell of him forgetting her,

goats or no goats. He picked up a log and placed it on the chopping block. 'Go inside.'

She blinked. 'Why?'

'I can't control which direction the wood flies in.' Yes, he was aware of how ridiculous he sounded.

'Are you joking?'

He looked tiredly in her direction. 'Am I laughing?'

She rolled her eyes before wandering indoors.

In the afternoon, Harlan saddled his horse and took Blake a few miles downstream to a good fishing spot. He taught her how to fish with a bow and arrow, and although she missed every time, he could tell she was having fun, so he let her go until she tired. Only once she had completely given up did he take over the task. They left the creek with a small trout, which they cooked on the hearth that evening.

'Of course the creek is on this side of the wall,' Blake said as they ate. 'We could have really done with some fish.'

'You have the port.'

'The bay is completely depleted, as you well know. You need a boat to catch anything worth eating.'

Harlan lay down in front of the fire and guided her head to his chest. 'And the creek would have been the same. The merchants would fish until there's nothing left.'

She turned her face up to look at him. 'You make it sound like we're lacking in good sense and restraint.'

'It's not an attack. I understand why.'

She settled her head once more. 'You can't possibly understand. *Your* kind live like kings.'

'*My* kind?'

'I feel guilty sitting here with a full stomach when I know my sisters and mother are hungry.'

He looked down and watched her thoughts play out. 'I can organise some food for them next time I'm in the borough. All you need to do is ask.'

She sat up, visibly irritated. 'More charity.'

'What's the matter with you?' he asked, sitting up too.

'Nothing.'

He had no idea what to do when she behaved like other women. 'Am I supposed to guess?'

'No.' She busied herself stoking the fire.

Grabbing her by the back of her dress, he pulled her to him. She crashed against his chest.

'What are you doing?' she said. 'I could have fallen on the floor.'

'As if I would let that happen.'

She threw an elbow into him. 'Let me go.'

He pinned her to him and brought his mouth to her ear. 'Not until you tell me what the hell is going on in that head of yours.' She doubled her efforts to free herself, but he held tight. 'Stop it.'

'Let go!'

'Not until you talk to me.'

She struggled for a full minute before going limp against him, her breaths coming fast. Only then did he relax his grip on her. The moment he did, her hands went over her face, and he froze up.

'Are you… crying?'

'No.' Her voice cracked.

He pulled her hands away from her face and turned

her to him. His stomach twisted when he saw her tears. 'Shit. Tell me what's wrong so I can fix it.'

She looked up at the roof in an attempt to stop crying. 'You can't fix it.'

'I'll be the judge of that.'

She licked a tear from her lip and met his gaze. 'We have tomorrow. Then I leave the next morning.'

He stared at her. 'So this isn't about the merchants not having a creek?'

'Not entirely,' she admitted. 'Though my point stands.'

He let go of her and leaned back on his hands, finally understanding. 'What happened to an amicable separation?'

'Well, you know what they say: the more time you spend together, the higher the chance of forming an attachment,' she said, quoting him.

'Do you think picking a fight with me will make the separation easier?'

'No.' She swallowed. 'Maybe. I don't know.'

She was right. He could not fix this. She had to go back to her family, and he had to go back to the barracks. 'What do you want to do? Want me to take you home in the morning?'

Her face collapsed. 'How is that better?'

'It's better than fighting.' He was no good at this stuff. 'Better than being blamed for all the merchants' problems.'

When she went to draw back from him, he pulled her onto his lap and rested his forehead on her shoulder. He was not ready to be pushed away—not yet. That would happen soon enough.

'Sorry,' he whispered.

She sniffed. 'I lied to you.'

He lifted his head. 'What about?'

She hesitated. 'About the extent of my feelings.'

He returned his forehead to her shoulder and fought hard against the words on the edge of his tongue. Releasing them would only make the separation worse. Besides, there were other words he needed to say first.

I killed your brother.

Those words seemed more native from the mouth of a defender than "I love you".

'Can we pretend this conversation never happened?' she asked, hand going to his face.

He pressed his eyelids tightly shut before looking up. 'We'll skip straight to the making up.'

'The game is called *what?*' Harlan asked, watching Blake draw a large circle in the dirt with a stick.

'Barley Break.' She straightened to admire her work, then tossed the stick away.

'Maybe we should wait until the rain stops.'

Her eyes went to the sky. 'That might take years. Besides, I see you standing on the wall in the rain all the time.'

He crossed his arms. 'I'm used to it. You should be dry and warming yourself by the fire.'

'We both know what happens when we relax in front of that fireplace. Two minutes later we're naked, then napping.'

'You had me at "naked".'

She looked at him. 'Pay attention so you understand the rules, please.'

A heavy breath left him. 'Fine.'

'I cannot leave the circle.' She walked the perimeter, deepening the line with the toe of her boot. 'And you must run through the area without being tagged. If you're tagged, then you go into the middle.'

'That's it?'

'That's it.'

'How does one win?'

Blake looked around the circle. 'With more players, the last person to be tagged is the winner, so let's say the person who passes through the circle the most times in a row without being tagged wins.'

He stared at her. 'And you think you stand a chance?'

Her head snapped in his direction, the beginnings of a smile on her face. 'I stand a very good chance. I'm far more agile than you.'

His eyebrows rose. 'You think you're more agile than a defender?'

'Yes. Plus, I have the advantage of having played before.'

His gaze fell to the marked area. 'The advantage of having run through a circle?'

She did not bother answering him, just moved into the middle, knees bent as she eyed him. 'Ready when you are.'

He regarded her as she swayed from side to side— game ready. He normally grew bored of women rather quickly, but he could not imagine a time when he would ever bore of Blake. She just kept finding ways to deepen his affection for her.

Removing his tunic, he walked over to the chopping block and dumped it on top. 'Fine. One game.' He turned back, deciding on a strategy. 'Ready?'

'I was ready ten minutes ago, Commander.'

Shaking his head, he broke into a jog towards the circle. She moved towards him, ensuring her foot never crossed the boundary. He moved in a straight line, eyes ahead and gait even. Then, just as he reached the perimeter, he pivoted. She was ready though, pushing off in the direction he was going, arms pumping at her side, prepared for the chase. He spun, moving around her in the other direction. She was going too fast at that point to catch him. Her feet slid as she tried to correct herself. By the time she had, he was already jogging over the line on the other side.

He turned to her with a triumphant smile.

She leaned on her knees, nodding slowly. 'Clever. I'll be watching your feet next time instead of your face.'

He jogged on the spot, pretending to warm up for the next round. 'You can watch my feet all the way to the other side of the circle.'

'Oh, an arrogant defender. Who would have thought?'

He could not help but grin. 'Ready?'

'You probably shouldn't ask. That's technically an advantage, and I'd prefer to win fair and square.'

If his smile grew any wider, he was certain his face would crack. He took off at a run, faster this time. He could see by her expression that she had not been prepared. Just before he reached the circle, he pretended to pivot before continuing straight. Blake leapt after him, fingers reaching, missing him by mere inches.

He crossed the line.

'It's fine,' she called after him, breathless now. 'I'll get you on the third.'

She did not get him on the third, or the fourth, or the fifth. She got him on the sixth because he let her. The aim was to win, not completely crush her self-worth. He would get her on her first time through, anyway.

'Six is fine,' she announced confidently. 'I can beat six.'

'Can you now?'

'Absolutely.' She was really out of breath.

Harlan moved to the middle of the circle and clapped his hands together once. 'Let's do it.'

His training gave him a clear advantage in this game. He could tell which direction she was going to move by the angle of her body and the direction her limbs were facing. He had spent years learning how to predict his opponent's next move. His survival depended on it.

She ran straight at him, so he was expecting her to pivot at some point. He watched her feet for any hints and saw none. She picked up speed, and he wondered how on earth she planned to get around him without popping her knee joint. She was almost within reach, to the point where he thought they might actually collide, when she suddenly tucked her head and dove forwards, rolling once beneath his arm before getting back on her feet and continuing on. He looked under his arm as she crossed the line on the other side.

Blake turned with the smuggest of smiles and hair full of dirt and debris. 'You're lucky I wasn't armed or I would have sliced your leg open as I passed by and left you to bleed out.'

He turned. 'Is that allowed? Because that changes things considerably.'

She laughed. 'Ready for round two?'

'You're not supposed to warn me. That's technically an advantage, and I'd prefer to win fair and square.'

More laughter.

'Just so you know,' he said, 'you only get to pass me once.'

This time Harlan did not move one inch from the centre of the circle. He watched her closely, ready for whatever play she would throw at him. This time he noted the movement in her eyes, the way her hands balled up before she was about to make her move. This time he leapt at her before she had a chance, arms enclosing her. He angled his body so he would take the brunt of the fall and she would finish safely in his arms. He lay on his back on the ground, half laughing and half winded.

'You're right,' he said. 'It's a fun game.'

'I told you.' She was breathless from laughter.

He drew her closer and said into her ear, 'I win, by the way.'

CHAPTER 27

*B*lake woke to a light-filled room and a note on the pillow beside hers.

Catching breakfast. Back soon.
H

They had only fallen asleep a few hours earlier, because sleep felt like a waste of the precious time they had left. One more day playing together. One more night wrapped in his arms. A day later, she would be just another merchant wary of the commander strolling atop the wall.

Pushing the thought from her head, Blake rose, taking the blanket with her. Dressing was just another waste of their time.

After a quick wash, she made her way downstairs to tend the fire. She had just decided to go browse the books in the library to pass some time when she heard a horse out front. Her heart sped up, and a smile spread across her face as she ran to the front door. She tugged it open and rushed outside, pulling up with a gasp as she came face to face with Shapur Wright. Her lungs stilled, and her eyes widened. His eyes narrowed, then swept the length of her.

'Suttone. I thought I might find you here.'

She pulled the blanket tighter around her. 'If you're looking for Commander Wright, he's fishing downstream.'

He stared at her. 'Is he?'

She did not know if she was supposed to invite him in —into his own home—or if she should excuse herself to dress.

'That is all right,' he said. 'It is better we speak alone.'

It took her a moment to respond. 'About?'

He looked past her into the house. 'About this little affair of yours.'

She glanced over her shoulder, trying to remember where she had left her dress. They had started in the kitchen and finished in the chair by the fire. Though she could not remember seeing it there earlier. There was no way she could invite him in.

'Do not worry,' Shapur said. 'I do not plan on staying.'

She turned back to him. 'Nor do I. I'm returning home tomorrow, if that's why you're here.'

He rested his hands on his hips and glanced back at his tethered horse. 'And then what?'

'Excuse me?'

He scratched his face. 'And then what? What plans have the two of you made?'

Then despair, surely. 'We've made no plans, sir.'

'Do you expect me to believe that?'

'Perhaps this is a conversation better had with your son.'

He drew a tired breath and took a few steps back. 'Did he tell you what happened to his mother?'

She lifted her chin. 'Yes.'

'How she died?'

'Yes.' Her eyes went to the road, willing Harlan to appear. 'I'm very sorry for your loss. I understand it all too well.'

Shapur nodded. 'Did he tell you she was a merchant?'

No. He had not told her that very vital part of the story.

Reading her face, Shapur said, 'Not surprised given the situation the two of you find yourself in.'

Blake reminded herself to breathe.

'A merchant marrying nobility is challenging with its social divides. A merchant and a defender is a moral disaster. Problems cannot be ignored, negotiated, or worked through. Love is not an antidote.'

'I assure you there has been no talk of marriage.'

He was silent for a long moment. 'And yet you would run into battle for him without a thought of what it would do to your family if those sea warriors had killed you.'

She did not have a logical explanation for that.

'I cannot tell him who to marry, but I can warn you about what you would be stepping into.'

She should have shut the pointless conversation down, but she was curious what reasons he would give that she might not have considered. 'All right.'

'Take your brother's death, for instance.'

She flinched at the mention of Kingsley, surprised Shapur even knew of his existence. 'What of it?'

The warden hesitated. 'Has Harlan told you of his part in what happened that day?'

Blake held the blanket tighter. 'He was there when it happened. It was the first time I ever spoke to him.'

'And what exactly do you think happened?'

Her eyebrows came together. 'I saw what happened. The tunnels collapsed. My brother was still inside.'

He crossed his arms as he collected his next words. 'I only tell you this to help you see what a future together would mean for you both.'

She waited for him to continue, her heart thudding in her chest.

'It is Harlan's job to defend those walls at any cost,' Shapur went on. 'So when it was discovered that merchants were moving beneath them and jeopardising the small amount of livestock this kingdom has, it was his job to stop it.'

Blake was no clearer on what he was trying to say.

'He came up with a plan to locate every shaft and every tunnel. His men drilled holes to weaken them.' He paused. 'Harlan carefully coordinated their destruction.'

She inhaled and brought the blanket up to her mouth. Memories from that day poured in. She had been standing over one of the shafts when she met Harlan. He would have known it was there, known the entire time what she was doing. He might have even seen Kingsley enter.

She took a step back from Shapur and reached for the

door frame for balance. 'He knew there were people inside.'

It was not a question.

'His job is to stop people moving between the boroughs. He did his job.'

She held her stomach, and the blanket slipped down one shoulder.

'Your first moral dilemma, day one of meeting one another. Now imagine watching him discipline your friends and family, your community. Imagine the guilt if you left, moved into the nobility borough, and lived a privileged life. Imagine the distrust. Imagine trying to find new friends in a class above you. Imagine a lifetime of it.' He sniffed, staring at her. 'Now imagine the consequences for Harlan if he failed to do his job.'

Blake's fingers had turned white on the door frame.

'I am not completely without feeling,' Shapur continued, 'which is why I am here giving you the chance to end it before history repeats itself.'

She saw genuine grief on his face, but she was struggling to think past her own. 'Forgive me. I wasn't prepared for this conversation.' Especially not the revelations.

He nodded. 'You saved his life, and I am grateful for it. But whatever you feel, it will not be enough.' Shapur turned on his heel and strode back to his horse without a goodbye.

Blake backed her way inside, pushed the door closed, and pressed her forehead to it.

⁓

Blake made it to the gate in under an hour, having run most of the way. She had no idea what the defenders on duty would make of the lone merchant girl trying to get *out* of the nobility borough. It would be a confusing situation for all involved.

She was almost there when the light mist of rain turned to fat drops. Pulling the hood of her cloak up, she marched ahead.

'Halt!' a defender called to her as she neared the gate.

Of course he was suspicious of the woman on foot dressed in merchant clothing. Noblewomen travelled in carts and wore silk-covered shoes, not mud-soaked boots.

Blake stopped and pushed her hood back.

'Hands up where I can see them,' the defender called out as he approached.

She raised her hands. 'I'm returning to the merchant borough.'

He stopped in front of her. 'From where?'

'The Wrights' house.'

He gave her a doubtful look. 'Cloak off.'

'What? *Why?*'

'You'd be surprised what I find hidden beneath them. Now, *cloak off.*'

She blinked slowly but did as she was told. 'I didn't steal anything if that's what you're checking.'

'Ah, an honest thief.' He began patting her down. 'How did you get in here?'

Blake rolled her eyes. 'I travelled here with Commander Wright.'

'And now you travel alone?' He rose.

The sound of a horse approaching made Blake look

over her shoulder. It was Harlan coming at a gallop. Her hands were still raised when he pulled his horse to a skidding halt ten feet away and dismounted.

'Put your cloak on,' he told her, striding over. 'It's freezing.'

The defender's eyebrows rose in surprise. 'You know this woman, Commander?'

Harlan nodded before turning his attention to Blake. He looked far from pleased with her. She had left without so much as a note for him.

'That will be all, defender,' Harlan said, dismissing the man.

The guard turned and wandered back to the gate. Blake followed him. He would surely raise the portcullis for her now.

'Blake,' Harlan said behind her.

She kept walking. A few more steps and she would be in the merchant borough.

'Blake!'

The defender stepped into her path as she reached the archway, and her frustration bubbled over.

'What now? He's already confirmed he knows me. What else do you want? Should I take off my boots? My dress?' Those words should never have left her mouth, and certainly not spoken in that tone. The defender drew his weapon, and she took a step back from it—straight into Harlan's chest.

'Stand down, defender,' Harlan said, stepping around Blake, placing himself between her and the red-faced defender. 'I'll handle this.'

The defender glared at Blake a final time before

turning and leaving. Harlan began dragging her off towards his horse.

'I just want to go home,' she said, trying to anchor her feet.

'I can see that.' He gave up and released her once they were out of earshot. 'Want to tell me what the hell is going on?'

She forced her gaze up to meet his. 'Your father came to the house while you were out.'

Harlan let out a breath. 'I see. He said something that upset you.'

Tears prickled Blake's eyes. She had no idea how to say the things she needed to without losing it completely. '*You* upset me.'

'What did he tell you?'

She could not do it. Turning away, she began walking towards the gate.

He caught her in a few strides, holding her arm so tightly she knew she stood no chance of pulling free.

'If you walk away from me again before we're done, I'll tie you to the closest tree.'

She blinked up at him. 'I believe you. I know you're capable of all kinds of horrible acts.'

His face remained impassive, his grip bruising. 'If you have something to say, say it.'

She leaned in. 'You murdered my brother. You weakened the tunnels, knowing whoever was inside would never make it out. Then you hung him on the wall and pretended it was the fault of the hard-working men who sacrificed sleep to dig those tunnels under darkness. As if they don't have enough guilt, enough trauma to live with.'

His grip eased a little. 'So he showed up and painted me as the monster. Clever.'

'You knew where all the shafts were located. You knew I was standing right above one that day, that someone I loved was likely inside.'

'Yes, I knew. And you're lucky I didn't drag you off to the tower when you lied about what you were doing there.'

'No, instead you kept me around to enjoy the show.'

His eyes searched hers. 'I didn't even know you. You were just a merchant standing in the forest, covering up a crime.'

'Did you see him go in?'

'What?'

'Kingsley. Did you see him go in?'

He shook his head. 'No. The only thing I saw was you ready to fall down from hunger. I took pity on you.'

She tried to pull her arm free again, but his hand only tightened like a clamp around it.

'You want an honest conversation,' he said. 'Well, there it is. I felt sorry for you.'

'Let me go,' she said, struggling.

'We're not done.'

She shoved his chest with her free hand. 'We *are* done.' A tear escaped, blending with the rain. 'We're *finished*.'

'I was doing my job.'

Her blazing eyes met his. 'You should have told me the truth about that day. It would have changed everything. I would never have come here with you.'

He took hold of her other arm so she would stop

pushing him. 'I'm a *defender*. You're a merchant. There are rules.'

Shapur's words came back to her. '*A merchant and a defender is a moral disaster.*'

She stilled, her heart squeezing so tightly she doubted its ability to continue beating. 'I trusted you. I knew I shouldn't have, but I did it anyway.'

'You *can* trust me.'

She shook her head. 'I can't—and it's not even your fault.'

He looked down at his hands, as if noticing for the first time what he was doing to her. He let go. 'Come back to the house, and I'll tell you anything you want to know.'

'This is the problem. You're not allowed to tell me anything. Your father shouldn't have told me anything. This is what he was trying to explain to me. If we keep this up, you'll always have to choose between me and the oath you took when you became a defender. Every choice will cost you.'

He glanced in the direction of the gate. 'So now you're just going to walk away and pretend the past few days never happened?'

She licked rain off her lips and lifted her shoulders in a shrug. 'That was always the plan.'

He moved closer, keeping his voice low. 'What if I want to make a different plan?'

Rain splattered Blake's face. 'Then I would tell you to look to your parents and decide if that's really the life you want for us.' Her expression softened. 'Please. I want to go home.'

He searched her eyes for the longest time; then,

nodding, he called to the defender, 'Let the merchant through.' Turning away, he returned to his horse.

Blake's feet felt like they were shackled and weighted as she stood there in the rain, suddenly doubting her ability to leave. She wanted him to come back and take hold of her again, to crush her bones until they were dust in his hands. But before she could move in either direction, she heard his horse canter away.

CHAPTER 28

The lecture Blake endured from her mother upon her return was enough to make her wish she had remained at Harlan's house—and that was saying something.

Not one for drama, Eda went out into the courtyard, and Lyndal remained in the room as mediator.

'If you think your uncle will not find out about your little escapade, you are wrong.' Candace brought a hand to her brow, eyes closing. 'The thing that I cannot get my head around is that you are smarter than this. You must have known this affair would not end well.'

The word 'affair' did not seem to fit. To have everything they felt reduced to one cheap word was devastating. 'Can we not make such a big deal about this? It's done. Finished.'

Her mother threw her hands up. 'As are any future prospects. Word will travel. It is hard enough finding a suitable husband without these added complexities.'

Added complexities. That was what the past few days of playing, fishing, learning, and loving had been reduced to.

'Have you no shame?' her mother asked, close to tears now.

She had more shame than she could stomach.

Lyndal cleared her throat. 'I'm sure everything was above board and the pair were chaperoned throughout her stay.' She gave Blake an encouraging nod.

Blake looked out the shop window and sighed. 'Whatever I tell you won't change the facts, nor Uncle's opinion of me, so what's the point in lying?'

Candace released a breath. 'Reckless. Reckless and selfish. Has our family not suffered enough these past few years?'

The only person suffering was Blake. Not only had her heart been completely shattered, but now her mind was being picked apart. 'I'd like to change.'

Candace looked her over. 'I suggest you burn the dress. Your sister does not have the time or energy required to wash out that much sin.'

Blake closed her eyes and refrained from covering her ears, then walked off towards the bedroom. Lyndal followed, taking hold of her arm once they were out of sight.

Blake spun around. 'Don't grab at me!' She brought a trembling hand to her aching arm, where Harlan's hand had been earlier.

Lyndal gestured to the bedroom. 'Go.' She closed the door behind them. 'All right. Out with it.'

'Out with what?'

'All of it.'

Blake stared at the collar of her sister's dress. 'I made a mistake, and I don't want to talk about it.'

Lyndal crossed her arms. 'But the mistake was your choice, yes? He didn't take advantage of you, did he?'

'No, of course not.'

Lyndal looked her up and down. 'Then why do you look like death warmed up? Shouldn't you be glowing or something after your romantic rendezvous?'

'I really don't want to talk about it.'

Lyndal led her to the bed and guided her down onto it. 'Mother will get past it. You know she's not one for grudges.'

It was not her mother's feelings that Blake was worried about. She was more concerned that *she* would never get past it.

'Do you regret it?' Lyndal asked, taking Blake's hands in hers. 'Is that it?'

Even after everything, Blake could not bring herself to regret any part of it. 'No.' The word came out as a whisper.

'Is it over?' Lyndal asked quietly.

'Yes.' Blake's head fell to her sister's shoulder. 'Yes, it's over.'

Candace had been right. Lord Thomas found out about her little adventure into the nobility borough—and he was not happy.

He showed up at the house—with a groomsman to guard his horse—and burst through the shop door with such force the bell hit the wall opposite. Blake rushed into the shop to see what all the noise was about and stilled when she saw her uncle. His eyes narrowed on her.

'You little harlot.'

She felt cold, her feet frozen in place as the man stormed towards her. She knew he was going to strike her before it happened, and she did nothing to stop it.

Slap.

The force of it she did not expect. It sent her hurtling into Eda, who had just entered the shop behind her. Her youngest sister caught her in her arms.

Candace stepped in front of the girls, arms outstretched like a shield. 'Enough!'

Thomas drew a deep breath and began to pace.

'What on earth is going on?' Lyndal asked, rushing into the room. One look at Blake's burning cheek answered the question. Her eyes returned to Thomas, filled with accusation.

The funny thing was, Blake could have stopped it. She could have stepped back, caught his arm, or turned her head away. But a part of her felt like she deserved it—just not for the reasons he did.

'Hardly discreet,' her uncle began. 'You could have at least kept the scandal in your own borough. Chadora's nobility cannot be expected to keep your filthy secrets. Everyone knows there is only one reason the warden's son would take a woman to that dumping ground of a house.' He stopped pacing, jabbing a long finger in her direction. 'You do understand that you are *my* burden now? That you just whored away your future? The best you can hope for now is some tavern merchant with low standards.'

Candace lowered her hands. 'I think you have made your point.'

Thomas wheeled on her. 'What sort of daughters are you raising here? Criminal mutes and whores. You better hope Lyndal stays the course, because she is your only hope now.'

Turning on his heel, he marched out of the shop, slamming the door shut behind him. The four of them watched the window shutters rattle before falling still.

Harlan rarely drank, so on the rare occasions he did, he tended to drink a lot.

'We should slow down,' Astin said, seated on the stool beside him, 'or we'll never make it back to the barracks.'

They were seated at the open window in the tavern closest to the water, watching the ship merchants unload on the dock. Harlan knew Blake would be down at some point, which was why he was paying particular attention to goings-on outside. He needed a glimpse of her to put his mind at ease.

'Did you hear me?' Astin asked.

Harlan tore his gaze from the window. 'What?'

Astin assessed him a moment. 'You know I rarely side with your father, and by rarely I mean never, but I think he has a point this time.'

Harlan emptied his cup before replying. 'What point is that?'

'Your occupation is problematic. You're commander of the merchant borough, a position you worked hard for.'

'I didn't really have a choice. My father was always going to make me work harder than any other defender.'

'And there's every chance you'll be named warden when the time comes for your father to step aside,' Astin continued, eyeing the pretty barmaid as she passed by.

That was true. Shapur had always spoken as if Harlan would one day step up and replace him. Harlan had never considered alternative paths, because the defender lifestyle had been ingrained in him from such a young age; he knew he would be lost without the discipline and structure that came with it. But now there was Blake. 'I should have told her about the tunnels. I think it was hearing it from someone else that did the damage.'

'You think *that's* the reason? Not the being responsible for her brother's death part?'

Harlan didn't bother replying.

'Weird that your father told her. If *you* had told her, he probably would have disciplined you. I guess that's the point he was trying to make—whatever you do, you're in the shitter.'

Harlan sat up straight when he spotted Blake and Lyndal walking down the muddy path towards the wharf. Astin turned to see what he was looking at.

'Ah, so that's why you agreed to come.'

Harlan narrowed his eyes on what appeared to be a bruise on her face. His muscles grew rigid.

'The best thing you can do for both of you right now is remain exactly where you are,' Astin said. 'Just let her go about her business.'

Harlan's chair scraped the wooden floor as he rose,

drawing the attention of the room. 'I'll be back in a minute.'

Astin rubbed his forehead. 'I'll pay, then, shall I?'

Harlan was already out the door, striding towards her. A bitter wind swept off the ocean, hitting him in the face. 'Blake.'

She turned at the sound of his voice. He almost tripped over his own feet when he got a proper look at her face. A bruise covered one cheek and most of her eye. She brushed her long hair forwards over it, but it was too late by then.

Lyndal threaded a protective arm through her sister's as he approached. He was undeterred, marching straight up to Blake and lifting her chin with his fingers so the hair fell away and he had a clear view of her injury.

'I beg your pardon, Commander,' Lyndal said.

Blake stepped back and pushed her hair forwards.

'What happened to your face?' He spoke through clenched teeth.

'It's nothing,' Blake said absently.

'Nothing?' Harlan ran a hand over his head. 'Your mother do that?'

Lyndal's mouth fell open. 'Our mother has never hit anyone in her life.'

Harlan heard Astin approaching at a jog. A moment later, a hand landed on his shoulder. 'Just remember you're not on duty.' He leaned closer and whispered, 'And we've had quite a few ales.'

'Exactly,' Lyndal replied.

Astin looked at her. 'But he's still the commander of your borough. You would do well to remember that.'

Lyndal stared back at him, unblinking. 'You can spare me the empty threats, defender. What might actually be helpful is if you take your intoxicated friend and crawl back into the tavern you came from.'

A smile played on Astin's lips as his eyes swept the length of her. 'Shy little thing, aren't you?'

It came to Harlan's foggy mind then. 'Did your uncle do this?'

Blake said nothing.

He stepped back, because he was worried the waves of rage rolling off him might knock her to the ground. 'That bastard.'

'Just leave it,' Blake said, looking everywhere but at him. 'Don't make things worse for me.'

He stepped up to her again. 'He *hit* you.'

Her dead eyes finally met his. 'You think I care about one bruise on my face?'

His eyes searched hers, and he understood then. She was trying to hold all the other broken pieces together—like he was.

Lyndal cleared her throat. 'Ah, if you could just take one large step back, I know *I* would certainly feel a lot better.'

Harlan ignored her. 'He's lucky I don't go to his house and teach him a lesson of my own.'

Blake continued to watch him. 'Do you suppose that would help cultivate his affection for me?'

He looked out at the water.

'Please, just leave it alone,' she said tiredly. 'I really can't take any more visits from him right now.'

Harlan hated where they had ended up, but here they were.

'Right, well.' Astin clapped his hands together. 'Now that's all sorted, we should probably head off.'

'Let's go,' Lyndal said, pulling Blake in the direction of the ship.

Harlan watched them walk off. Then his gaze caught on a cart passing by carrying large stones.

'God,' Astin said. 'I hope that's not what I think it is.'

Harlan looked over at the wall where the stones were being unloaded. His stomach fell. 'They're closing the wall. You know about this?'

'I'd heard rumours.'

Harlan looked back at Blake, who was now greeting Odo. The sea merchant reached for her face, but she only waved him off as she had done earlier with him.

'The merchants won't like this,' Astin said, 'but it's Chadora's most vulnerable point right now. I suppose there's *some* logic in the decision.'

Harlan faced him again. 'Logic in completely closing the merchants in? Look at the volume of foot traffic passing through. Some are collecting supplies, and others are fishing off the rocks as the only means of food for their families.'

'And some are paying for sex at the taverns,' Astin said. 'Soon they'll be forced to bring fishing equipment along for show.'

Harlan did not smile. 'They'll riot.'

'More than likely. And you'll restore order to the borough, and life will continue as normal. That's what history has shown us.' There was resignation in his voice.

Harlan watched Blake hand the payment over to Odo. He knew better than to go offer his help in carrying the supplies home—and he would not be much help in his current state anyway.

'What are you two doing here?' came the warden's voice.

Harlan turned to see his father approaching. 'Did you know about this?' He pointed to the stones.

'The wall? Of course I knew.'

'You didn't think to inform me?'

Shapur stopped in front of him. 'Why? You are not commanding the borough at present.' He sniffed the air. 'Are you drunk?'

So drunk. 'This doesn't feel right. It feels a lot like we're taking from people who have nothing left.'

Shapur glanced at Astin, who was pretending not to listen in. 'No one cares about your feelings. The decision was made by our king, and it is our job to support him and ensure the people in your borough uphold the new rules.'

'They'll riot.'

'And we will stop them by using whatever force is necessary.' He glanced in the direction of the dock, where Blake and Lyndal were making their way back carrying rolls of fabric too heavy for them. 'She has gotten in your head. You need to find a way to expel her.'

Harlan frowned. 'It was *you* who got into *her* head.'

'You should thank me for stepping in. Her uncle came to see me, Lord Thomas.'

Harlan tensed at the mention of him. 'What did he want?'

'What do you think?'

Harlan rubbed his forehead. 'Whatever you told him did her no favours. You should see her face.'

'What *I* told him? The two of you were hardly discreet.'

'I have a mind to pay him a visit.'

Shapur pinned him with a stare. 'And who do you think will pay for that visit? Use your head. You want to help her? Then stay away.' He looked between Harlan and Astin. 'I suggest you both go back to the barracks and sleep off the ale. You have a tough couple of weeks ahead of you.'

Harlan frowned. 'Not me. I'm stood down until further notice.'

Shapur turned away. 'Consider this your notice, Commander.'

Harlan watched him walk off.

Astin clapped him on the back. 'Well, that's good news. Back on the job.'

Harlan had quite enjoyed training the new recruits, and he would have been happy to continue doing that instead.

Blake glanced in his direction as she strolled by. The hurt in those pretty eyes of hers made him look down.

'Let's go,' he said, his head a mess of emotion and ale. 'I need to lie down before I fall down.'

Blake could not tell if she was avoiding Harlan in the weeks that followed or if he was avoiding her. Both, maybe. He was not on the ground, not on the wall, not amid the trees when she took walks. She knew he was back commanding the borough—just nowhere near her.

A week after her encounter with Harlan in the port, Astin showed up with a parcel of food for the family. Blake tried to refuse, but the defender reminded her that there was a time and place for pride, and they were in the middle of a famine.

'Tough times are coming,' he told her.

She looked up at him. 'How much tougher can things get?'

His non-response spoke volumes.

It was the sight of her hungry sisters watching through the window that eventually made her reach out and take it.

'How is he?' The question spilled out despite her best efforts to hold it in.

'Broody' was Astin's reply. He glanced in the direction of her sisters. 'Good day, merchant.' He stepped off the veranda and walked down the street.

Blake knew she needed to find a way to be independent of Harlan—for both their sakes. She needed to replace the food he was sending so she could comfortably cut ties without depriving her family.

'I heard rumours they're digging more tunnels,' Thea told her the following morning as she swept her veranda. 'Though if any defenders come knocking, you didn't hear it from me.'

Even if Blake could find out their location, she knew she would not make it past the shaft. Her hands turned clammy at the mere thought.

Thea paused and leaned on her broom. 'I told Birtle no way, not after last time. Safer to climb over the thing.'

'And just stroll past the guards?' Blake asked with a smile.

Thea resumed sweeping. 'They can't be everywhere at once, and all eyes are on the ground right now.'

Blake's smile faded. 'I suppose you're right.'

That afternoon, she walked to the east end of the forest. She sat with her back against a tree, watching the defenders atop the wall. She made mental notes of how far they walked and how long they were stationary at each turret.

The walls were sixty feet high, a little more than some of the larger trees the girls had climbed as children. While there were no branches to hold on to, the oddly shaped stones created small footholds for an experienced climber on the lighter side.

But there were reasons why merchants did not go over. The risks were enormous. Using a rope would guarantee you were caught, and not using a rope dramatically increased your chances of falling to your death.

Blake rose and brushed off her skirt before starting the long walk back to the village.

When she arrived, she found people standing in groups in the square, speaking in urgent, angry tones. Others were marching off in the direction of the port.

'What's going on?' she asked a young boy jogging past.

He turned, running backwards for a few paces. 'They're closing the wall.'

Blake's entire body went limp. She stared after the boy for a moment before collecting herself and following him.

It was chaos at the port. Men ran back and forth between stone masons chiselling raw stone into tidy blocks, which were then hoisted into the air to the newly built scaffolding at the end of the wall. Below, men made mortar from lime, soil, and water. She had seen the supplies being delivered the day she was in the port but had naively thought they were for repairs.

A hand on her arm made her jump. It was Eda.

They're walling us in, her sister signed.

Blake ran a hand over her sister's hair. 'It'll be all right.' Though her gut told her otherwise.

'You can't do this!' shouted a nearby merchant. He approached one of the defenders, hands curled into fists at his sides. 'We'll tear the bloody thing down.'

The defender grabbed hold of his arm, twisted it until

there was a loud pop, then released him with a shove. The merchant staggered around in circles for a moment, swearing through gritted teeth. It was supposed to be a warning to others, but it had the opposite effect. Merchants moved in on the defender.

'You going to break all our arms?' one woman shouted.

More defenders arrived, backs tall and hands on their weapons. The answer was, of course, yes. They would break every arm there if they needed to.

More merchants arrived, prompting the defenders to draw their swords.

'Let's go,' Blake said, taking her sister by the arm. 'It's about to get ugly.'

Eda did not move.

'Now,' she ordered.

Every merchant must take a stand, Eda signed. *How else will we stop this?*

Blake knew there was no stopping the king once he made up his mind about something.

A nearby defender shoved a woman so hard she went hurtling into Eda, knocking her to the ground. Blake pulled her sister to her feet before turning to him. 'You feel like a big man now?'

His eyes narrowed on her. 'Go about your business, boor.'

But the anger had taken hold of her. 'You can't lock us in here. We're not prisoners.'

The sound of a horse approaching made them all stop and look. There was Prince Borin on horseback, flanked by Astin and a handful of other guards. Her face fell when she spotted Harlan wearing his serious defender expression.

'Can we have some calm, please?' the prince shouted as he moved between the merchants. 'Let me be very clear. This wall is not to keep you in but to keep intruders out. It is being built at your king's expense to keep you safe.'

'So we're supposed to thank him?' Blake muttered to her sister.

Harlan's eyes shot to her. She tried not to wilt beneath the intensity of his stare. Seeing him was like tearing off a scab that had barely had a chance to form.

'We don't need your protection,' someone called out. 'We need freedom to come and go from the port without being questioned or detained by your men.'

'You want the sea warriors to enter freely also? Want them to burn down your homes? Slaughter your families? Take your food?'

Blake could not help herself. 'What food? There's no food.'

The prince found her in the crowd. 'Patience, merchant.'

'She's right,' someone else shouted. 'Your defenders are standing on the wrong side of the wall.'

'You people do not get to decide what is best for the entire kingdom,' Borin shouted.

'But we should get to decide what's best for us,' Blake shot back. She pointed at the wall. 'This further reduces our freedom and you know it.'

The defender closest to her made a move in her direction, but before he reached her, Harlan's horse pushed between them. She looked up. The smallest shake of his head warned that she was crossing a very dangerous line.

'Let's go,' she said, taking Eda's arm and turning away from the prince.

The horse followed her.

'Blake,' Harlan said.

It was not the voice he had used with her in front of the fireplace, the one whispered against her bare skin. It was the voice of the commander who had killed her brother.

She did not turn around.

Harlan dismounted and caught up with her. 'So you'll take my food but won't even reply when I call your name?' He spoke quietly so as to not interrupt the prince.

She stopped walking. 'I tried to refuse your food, but your friends are as pushy as you.'

His eyes moved between hers. 'Go straight home. Stay away from the port for a few days. Understand?'

There was that anger again, simmering away in the pit of her belly. 'What's the matter, Commander? Having a tough time caging us in?'

His expression did not change. 'Don't make me assign a defender to your front door.'

She shook her head and resumed walking.

'You'll still be allowed to conduct business as normal,' he said, following her.

'Allowed?' She laughed. 'I'd fall at your feet with gratitude, but the street's a little muddy.'

He looked over his shoulder, then closed the distance between them. 'I don't want the wall either, but since there's not a damn thing either of us can do about it, best we both keep our thoughts to ourselves.'

It was one of those torturous moments where Blake was torn between shoving him and burying her face against his chest. Was it wrong to miss that earthy scent of his? 'Better get back on your horse, Commander.' She kept her eyes ahead. 'I suspect the prince is going to need you.'

CHAPTER 31

*D*on't go, Eda signed to Blake. The dying embers from the main room cast light through the open door over Eda's bed.

Blake had thought her sister asleep as she tried to sneak from the room, but Garlic flapping around the place must have woken her. At least Lyndal had slept through the commotion. She could sleep through just about anything.

'Go back to sleep,' Blake whispered.

I saw the bag, Eda signed, referring to the one Blake had stuffed into the waist of her skirt. It was one of the canvas bags Kingsley used to take when he went through the tunnels. *You're going under the wall.*

She was going *over* the wall, but the less Eda knew the better. 'Go back to sleep, and don't say a word to anyone.'

Eda's worried face was the last thing Blake saw as she fled the room.

As she stepped down onto the street, her mind went to the last time she had seen Kingsley. His final words had been equally as dismissive. She wondered if he regretted them as the roof of that tunnel collapsed on him.

This was different.

That was what she told herself as she headed into the forest. This was careful, considered. Carried out under the cover of darkness. If she was discovered, she could run and disappear into the trees. The defenders would never be able to identify her.

Unless they caught her.

Then they would display her on the wall.

But if everything went to plan, she would have a way to provide for her family that was not dependent on Harlan. Perhaps the food would finally stop sticking in her throat every time she swallowed.

Blake moved quietly through the forest, always alert to her surroundings. When she reached the edge of the trees, she stopped behind a wide trunk and peered up at the wall. She watched for over an hour, studying the movements of the defender on duty. She counted out the time it took him to walk from one turret to another. He was slower than the daytime guards she had observed. That would work in her favour.

Removing her boots, she hid them out of sight. Her bare feet ached in the cold. She waited for the defender to pass by again, then took off at a sprint towards the wall. When she reached it, she flattened her body against the cold stone, grateful for the cloud cover. She counted out the time in her head, allowing for the guard to return and leave again, then started to climb.

She pressed her fingers into the protruding edges of the stone, her face brushing the wall as her toes felt their way up it. There were times when a single toe held the full weight of her while she figured out her next move.

At the twenty-feet mark, her limbs began to tremble, every muscle in her body working to keep her attached to that wall. Progress was slower than she had anticipated, which meant she would have to wait for the defender to pass again before climbing over the embrasure.

She was ten feet from the top when her right foot slipped. Her face smashed into the stone wall, and fear pounded in her ears. If she fell from that height, she would most definitely injure herself, but worse, she would not be able to run from the defenders. Her misplaced foot scrambled for an edge, her arms shaking violently as they struggled to hold her weight. Finally, she found a toehold. She breathed out, not daring to look down.

Gritting her teeth, Blake dragged and pushed herself up the last few feet, pausing at the top when she heard footsteps. She held her breath, waiting for the defender to pass.

But he did not pass.

With a loud sigh, the defender leaned against the wall for a rest.

Of all the places for him to stop.

Blake dared a glance under her arm at the ground below. She did not have it in her to climb down again. Her body was about to give out. Her palms were sweating despite the cold air. She struggled to keep her breathing quiet as she swallowed down the scream sitting in her throat.

She had two choices: fall or reveal herself to the defender. Neither was particularly appealing, but a broken back was the less appealing option at that moment. If she surprised the guard, she stood a chance of fleeing without being caught. But flee to where? There were more defenders in the turrets.

Her toe began to slip, and she knew she had only moments to act. Reaching, she took a firm hold of the embrasure and, with all her remaining strength, pulled herself up. The effort was enormous. Just as her knee landed on top of the embrasure, she came face to face with a very young, very confused defender. He looked past her as if trying to figure out where she had come from. That was her opportunity, while his mind was still playing catch-up.

She leapt at him, knocking him backwards before he had a chance to draw his weapon. She heard the air leave his lungs as his back slammed into the wall walk, and then she was scrambling off him. If she could make it to the turret without being seen, she stood a chance. But when she went to run off, he grabbed hold of her ankle, sending her sprawling forwards. She put her hands out just in time to prevent her face from hitting the ground. She kicked wildly until she finally freed herself. Adrenaline coursed through her as she focused on the turret ahead of her, preparing to run.

But the man was too fast and too well trained.

He was standing once more with an arm secured around her waist before she was back on her feet. Desperate, Blake threw her head up, making contact with the man's nose. He roared and threw her down onto the wall walk, drawing his sword. She rolled onto her back and fumbled for her knife as he raised his weapon above her.

Stomach? Chest? Throat? Where would he strike? She had seen men disembowelled while conscious, forced to watch their insides exit their own bodies. She closed her eyes, bracing.

There was a soft thud as something hit the ground beside her. Blake opened her eyes. The defender lay just inches from her face, his eyes closed and mouth slack. Confused, she looked up and found a panting Harlan standing over her. His eyes were two pools of fire.

She was in so much trouble.

'Get up,' he growled, pulling her to her feet with such force her head snapped backwards. 'Stay directly behind me, and don't make a sound.' He pointed to the closest turret.

Her legs were not cooperating, and Harlan was already out of patience. When she struggled to run, he took her by the wrist and began dragging her. When she stumbled, he pulled her to her feet without slowing down.

'Wait,' she whispered when he sped up.

He still did not slow down. 'If we wait, you hang.'

She willed her legs to work better.

They were almost at the turret when voices drifted out. Harlan stepped sideways, tucking himself into the outer wall of the turret and pulling Blake to him. He pressed her head to his chest and turned his face to the shadows. Two men exited, and she held her breath. Harlan had crossed a line there was no coming back from —and she had forced him across it.

The two men continued past them.

Harlan wasted no time, pushing off the wall and dragging her with him as he entered the turret. He led her to the stairs, then hurried down them, taking them two at a time and forcing her to do the same. When they reached the bottom, he paused and listened.

Silence.

A moment later, they were through the door at the bottom. Blake's first instinct was to run, but Harlan kept a firm hold of her wrist as he looked around. His hand was like an iron cuff, but she did not dare complain. His eyes went to her bare, filthy feet.

'Please tell me your shoes aren't back there,' he whispered.

She shook her head, too afraid to speak.

Harlan looked up, watching and listening to the movement above him. It was only a matter of time before the two men came across the unconscious defender lying in the middle of the wall walk.

'When I say go, you're going to run as fast as you can. Understand?'

She nodded.

There were shouts overhead, then men running.

'Wait,' he commanded, ear to the wall. When the men entered the turret, he said, 'Go.'

Blake took off at a sprint through the mud towards the trees. Her hand pulsed as blood returned to it. Harlan's feet pounded behind her, pushing her faster still. She did not slow when she reached the trees, navigating the trunks as best she could in the dark. He moved like a demon in her peripheral vision, his pace even and his breath quiet in comparison to her raspy inhales. They maintained that speed all the way back to the village, and then he took hold of her wrist again as they broke free of the trees. Somewhere behind them, dogs barked. She flinched at the noise and heard Harlan curse.

'This way,' he said, leading her to an abandoned shop. Instead of going inside, he nodded to the roof. 'Up you go.'

Blake looked up, panting. 'You want me to get on the roof?'

His reply came in the form of grabbing her by the waist and throwing her up in the air. She took hold of the edge of the thatched roof and dragged herself onto it, then turned to help Harlan, but he was already up. He carefully navigated the timber support beams so he would not fall through.

'Lie down,' he said, reaching into his pocket. He pulled out a piece of folded cloth. The smell of pepper hit Blake's nostrils.

'What's that for?' she whispered.

He began sprinkling pepper on the roof around them. 'The dogs have our scent. It'll buy us time.'

'Do you normally carry pepper around with you?'

His dark eyes flashed at her, but before he could reply, dogs burst from the trees a hundred feet away, pulling their handlers along in excited leaps. Blake held her breath. She had seen merchant men torn apart by those dogs. The handlers had control over them to a point, but then instinct seemed to take over.

She began shivering, and Harlan rolled his head to look at her.

'Eda came to the gate,' he whispered.

Of course she had. Blake looked up at the sky, trying

to remember the last time she saw stars. It had been years. 'I don't know whether to thank her or scream at her.'

'Thank her.'

Her eyes closed when a dog barked nearby. They were both still as feet ran past.

'I guess that explains the pepper,' she whispered when the footsteps faded. 'Did anyone see you up there?'

Harlan shook his head.

She swallowed down her guilt. 'Good.'

More silence.

'Why did you do it?' he asked, sounding angry again.

'Food.'

He looked away, staring up at the clouds too. 'You risked your life for a bit of grain even though I've been sending you eggs and butter.'

A tear slid into her hair. 'I can't rely on you anymore. Surely you understand why.'

'And surely you understand why I can't stand back and let you go hungry.'

She brushed away the next tear. 'For the first time in my life, I'm doubting my ability to survive.'

'Don't say that.'

'I don't know what I'm supposed to do.'

His fingers brushed the back of her hand. 'You accept my help until you figure it out.'

They were silent for a moment.

'I miss you,' she said to the sky. 'But I'm so angry.'

He nodded. 'That's all right. Hate me if it's easier.' He turned his head to look at her again. 'Just don't let it make you reckless. I need you alive at the end of all this.'

She turned to meet his gaze, then brought her lips to

his uniformed shoulder. 'This is so much bigger than us now. That new wall will change everything.'

'I know.'

'Do you?' She tilted her head up to read his face. 'We won't die quietly. This is no longer about what the king is keeping out but who he's trapping inside.'

Bringing a hand to her face, he kissed her forehead so gently she wondered if she had imagined it. What a contradiction he was. Breaking her one moment, then gathering up all the pieces of her the next. She never doubted his feelings though, not even when his fury burned holes in her skin.

'My orders are to protect that wall at any cost,' he whispered.

'I know.'

'Any man, woman, or child who removes a single brick from that wall will pay.'

More silence as dogs whined in the distance. At least they were getting farther away.

'The day your sister was lashed,' Harlan said, 'you signed something to her. It made her stop crying. What was it?'

She thought back to that day, then realised what he was referring to. Lifting her hands, she signed and spoke the words. 'Stand tall and strong, warrior.' Her hands fell to her stomach. 'My father used to say that to us when we were children. Whenever we scraped our knees playing gameball or returned home in tears because the boys were being mean to us. He wanted his daughters to be resilient. It was like he knew what lay ahead of us.'

'Resilience is probably the greatest lesson a merchant father can teach his child.'

She studied his face in the dark. 'Would you save him for me if you had your time over again?'

His eyebrows came together. 'Kingsley?'

She nodded.

'I see you suffer every day because he's not here. What do you think?'

She let out a breath, thoughts drifting again. 'Lyndal said I should forgive you for everything that happened before us.'

'Maybe.' He watched her in the dark. 'I think the question is, can you forgive me for everything that happens *after* us?'

'I don't know.' She pressed her forehead to his. 'I hope so, because I don't have the energy to hate you anymore. This existence is exhausting.'

His eyes searched hers. 'You keep your head down, but you don't give up the fight. You hear?'

Another nod.

They listened as the dogs and their handlers gave up their search and disappeared into the trees.

'Promise me you won't try anything like that again,' Harlan whispered.

Blake swallowed. 'I promise.'

'Where the hell were you last night?' Shapur called as he marched towards his son.

Harlan was on his way to the mess hall after training. He had managed to avoid his father for most of the day. 'Sleeping, until I was called to the gate.'

Shapur crossed his arms. 'Because of the breach?'

'A personal matter.' He was not obligated to explain to his father what he did while off duty. 'I did hear about the breach though. But don't worry. They never made it over the wall.'

'They were never caught either.'

Harlan continued walking, his father falling into step with him. 'She won't be the last person to try.'

'She?' Shapur's brow creased. 'Well, *she* scaled the wall without so much as a rope.'

Harlan blinked away the image of Blake falling to her death. He had not asked her how she had gotten up there, maybe because he was afraid of the answer. 'I've put some extra men on that wall.'

'The merchant needs to be found and disciplined.'

Harlan looked heavenward. 'And how do you suggest I do that when even the dogs couldn't find her?'

Shapur grabbed his arm, forcing him to stop. 'What the hell is going on with you? Someone breaches the wall and you just shrug and say, "Oh well"?'

Harlan pulled his arm free. 'I just told you I put extra men on the wall. You know, this is what happens when you cage people in. Stop acting surprised.'

'These are orders from our king.'

'And he doesn't make mistakes?'

Shapur looked around to ensure no one had heard. 'Careful. Men have hung for less.'

Harlan was done with the conversation, with the threats, with all of it. He did something he had never done in his life. He walked away from his father first.

'Commander!'

'I need to eat.'

'I want you knocking on every door in that borough. Find out what people know. You hear me?'

Without looking back, Harlan saluted his father. 'Loud and clear, warden.'

'Of course you must be the one to do it,' Lyndal said, thrusting the knife towards Blake. 'It's *your* duck.'

Blake took the knife and looked down at Garlic. He was napping on her foot. The fact that he had time to nest showed how long they had been arguing. 'But you're the cook in the household.'

'So?'

'So he's an ingredient.'

Lyndal sighed. 'He's food only once slaughtered and plucked. Right now he's still your pet.'

Eda was leaning against the wall watching the exchange. When Blake glanced in her direction, her sister looked away. She had not forgiven Blake for attempting to go over the wall.

Candace walked into the courtyard and looked between the three girls, then down at the knife in Blake's hand. 'Oh. Well, I suppose it's time.'

'If you hadn't named him, this wouldn't be so difficult,' Blake said quietly.

Lyndal's mouth fell open. 'And is it my fault he sleeps in your bed too?'

The sound of the shop bell hitting the ground made the women all look in that direction.

'Anyone here?'

Harlan's voice had Blake's feet moving before her thoughts could catch up. She froze in the doorway of the shop, her sisters and mother on her heel.

Harlan stood in the middle of the room with the young recruit who had been in the water with him the day the sea warriors attacked.

'We need to speak with every member of the household,' said the defender.

Blake stepped into the room. 'What is it you need to talk to us about?'

'We need to know where you were last night.'

Lyndal immediately looked at Blake, who did not dare meet her gaze.

'We were here,' Candace said. 'All of us were early to bed.'

'Did you hear or see anything unusual throughout the night?' Harlan asked.

That was when Blake realised they were looking for the person who had breached the wall. They were looking for *her*.

'Is this about the breach?' Candace asked. 'Because I assure you we know nothing of it.'

Lyndal straightened. 'What breach?'

'Someone tried to go over the wall last night,' Blake said, keeping her tone as casual as possible.

'Over?' Lyndal questioned. 'Goodness. They must have been quite desperate.'

Harlan's eyes went to the door, where Garlic had just appeared. 'You still have the duck?' He sounded annoyed. Not entirely surprising given recent events.

'Actually, today is the big day,' Lyndal said. 'Blake was just about to do the honours.'

Blake crossed her arms against the cold air blowing in through the open door. 'I think we should wait until tomorrow.'

'Why?' Lyndal asked.

She knew exactly why. Because there had been enough death in their family, and this felt a lot like the death of another sibling. 'Because... tomorrow is better.'

'I'll do it,' Harlan said, reaching for his sword.

Blake bent down and grabbed the duck. 'Thank you, Commander, but I don't want to delay your important work.'

His eyes moved to hers. 'If you hear anything, you're obligated to come forwards with the information.'

Blake was grateful that Garlic was covering her thudding chest. 'I know.'

Candace went to the door, opening it wider for them.

The young defender looked between them, then gestured to the bell on the floor. 'You should fix that.' Then he walked out.

Harlan nodded once at Blake before following him.

Pushing the door closed behind them, Candace exhaled. 'He acts like he did not ride off with you on horseback and completely ruin your future.'

Blake did not reply; she simply waited for her mother and Eda to disappear into the house before turning to Lyndal. 'I can feel you glaring at me. Come on. Out with it.' She set Garlic down and walked over to pick up the bell.

'I was just thinking about how filthy your feet were when you rose from bed this morning,' Lyndal said, wandering closer, 'despite all of us washing before retiring.' She paused. 'I was also wondering why you wore your good shoes out of the house this morning and returned wearing your boots.'

Blake fiddled with the bell in her hand. 'Kingsley was supposed to fix this.'

Lyndal looked down at the bell. 'I remember. It was the last thing he said before he went off and got himself killed.' She glanced away. 'If you follow in his footsteps and die trying to play the hero, I shall never forgive you.'

Blake looked at her sister. 'I know.'

'Do you? Do you know what it would do to us if we lost you?'

She knew. 'I'm not going anywhere, I promise.'

Lyndal looked down at the bell again, then disappeared into the house.

Blake turned the bell over and over in her hands, then went to fetch the bag of tools from the cupboard. She grabbed the stool from behind the table and placed it next to the door. Bell in hand, she stepped up and finished the job her brother never could.

CHAPTER 33

'I want five archers in each turret along the south wall,' Harlan said. 'Out of sight so the merchants don't feel threatened.'

He had objected to the unveiling of the new wall, but his reasons had fallen on deaf ears. The king insisted it would reduce tensions and turn the narrative to a more positive one. According to Astin, Prince Borin was in complete denial about the merchants' feelings. He believed any conflict would blow over once they realised they were better off.

'I want forty men behind the crowd,' Harlan continued, looking around at his men. 'Ten more archers along the east wall to ensure the royal borough is protected. The rest of you will be in the port, also out of sight. We're taking precautions, not provoking civil war.'

They were standing outside the armoury, Shapur listening at the back. He was not interrupting for once.

'The king will speak from atop the wall,' Harlan said. 'That's the safest place for him. You'll be focused only on the crowd. If anyone becomes vocal, you remove them with minimal fuss. It only takes one defender to remove a merchant, not five—remember that. If you start ambushing people, others will step in. Seen it happen a hundred times before.' He looked around at their faces, making sure they understood.

'Will the gate be open or closed?' Roul asked. He was standing at the front with his arms crossed.

'Closed.'

Roul shifted. 'Won't that provoke them?'

Shapur spoke up at that. 'We cannot have them wandering into the port borough for no good reason.'

Roul turned to the warden. 'Who decides which reasons are valid?'

'Careful what comes out of your mouth next, defender,' Shapur warned.

Roul faced forwards again.

Harlan had grown rather attached to the new recruit. He had been quick to poach him at the end of his training.

'Right. Everyone clear?' Harlan asked.

The men nodded.

'Good. Let's move out.'

'I've no interest in going,' Lyndal said. She was seated in the main room with her legs tucked up and Garlic on her lap.

Yes, the duck was still alive.

'I'm with Lyndal,' Candace said. 'Attending the

unveiling will be taken as a sign of support, and I'm against it.'

Every merchant is against it, Eda signed.

Blake knew Harlan would be there. She also knew there would be trouble. Thea had told her there were many attending who had a clear message for the king regarding his new wall. Blake did not know who she was more worried about, the merchants or Harlan. 'Eda and I will go, then.'

'If you must,' Candace said, 'but stay at the back, away from any potential trouble. And make sure you come straight home afterwards.'

Blake and Eda went to the bedroom to fetch their cloaks. The sight of Eda holding her shirt up with her teeth while she strapped on her dagger made Blake smile. Her sister's sixteenth birthday had come and gone. Harlan had somehow found out and sent a food package with black bread for the occasion. Blake had wanted to thank him for making it special, but she never saw him. All she got were glimpses of him atop the wall. He was rarely inside the borough anymore.

Probably for the best.

Every time she saw him, it took her a few days to rebuild her immunity.

'Ready?' Blake asked, lowering her skirt.

Eda finished tucking in her shirt. *Ready.*

Around half the merchants were present for the unveiling. Men stood in groups, their expressions far from celebratory. Blake and Eda stood with the other women at the back, where young children dashed between skirts, lost in their games.

Blake noticed the defenders were scattered amid the crowd, their sharp gazes shifting from person to person. Her eyes travelled up to the archers along the walls. Not as many as she would have predicted given the situation, but she suspected there were more hidden in the turrets. Harlan was not a man who took risks.

It was a long wait before King Oswin finally appeared on the wall, Prince Borin marching at his side. Eight defenders surrounded them, Astin among them. Prince Becket was nowhere to be seen. It was common knowledge that he had no interest in such things and preferred the quiet of the castle.

When the king and prince came to a stop above the new portcullis, the defenders formed a circle around them. They were not taking any chances.

'What a proud day for Chadora,' King Oswin began, his booming voice reaching all corners of the borough. 'To see our most vulnerable now completely protected from the harsh realities that face those outside of Chadora's walls. Let your minds be at ease.'

Not a single noise came from the so-called vulnerable crowd standing before the king. Hard faces stared back at him.

'No sea warrior will be foolish enough to come ashore now,' he continued. 'They will not make it past the port.'

The only noise was the shuffle of merchant feet.

'I know some of you have concerns,' King Oswin went on. 'However, let me assure you that any man standing before me who needs to conduct business in the port will be able to do so.'

Blake leaned closer to Eda. 'I really hope he means "man" in a figurative sense, or he's going to have a lot of angry women on his hands.' She spotted Harlan atop the wall and straightened. She had come to recognise him like her own shadow. Those broad shoulders. The curve of his neck. Those perfectly formed lips that she imagined on her skin at night. He was concentrating hard on the scene below. If he knew she was there, he did not acknowledge it.

The cover was pulled back, revealing the same portcullis merchants faced at every wall. It was the most depressing sight Blake had ever seen. They could just make out the water through the latticed wood.

When no one applauded, the king stepped forwards to speak. 'May this day mark—'

His words were cut short when an arrow pierced his neck. There was a collective gasp from the crowd as the king's defenders burst into action. Astin stepped in front of Prince Borin, ushering him back to the other side of the wall.

Blake's eyes shot to Harlan, but he was no longer there.

'We have to go,' she said, grabbing Eda by the arm and dragging her off.

But the defenders at the back had drawn their swords and were not letting anyone through.

'Arms up!' they shouted. 'Hands where we can see them—all of you!'

Blake and Eda raised their hands, planting their feet as

the defenders shoved past them in search of the shooter. There was panic as the merchants were driven into a tighter circle.

'Hands up! Now!' the defenders continued to shout, shoving people in all directions. They began tearing cloaks off the backs of merchants and patting them down. They confiscated every weapon they came across, even though the daggers they were taking had nothing to do with the arrow wedged in the king's neck.

'Keep your hands up,' Blake whispered to Eda when a defender approached them. 'Don't resist.'

Eda stared ahead as her cloak was torn off. Large hands slid down her body. Blake knew the moment he found the dagger, because he stilled. Eda flinched as her shirt was torn open, her weapon taken. It took all of Blake's strength to remain still and silent.

'Face down on the ground,' the defender shouted.

Blood pounded in Blake's ears now. 'Do it,' she said when her sister looked at her.

Apparently Eda was not fast enough, because just as she got to her knees, the man kicked her in the back, sending her hurtling to the ground.

'Careful,' Blake said.

The defender responded by grabbing her neck and pushing her down onto the street too.

Screams rang out around them as the defenders tore through the crowd. The violence grew, the merchants no longer willing to stand idle while they were stripped and beaten.

Blake turned her head to her sister. 'It'll be over soon.'

The sound of a blade slicing through flesh made the

girls flinch, and then blood sprayed Eda's face. Blake jumped when a merchant man hit the street in front of them, blood gushing from his open neck. It ran towards Blake and soaked into her dress. Her breaths came shorter. She needed to get her sister out of there but knew any non-compliance would be met with deadly violence.

Chaos swelled around them, defenders unable to focus on a person for longer than a few seconds before another came at them.

'Get ready to run very fast,' Blake said, eyes on a nearby defender. The second he was distracted, she said, 'Now.'

The girls sprang to their feet and fled.

'Halt!' someone shouted behind them. But they did not stop.

'Head for the forest,' Blake told her sister. They could disappear there.

But as they reached the edge of the square, more defenders spilled out of the royal borough, blocking their only exit. Blake had just a few seconds to decide their next move.

She grabbed Eda by the arm.

'Put your hands up,' she said. 'We're unarmed. They won't hurt us if we comply.'

She was wrong.

The men approached with weapons in hand. One defender marched straight up to Eda and smashed the hilt of his sword into the side of her head, sending a spray of blood over Blake. Eda's eyes rolled back, and she sank down onto the muddy street. Blake stood frozen, her mind screaming. She had done exactly what Harlan would have wanted her to do. Submissive, obedient, cooperative. And now her sister was unconscious on the street.

Something snapped inside her.

She reached into her pocket for her dagger, and when the same defender came for her, she sliced his sword arm.

No, she would not stand helpless while these men knocked women to the ground. She would not play the merchant while they abused the power handed to them.

When the defender came at her again, Blake ducked to avoid being caught and punched him as hard as she could in the groin. The weapon fell from his hand as he folded in half, and she snatched it up, moving to stand in front of her sister. Panting, she glanced over her shoulder and sucked in a breath at the sight behind her. It was like the scene from the beach when the sea warriors had attacked, but this time it was merchant against defender.

While the defenders had a clear advantage with their training and weapons, what they did not have was years of pent-up anger, a heightened prey drive fuelled by starvation, and an unholy need to protect the people they loved.

More merchants joined the fight, spilling from nearby shops and houses. The defenders stopped using the hilts of their swords and started using their blades, cutting, slashing, and driving their weapons through any man or woman who stepped into their space—armed or not.

Blake gripped the sword, daring the defender on his knees before her to take it back. 'We had our hands up, for God's sake,' she screamed. 'Why did you do that?'

He got to his feet, eyebrows fused together in one angry line. 'Drop the sword.'

'No.'

He drew his knife and lunged, thrusting the blade at her neck. She ducked and swung the sword, forcing him back. He came at her again and again, and she just kept swinging, her lungs emptying with the effort. Eventually he caught hold of her arm and moved to stab her through the stomach. But she was ready. She kicked his front knee so hard she felt the crunch in her own bones.

The defender roared, hands going to the knee, which was now turned at a strange angle. Somehow he kept hold of his weapon. She wondered if she had it in her to kill him. Before meeting Harlan, she would not have hesitated, but now taking the life of one of his men felt a lot like betrayal.

She cut his leg instead, the way she had seen Harlan do on the beach that day, and prayed it would be enough.

She felt someone behind her. Fuelled by adrenaline and fear, she spun, swinging her weapon, not caring this time if she sent a head rolling as long as her sister was alive at the end of it all.

A sword met hers just inches from the defender's neck. Her hands slackened around the hilt as she recognised Harlan. Blood covered one side of his face.

'Blake.'

She let her weapon fall to the ground and bent to her sister, who was getting trampled. She knew as long as Harlan was standing above her that no weapon would touch her. She dragged Eda to her feet, and the younger girl's head rolled back. Her stomach clenched at the sight of her sister in that state.

Harlan tucked them both under one arm and led them through the maze of fighting, shoving any merchant who stood in his way and yelling at his own men to move. A man stepped into their path, carelessly swinging his weapon around. It almost hit Eda. Harlan bashed him in the face with the hilt of his sword and shoved him aside.

'Clear a path,' he called to the defenders lined up ahead of them. 'Move!'

The men stepped aside to let them through.

Eda groaned as they slipped between the defenders. Relief flooded Blake.

When the line sealed behind them again, Harlan said, 'I can't come with you.'

She adjusted her grip on her sister, knowing he had already done too much. 'We'll be fine.'

Running a hand down his face, Harlan nodded and turned back to the line. 'Open up.'

The defenders moved aside.

Harlan's sword turned in his hand as he marched through, swallowed up by the fighting. Blake closed her eyes and turned away, pressing her lips to her sister's bloodied head for a moment before lifting her into her arms and carrying her home.

CHAPTER 34

The smell of alcohol and blood was so thick in the air inside the infirmary, Harlan was forced to cover his nose and mouth as he made his way through it. While far more merchants had been injured and killed, the defenders had certainly not left the borough unscathed.

Shapur walked next to Harlan. 'It is possible the archer was inside one of the houses.'

The commander shook his head, pausing to watch a leg being stitched. 'Even an experienced archer couldn't manage that distance. Certainly not with that accuracy.'

Shapur looked around, scowling. 'You will need to search every shop, every house, and every inch of that forest. Confiscate every weapon. The last thing we need is armed merchants as they count the dead.'

Harlan resumed walking towards the door, in need of air. 'Every household has a bow of some kind, along with many other weapons. It's perfectly legal.'

'Well, that is about to change,' Shapur said quietly as they stepped outside and drew a lungful of clean air.

Harlan turned to his father. 'What are you talking about?'

'King Oswin is dead,' Shapur said, crossing his arms. 'Prince Borin is understandably angry. He wants justice.'

'Well, he needs to leave that to his defenders and focus on his family. The queen will need to be told. We're going to need Queen Fayre here to keep her son in line.'

'Prince Becket departs for Toryn in the morning, but it will be at least two months before they return. The seas are rough this time of year and the ships irregular.' Shapur looked out at the empty training field. 'In the meantime, our new king wants the merchants stripped of their weapons and the killer on the wall by the end of the day. Those are his orders.'

Harlan blinked. 'He's putting a time limit on it? Does he realise half his military are in the infirmary?'

'Who is going to tell him no?'

'You could. Or the king's advisors.'

'He cannot see past his grief right now.'

Harlan shook his head and brushed a hand down his face. 'Families require weapons for hunting.'

'Then lucky for them there is nothing left to hunt.'

'What about family heirlooms? Are we stripping merchants of their histories now?'

Shapur was not shutting him down like usual, which meant Harlan was raising valid points. But because the warden was loyal to a fault, he would follow the prince's orders.

'Take what is left of your men and split them into four

groups,' Shapur said. 'Start at both ends of the main roads. We do not want people warned of your arrival. That will give them time to hide their items. Every shop is to be turned upside down, every weapon, including things that can be used as weapons, confiscated.'

Harlan tried to relax his jaw. 'You do this, you take away what little these people have left, and you'll have men carving knives from sticks and killing defenders on the street.'

Shapur's eyes darkened. 'You are a defender of the king. Do not stand before me on the day of his death protecting those responsible.'

'One person fired that arrow. *One*. You cannot punish an entire borough.'

Shapur leaned closer. 'Tell that to your men in the infirmary. What we witnessed today was an uprising. If you think they will make daggers out of sticks, then take away their sticks.' He straightened. 'Go do your job, Commander.'

They heard the defenders before they reached their home. Blake, Lyndal, and Candace watched from the shop window as the men marched onto the street. Eda was recovering in bed, five stitches in her scalp.

'What are they doing?' Lyndal asked as men stormed into the shop opposite, shouting instructions.

Candace drew back from the window. 'Looking for the killer.'

The defenders exited the house, tossing a crossbow,

two daggers, and a quiver of arrows into the centre of the road.

'There's no way the king was killed with a crossbow,' Blake said. 'This is ridiculous. And why are they confiscating people's knives?'

More defenders appeared, tossing weapons onto the growing pile. Some merchants tried to lock their doors, but the soldiers kicked them open and marched straight inside.

Screaming ensued.

Blake backed away from the window, head shaking. 'Open the door so they don't break it.' She rushed out back and gathered the two bows they owned, placing Kingsley's in plain sight before taking the other one to the bedroom. It had belonged to their father, and it meant more to Eda than anything else in the world.

Blake looked around. Time was running out.

Eda sat up, eyeing the bow. *What's wrong?*

'We need to hide it,' Blake said. 'They're coming.'

Who?

'The defenders.'

Eda swung her legs over the edge of the bed, eyes closing momentarily with dizziness. She opened the drawer where her underthings were kept and pulled out a small knife.

Of course she had knives hidden around the place.

Crouching beside the bed, she lifted the linen and plunged the blade into the side of the mattress, making a hole wide enough for the bow.

'Good idea,' Blake said. She knelt and began tearing

handfuls of wool out. It took her a minute to get the bow in, and then she had to restuff the mattress.

Lyndal burst into the room. 'They're coming.'

They all looked at the quiver of arrows sitting on the floor, each one handcrafted by their father. Blake took a single arrow and poked it into the mattress before kicking the quiver to Lyndal. It slid across the floor, where it was snatched up.

'Put it with the other bow,' Blake said, her heart like lead in her chest. She did not dare look at Eda.

Men's voices reached them from the shop.

'Lie down,' Blake whispered, scooping up a rogue tuft of wool and hiding it. 'And for God's sake, look sick.' She tucked the sheet over the damaged mattress just as heavy footsteps stopped in the doorway.

Rising, Blake turned to see Harlan. She stopped breathing for a moment. His face was covered with cuts and bruises, and dark circles enclosed his eyes.

They stared at each other, not speaking.

A second defender entered the room and looked around. He went to the dresser and began opening the drawers and emptying the contents onto the floor, efficient and thorough.

Harlan stared at the floor.

Panic rose in Blake as the defender began lifting the other mattresses. When he reached Eda's bed, Blake stood in his way.

'Move,' the defender said, staring her down.

Blake looked over at Harlan, expecting him to come to her aid like he always did.

He lifted his eyes to her, nothing but defeat and resignation in them. 'Move your sister to another bed.'

Blake's eyebrows came together. She turned to Eda, helping her out of the bed and walking her into another one. She held her breath as the defender lifted the mattress and let it drop back down onto the creaky wooden frame. As it landed, the sheet flitted up, revealing the cut with wool bulging from it. The defender doing the search had already turned away, but Harlan saw it. His eyes met Blake's, and she waited to see what he would do.

'Check the kitchen,' he told the defender.

The soldier left the room, and the sound of items being thrown around the kitchen followed shortly after.

Blake walked over to Harlan, studying the injuries on his face.

'This isn't the way,' she whispered.

He dipped his head closer to hers. 'You said you would forgive me for whatever comes next.'

She swallowed, tentatively reaching up to touch the large cut above his eye. The wound had crusted over already. 'But what if you can't forgive yourself?'

Eyes closing, Harlan leaned into her touch for a moment, then turned and left the room.

CHAPTER 35

'What do you mean, you did not find his killer?' Prince Borin asked, fingers pressing into the arms of his father's chair.

Harlan was still adjusting to the sight of him seated on the elaborate throne. He looked too small for it, like a child playing king.

Shapur answered that. 'None of the arrows confiscated in the borough today matched the one taken from your father.'

Prince Borin's mouth twisted. 'Or Commander Wright failed to find it.'

Harlan drew a breath. 'We turned the entire borough upside down, Your Highness.'

'Well, it came from somewhere, Commander.'

Harlan had not been a huge fan of King Oswin's, but he was even less of a fan of his firstborn son. 'It's possible the arrow used was made for the job. A single arrow that can't be traced.'

Borin regarded him, one finger tapping. 'If the defenders cannot weed out my father's murderer, then we shall leave it to the merchants.'

Harlan snuck a look at Astin, who was standing by the wall. The bodyguard looked as defeated as Harlan. 'Can you clarify what you mean by that?'

Borin rose and walked over to him. 'Get your men out of the borough. Close the gates. And keep them closed until the killer is handed over.'

King Oswin's advisor, who had remained silent until that point, took a small step forwards. 'I do not think that is wise at such a time, Your Highness. I suggest you focus on the funeral arrangements and the upcoming coronation.'

Borin spun around. 'My father is dead! The very least we can do is bring his killer to justice.'

Shapur cleared his throat. 'If I may, Your Highness. I served under your father his entire reign, and I never knew him to be a vindictive man.'

'Are you calling me vindictive, Warden?' Borin asked, eyes shooting to him. 'If your loyalty is as deep as you claim it is, then you should be the first person backing me on this.'

Harlan's eyebrows lowered. 'How will the merchants source food and access supplies?'

'They won't,' Borin shot back. He wandered back to the throne and took a seat. 'That is the point of the exercise. No one in, no one out. You will be amazed how quickly the killer will be revealed.'

'What if there's trouble in the borough?' Harlan asked.

Borin narrowed his eyes on the commander. 'No one in. No one out. They might finish with a new-found appreciation for law and order.'

Shapur shifted. 'There are times my men need to—'

'Did I stutter, Warden?' the prince asked, making his voice as loud as possible without actually shouting.

Shapur stared at him for the longest moment, then bowed. 'No one in. No one out.'

The square was packed so tightly that the girls could not get near the notice. Word was spreading though, drawing every merchant to the square to read the news with their own eyes.

'All it takes is one person spreading misinformation to cause blind panic in an already fragile borough,' Lyndal said as they waited.

A woman with a young baby pressed to her chest squeezed past them. Her eyes met Blake's, and Blake saw the same hopelessness in them she had seen in Harlan's the day before. That was the moment she knew the rumours were true.

'Almost there,' Lyndal said, holding onto her sisters. They could not afford to be separated.

After what felt like an eternal wait, they reached the notice. They read it once, then twice.

March 4, 1327
By royal decree, the merchant borough will be closed until King

*Oswin's killer is brought forward. No one, including members
of the king's army, will be permitted to enter or exit the region.
Anyone with information regarding King Oswin's death should
present themselves at the royal gate.*

'Closed?' Lyndal said, her face screwing up. 'How can
you close a borough?'

Blake looked up at the defenders watching them from
atop the wall. They had not passed one guard on their
walk there. She wondered where Harlan was and what he
had said on the matter. She found it hard to believe that
anyone would be in support of such a lockdown.

'What if the killer isn't found?' Lyndal asked as they
turned away and weaved their way back through the
crowd. 'Are we to be left to starve?'

The answer was yes.

Prince Borin wanted justice for his father's death.
Blake knew only too well what grief did to a person. It
could consume every part of you if you let it—and his
grief was only a day old.

Once home, the Suttone women gathered around the
small table in the main room. Garlic was on Candace's
lap. Their remaining food sat in front of them: four
carrots, a turnip, two leeks, two spoonfuls of butter, a
duck no one had the heart to slaughter, and one of the
saddest cabbages Blake had ever laid eyes on. All of it
provided by Harlan.

'Some of the vegetables can be regrown with enough
daylight.'

Blake closed her eyes against Lyndal's optimism. She

just needed a few minutes to wallow. Not just for the loss of food but the loss of Harlan. Her memories of those precious days spent together were beginning to age, and she was so angry at herself for cutting that time short. Where had it gotten her?

Not fed.

Not pieced back together.

Happiness seemed so far out of reach at that point she doubted it would ever come again.

'Soup is the most logical meal plan,' Lyndal continued, 'because we can just keep building on it as more food arrives.'

'Arrives from *where*?' Blake asked, tone blunt.

Lyndal looked between them all. 'We shall get it from somewhere.'

Blake rose, unable to take it any longer. 'The food sitting on this table is a joke. It's barely enough for one week. This could drag on for months. Or perhaps they'll never find the killer and we'll all die.'

'For goodness' sake,' her mother said, eyes closing.

'At least the birds will finally return to the borough,' Blake went on, unable to stop, 'if only to pick at our corpses.'

Candace's eyes snapped open. 'Enough. How is that helpful?'

'It's not,' Blake replied. 'Nothing can help us now. Don't you see? This is how it ends for us.'

Eda stared down at her lap, and Lyndal's eyes welled up despite her stoic expression.

'The killer might be handed over by the end of the day,' Candace said. 'Now, you can either sit down and contribute something constructive to the conversation or *leave.'*

Eda looked up, eyes pleading. But Blake could not be strong for her in that moment. Stepping back from the table, she left the room.

$\mathcal{A}$ persistent hunger plagued Blake in the days that followed the announcement. She found herself thinking about the evening meal while consuming the morning one. They had halved their portions to make what they had stretch further, but it had already not been enough food to begin with. Now they were on a slow path to starvation.

Two weeks into their sentence, Blake was on her way back from the well when she spotted Harlan atop the wall, watching her. She had a full pail of water in each hand as she navigated the slippery stones. Water sloshed from the bucket as she came to a stop in the middle of the street. He looked around, then gestured for her to come to him. Abandoning the pails, she made her way over. But when she arrived, all he did was drop a tightly folded piece of parchment over the edge of the wall before striding off.

Not one word spoken. She would have done anything to hear his voice.

Picking up the parchment, she stuffed it into her

pocket to read in private, away from the prying eyes of the defenders above. She returned to the abandoned pails, picked them up, and continued home.

Only when she was in the privacy of the bedroom did she pull it from her pocket and read.

I'm going to bring you some food. Return to this spot at noon. Burn the note.

There was no name at the bottom, not even a letter she could run her finger over.

Blake found an excuse to leave the house by herself before noon, not wanting to risk missing him. She waited out of sight beneath a tree, eyes trained on the wall. She had been there for close to half an hour when a small cloth parcel landed on the ground twenty feet away. Her eyes travelled back up the wall, and she saw Harlan striding away without so much as a backwards glance.

The empty space inside her grew. She just wanted to lay eyes on him for a few seconds longer, but he was not taking any chances.

She moved out to retrieve the parcel, but a woman came from another direction and got to it first. Snatching it off the ground, she shoved it into her dress. She likely saw Blake waiting and stuck around to see what would eventuate from it.

'Hand it over,' Blake said, being as intimidating as she could be in her state.

'I have children,' the woman replied, backing away.

'And I have sisters and a mother.'

'He'll bring you more,' the woman said, tearing up. 'No one will bring me anything. I'm not a bad person.'

Blake knew that. She could smell the desperation coming from her. Swearing loudly, Blake said, 'Steal from me again and I'll strangle you with my bare hands. You hear me?'

The woman nodded and took off at a run.

When Blake arrived home, empty-handed, she heard a commotion out in the courtyard and rushed out to see what was going on. Her mother sat against the wall, bleeding from the head. Lyndal was crouched down beside her, clutching Garlic to her as she tended to Candace. Eda stood in front of two boys, holding a small log in one hand.

'What the hell is going on?' Blake asked, walking over to stand beside Eda.

The two boys were no older than twelve. It took Blake a moment to recognise them due to their sunken faces. She had played gameball with them a few times.

'They tried to steal Garlic,' Lyndal said, glaring at the boys.

Anger pulsed through Blake. 'Did you do that to my mother? Did you make her bleed?'

The boys were too hungry to be fearful, their dull eyes fixed only on the duck. There was no reasoning with children in that state. A conscience was just another luxury no one could afford.

'You better get out of here before I let my sister beat you,' Blake said.

Lyndal rose. 'You're just going to let them go?'

'As opposed to *what*?' Blake snapped over her shoulder.

The boys took advantage of her distracted state and darted off, leaping over the fence. Eda lowered the log and did not give chase. No one had the energy for that.

'They pushed our mother into a stone wall,' Lyndal said.

Blake pressed her eyes shut. 'And nobody cares except us. There's no one to tell, no one to protect us from ourselves. What would you have me do? Hang them from the wall?'

Lyndal was silent.

'This is probably the only living animal in the entire borough,' Blake said. 'They'll come back for it, because that's what desperate people do.' She tore the duck from Lyndal's grasp and walked into the kitchen to fetch one of the knives the defenders had not confiscated.

'What are you doing?' Lyndal asked when Blake returned outdoors holding the knife.

The duck flapped in protest as Blake held it down on the paved ground.

'I'm doing something we should have done a long time ago.'

Lyndal covered her eyes, and her mother looked away. Eda stood motionless as Blake raised the pathetic excuse for a knife above her head. The defender had taken their axe that day—and Harlan had let them. Her hand trembled, and Garlic stilled beneath her grip as if accepting his fate. Killing him would solve two problems: they would have some proper food for once and nothing left worth stealing.

Harlan could not help them anymore.

Blake blinked against the sting in her eyes. Tears

escaped, running down her nose and dripping onto the submissive bird. She could feel its heart beating beneath her hand.

A roar climbed up her throat and tore from her mouth. She threw the knife as hard as she could at the fence. It bounced instead of sticking, narrowly missing Eda, who stepped back from it in shock. Blake released the duck and shoved it towards her mother, much too hard judging by the way it tumbled.

Panting, Blake rose and wiped her face. 'Keep that log by the door. If those boys return, or anyone else for that matter, use it.'

The ship carrying supplies for the merchants came and went. Prince Oswin bought all the supplies and had them transported into the royal borough to be distributed to the other boroughs.

Harlan watched the whole thing from atop the wall, wondering how one foolish boy had the power to eliminate an entire class of people from the supply chain. His agitation grew with each passing day. He could not even buy food on the black market for Blake and her family because his father had eyes everywhere ensuring orders were followed.

'The sooner they hit rock bottom, the sooner this ends,' Shapur had said.

Harlan had stolen food from the mess hall for Blake, then watched from the shadows as it was stolen from her. He had not accounted for thieves in his plan. Seeing her grow thinner and weaker by the day was a special form of torture that kept him awake at night.

Three weeks into the lockdown, Shapur entered the mess hall and sank into the seat beside Harlan. He looked across at Astin, who was eating his morning meal, and cleared his throat. Astin looked between them, then picked up his bowl and rose from his chair, moving to another table.

'You need to discipline Thornton,' Shapur said as soon as they were alone.

Harlan dropped his spoon into his bowl and turned to look at his father. 'For what?'

'I was passing the port gate this morning, and I saw him throw a handful of mussels through the portcullis to some merchant children.'

Harlan blinked and returned to eating. Even liquid meals stuck in his throat nowadays. He scooped lentils and vegetables into his mouth before responding. 'The children wait at the gate, arms so thin they can fit through the gaps when they beg.'

Shapur let out a heavy breath. 'You think I do not see them? That I do not feel pity?'

Harlan slurped on his soup. 'I know you walk straight past.'

'We *all* must walk straight past. Those are our orders, as difficult as they might be.'

Harlan nodded and set his spoon down. 'Tell me, what's the punishment for throwing mussels to malnourished children these days?'

'Careful, Commander.'

'What would you have me do to the young defender

who's excelled in his role from day one? Want me to cut off a few fingers? Lock him up? Make sure next time we face sea warriors together he doesn't care if I live or die?'

'You are commander of that borough. You will think of something. We are near the end. Do not lose faith in the plan now.'

'I didn't have faith in the plan to begin with.'

'There is very little food left in the borough. Survival will beat secrecy. Someone knows who killed the king. And if that person has any decency, he will turn himself in before more people start to die. We are reaching the tipping point. That is why you must deal with Thornton.'

Harlan watched his father leave the mess hall before shoving his bowl away.

'Everything all right?' Astin asked, returning to the table.

Harlan rose and shook his head. 'Nothing's right in this fucking place.' With that, he left the mess hall and went in search of Roul.

He found the defender on the port wall, looking out at the merchant borough. He stood to attention when Harlan approached.

'At ease, defender.' Harlan stopped in front of him, eyes going over the wall to where a man lay in the street. 'Is he dead?'

Roul nodded. 'They've been stepping around him all morning. Seems too soon for this kind of thing, doesn't it? Easy to forget that they were already starving long before we closed the gates.'

Harlan blinked away the image of Blake lying in the street, her sisters too weak to move her. He had not thought about where they would put the dead—and there would be more. His eyes returned to Roul. 'The warden tells me you've been giving mussels to merchant children.'

Nothing changed on Roul's face. 'Yes.' There was no remorse in his voice.

'I don't want to stand here and tell you to stop, but you're no good to anyone locked in the tower.'

Roul nodded and looked down at the corpse again. 'I became a defender to protect the people in this kingdom, not contribute to their suffering. Now we have children caught up in games they don't understand living with consequences they don't deserve.'

Harlan ran a hand down his face and swallowed. 'You're a good man, but I need you to be discreet. If I don't discipline you, then someone else will.'

Roul frowned. 'This lockdown is a mistake. I think you know that. It'll be one of those points in history we'll look back on with shame.'

It was like having a mirror held up to him. Harlan had no choice but to look at himself. Not liking what he saw, he stepped back. 'That's all, defender. Back to work.'

It was week four of lockdown when Blake saw Harlan again. He was watching her from atop the wall. She could not read his face from that distance, but she felt his mood. It was as dark as her own. She could tell he needed something from her, but by the time she wandered over, he was gone. The only evidence he had been there was a note sitting on the ground. She bent to pick it up, unable to wait until she got home to read it.

Come back when it's dark. Signal with a whistle so you aren't waiting around drawing attention.

Blake did not tell her family about the letter as she did not want to get their hopes up. After dinner, she told them she was going for a walk to get some air.

I'll come with you, Eda signed.

Blake shook her head. 'It's too cold out. Stay here.'

She returned to the same spot she had found the note

and whistled softly. A noise behind her made her turn, and for one naive moment, she thought Harlan had come in person.

But he was not there.

A white linen parcel tied with string landed in the mud a few feet away. She ran to it, grabbing it off the ground and tucking it inside her cloak. Only then did she lift her gaze, expecting to find the wall empty. But there was Harlan, leaning on the embrasure, looking straight at her. She took a few steps back from the wall so she could see him better. They could not speak or do anything that would draw attention to them. So they just… looked.

She wanted so badly to hear his voice, touch his stubbly face, to glimpse a rare smile.

When Harlan straightened, her chest pulled. She was not ready for him to leave. But he was not leaving, he was looking at something. He was looking behind her.

She turned and found three men around her age standing there.

'What did he give you?' asked the tallest of the three.

Blake's hand went protectively over the parcel. She should have left while she had the chance, but Harlan was not easy to walk away from. Her heart sped up as she ran through all the possible ways the situation would play out. The men would not leave without the food, she knew that for sure. She also knew Harlan would not stand idle while three men robbed her.

The best thing she could do for everybody involved was run.

She took off as fast as she could in the opposite direction. If she could make it to the village, they would be less likely to assault her in view of others. Feet pounded behind her. She could hear the laboured breath of the men as they drew closer. The soft thud of an arrow piercing flesh followed by a cry of pain made her stop.

Blake turned to see an arrow protruding from one of the men's thighs. His two friends stared in stunned silence. It was clear Harlan had been trying to stop him, not kill him. One of them looked at her, eyes filled with accusation, as if she had shot the arrow herself. The other went to help his injured friend.

'Give me the package,' said the man staring at her.

She shook her head and backed away, annoyed at herself for stopping when Harlan had gifted her time.

The man approached so quickly she did not have a chance to run. He went to grab her, and she punched his hand away. He reached for her again, catching her by the arm this time. Not only did she not have a weapon to fight with, but she barely had any strength. Before she could swing a leg at him, he threw her to the ground and reached inside her cloak, searching for the parcel.

She struggled beneath him. 'He'll kill you.'

Just as he took hold of the parcel, an arrow struck her attacker's temple. He did not cry or make a sound.

That shot had definitely meant to kill.

The man tipped forwards, and with her remaining strength, Blake shoved him off her. She lay there panting and trying not to cry while the other men stared wide-eyed at their dead friend.

'Run,' she said, 'before he kills you.'

The injured man held tightly to his remaining companion, and the pair hurried away.

Blake turned to look at the man dead beside her. His cheeks were as sunken as her own. His family would expect him to return home. At what point would they start to worry?

When she looked back at the wall, she saw only the faint glow of torches. How Harlan had hit the man in the dark from that distance she had no idea. She could feel him watching her though, an arrow trained in her direction just in case. He needed to know she was all right. He needed her to get up.

She could give him that.

Blake rose slowly, forcing her legs to work. She stuffed the parcel back into her cloak with numb fingers and tried not to sway on her feet or do anything that would make him question her ability to make it home. He could not afford to take more risks than he had.

He had brought her food.

He had killed so she could eat.

So with strong, steady steps, she turned away from the wall and walked home.

'What happened?' her mother asked the second she walked in. 'You're so pale.'

Blake sank down into a chair and pulled out the parcel, placing it on the table in front of her.

'What is that?' Lyndal asked.

Blake blinked back tears. 'Food.' She closed her eyes to block out her mother's concerned expression. 'Harlan dropped it over the wall.'

Lyndal unwrapped the parcel just as Eda stepped into

the room to see what was going on. They all stared down at its contents.

A chunk of butter, two green carrots, and a piece of black bread. That was what the merchant's life had been worth.

Blake did not return to the wall again.

CHAPTER 38

Ten days after the wall incident, when every scrap of the food was gone, Blake sharpened an old kitchen knife into something of use and went out into the forest to hunt for the only thing available to them —aureate grubs.

She moved from tree to tree, carving and hooking, dragging the insects out and dropping them into a piece of cloth so she could take them home to her family.

Five grubs in, she heard a twig snap behind her. She spun around, pointing the embarrassing knife at the intruder. Her hand fell. 'Mother.' She looked past her to see if she was alone. 'What are you doing all the way out here by yourself?'

Candace pulled her cloak tighter around her. 'You are all the way out here by yourself.'

'Yes, but I'm armed.'

Her mother eyed the knife in her hand. 'Bit of a stretch.' She looked down at the moving pile of grubs on the ground. 'Are you collecting bait?

Blake followed her gaze. 'Actually, I'm gathering our next meal.' She bent, picked up one of the wriggling grubs, and popped it into her mouth.

Her mother flinched at the sound of her chewing.

'Don't worry, I had the same reaction the first time I saw Harlan eat one.' Blake picked up another and held it out for her mother. 'They're best eaten fresh and raw.'

'The commander told you they were safe to eat?' her mother asked, not taking the grub.

'Yes. Defenders are taught ways to survive off the land as part of their training. Pity they don't teach merchants, really.'

Candace drew a breath, her face determined, and took the grub from Blake. She closed her eyes as she put it in her mouth, chewing quickly. Her eyes opened as she swallowed. 'You know, I think it is the idea more than the taste.'

Blake smiled. 'Agreed.'

Candace reached out and took the knife from her daughter's hand. 'Could you show me how to find them?'

Blake tilted her head. 'Why? What's going on?' When her mother teared up and looked away, Blake stepped closer and placed a hand on her arm. 'Whatever is the matter?'

Candace took a moment to collect herself. 'It should be me.'

'What should be you?'

Candace pressed her lips together. 'Out here, scavenging for food. I should be begging at the gate if that is what it takes.'

Blake watched her mother struggle to get the words out.

'I stopped being the parent,' Candace said.

Blake understood then. 'Is that what's upsetting you? You lost your husband. Then you lost your son. You were grieving.'

'We were *all* grieving. Every one of us. But only I fell apart. You were just a child when your father died. You needed your mother to get out of bed.'

'And you did.'

Candace gave her a knowing look. 'I was no use to anyone, so you sat me in a chair with a needle and thread.'

Blake swallowed.

'The night you returned from the wall. The night Harlan dropped the package. I saw your face when you walked in,' Candace continued. 'I asked you what was wrong, and you said nothing. You were protecting me like one does their child. That was the moment I realised how severely I have failed you all.'

Blake sighed and looked around. 'I simply did not wish to add to your suffering.'

Candace brushed a tear from her cheek. 'Well, I refuse to see you worry and suffer alone from this point forwards.' She sniffed. 'And you should know that I am very sorry for the things I said to you the day you returned from the nobility borough. I was not angry at you but frightened for you.' She brushed another tear. 'I am very sorry for the things I said to you that day, but I am more sorry for all the things I did not say.'

Blake tucked her hair behind her ears. 'What did you not say?'

'I did not say how happy I am that you got to experience that kind of love. It is such a rare and precious thing. I see now that your feelings for one another were genuine. I truly hope that kind of love comes again for you, but the reality of our situation is that it probably will not. So I stand before you now, a little late, and say hold tight to those memories.'

Blake bit her lower lip. 'If you had your time over, would you have done anything different?'

A smile spread across her mother's face. 'I might have married your father sooner if I had known our time together would be cut short.' Her smile faded. 'And I would have forced myself to keep living after his death. Perhaps if I had, I would not have lost my son too.'

Blake's heart twisted. 'It's not your fault he died that day.' She looked down. 'I was right there, and Harlan...' She could not finish.

Her mother waited for her to look back up. 'Lyndal told me about his part in that day. The defenders made no secret of the fact that they would act in the best interest of the borough, not a handful of individuals.'

'You aren't angry?'

'Of course I am angry. But not at the commander.'

Relief filled Blake. 'He's a good man. I know he's a defender—'

'I see it.' Candace reached out and squeezed her hand. 'I see it.'

Blake gave her mother a weak smile before looking down at the grubs. 'Do you really wish to know how to hunt for these majestic insects?'

A nod. 'I really do.'

Blake turned to the tree behind her and crouched down. 'Then join me in the dirt.'

'I'm going to get water,' Lyndal said, rising from the table, 'to wash down that delightful meal you just fed us.'

Candace returned to her chair by the fire and picked up her sewing. 'I am rather tired after today's hunting efforts.'

Lyndal emitted a weak laugh. 'Hunting? Is that what the two of you are calling it?'

'There is *some* skill involved in finding the grubs,' Blake said. 'I'll come with you to the well. Eda, you're on duck guarding duties here.'

Fetching the empty pails, Lyndal and Blake stepped out onto the quiet street and made their way to the well near the square. They were attaching one of the pails when they heard children squealing at the port end of the borough. It was such a rare, happy sound that it made the girls pause and listen. Curious, they wandered towards the gate to see what was going on.

Fresh mussels scattered the ground. The delighted children were running in circles, picking them up and showing them to each other before shoving them into pockets.

'Prince Borin is not going to like this,' Lyndal said. 'Do you think the defenders threw them in?'

Blake's gaze travelled up to the top of the wall, and there was Harlan resting on the embrasure, watching the scene below. 'Yes, I think it was the defenders.'

Harlan straightened when he caught sight of Blake. Her eyes welled up as they stared at one another. He looked around, then raised his hands, signing something to her. She squinted to see better.

Stand tall and strong, warrior.

Her breath caught. He had remembered. Swallowing back tears, she signed back, *I love you. I miss you.*

Of course, Harlan had absolutely no idea what she was saying.

Lyndal slipped her arms through Blake's. 'Yours might be the most tragic love story this kingdom has ever known.'

Blake was so lost in the moment she had forgotten Lyndal was standing beside her. She turned to her sister. 'Must it be a tragedy?'

Lyndal searched her eyes. 'I think I'm losing hope.'

That was a terrifying admission from her sister, who was the epitome of hope. 'Don't say that.'

'And I'll die having been admired but never loved.'

Blake took her icy hand. 'What are you talking about? You're wholly loved.'

Lyndal nodded towards the wall. 'Not the way you are.' She gave Blake a weak smile. 'Let's go get the water. I'm so tired.'

Blake smoothed back her sister's damp hair. 'Don't lose hope just yet, all right?'

Lyndal turned away.

CHAPTER 39

*B*lake continued to open the shop every morning, but nobody came. The only time merchants left their houses was for water or to scavenge what they could from the forest. But even the forest was starving. The merchants had stripped it bare.

Every morning Blake and Thea continued to sweep their verandas, determined to keep some routine and purpose in their lives. They would lean on their brooms and talk about the latest deaths, which families had managed to successfully grow food, and which families had nothing. But seven weeks into the lockdown, Blake stepped out onto the veranda with her broom and found Birtle sweeping the veranda in place of his wife.

'Is Thea all right?' she asked.

Birtle gave her a smile that was not very reassuring. 'Just a bit tired.'

Everyone was tired. It did not matter how much they slept, their bodies just seemed to be giving up. The day before, Blake had tried to give her neighbour some of the grubs, but Thea had turned green at the sight of them and insisted she focus on keeping her sisters fed.

'How's Eda?' Birtle asked.

'No better, I'm afraid.'

Eda had developed a cough days ago that seemed to be getting worse. They had sent for the physician only to be told he had died. It would not have made a difference anyway, because the medicine she needed was food.

'I hope Eda's not keeping Thea awake,' Blake said. The cough was worse at night, and Blake had started staying up with her, propping her up in front of the fire and dozing at her side.

'Your sister's not the reason she's tired,' Birtle replied before resuming sweeping.

Blake made a mental note to check on Thea the following day, but she never got the chance. Birtle showed up at the shop early the next morning, head stooped and eyes red. Blake froze when she opened the door and caught sight of him.

'I wondered if your mother might sew a body bag for me.' His voice barely carried over the rain falling behind him.

Blake pressed her eyes shut and took hold of the door frame. When she opened them, she forced a smile. 'Of course she will. Come in. The fire's lit. When the bag's done, we'll go back to the house together.'

Birtle's mouth wobbled as he stepped past her and walked into the house.

After hearing the news, Lyndal gave Birtle a small bowl of soup, which was just leek and water with a little salt. Sometimes the warmth tricked the mind into thinking it was enough.

Candace sewed the body bag and handed it to Blake, who returned next door with Birtle.

'What would you like to do with her?' Blake asked, swallowing down her rising nausea.

Birtle sighed. 'Neither of us has the energy required to dig a grave. I guess we'll lay her along the wall with the others.'

The piles of corpses were growing. It was not just because the walls were the farthest point from the village but that merchants wanted people to see what was happening. But the only people who saw were the defenders guarding them. Still, there was a small amount of satisfaction in seeing them walk the walls holding handkerchiefs to their noses.

They took one end each, Blake recoiling inwardly as she held Thea's limp, bony ankles through the fabric. The walk felt eternal, and her arms tired out before they were even halfway there. She looked anywhere but down, even braving the walls which she had managed to avoid since her last encounter with Harlan. She was afraid he would summon her, try to feed her.

She was afraid of more people dying because of her.

'I need to rest,' Birtle said, gently placing his wife on the road and wiping his brow with a shaky hand.

Blake leaned on her knees, reminding herself there was no point in being sick because she had nothing to bring up. 'Ready?' she asked, grabbing hold of the ankles once more.

Birtle bent and lifted his wife.

The closest wall was the north one that separated them from the nobility. Unfortunately, they had to make their way through a quarter-mile of mud to reach it. By the time they got there, they were soaked through from the rain, and the body bag was splattered with mud. Blake paused when the wall came into view, eyes moving over the bodies, many of them not even covered.

So much death.

'Do you want to put her on top of the others or next to them?' Blake could barely believe what she was asking.

Birtle's gaze swept the length of the wall. 'It might be warmer on top.'

Who was she to poke holes in his statement? If he wanted his wife off the cold ground, that was what they would do. 'Good thinking.' She used her remaining energy to lift Thea on top of another corpse that had been wrapped in a sheet.

The pair stepped back, breathing hard from their efforts while trying not to breathe in the stench of rotting flesh. There was no priest in the borough to say a prayer or offer any words of comfort.

'Would you like to say anything?' Blake asked. 'Or do you want me to say something?'

He shook his head and scratched the silvery growth on his chin. 'No, you've done enough. Let's get you out of the rain before you end up sick like your sister.' He turned and trudged back through the mud towards the village.

With a heavy heart and tight chest, Blake followed him.

CHAPTER 40

Prince Becket and Queen Fayre sent word that their ship had docked due to bad weather and they would not make it to Chadora in time for the funeral, so King Oswin's funeral went ahead without them.

Since the nobility could not travel through the merchant borough, the defenders set up an alternative route through the farming borough. Harlan and his men were assigned the tedious task of accompanying groups between gates, because apparently they had nothing better to do than ensure rich families were not disturbed by grazing oxen.

When Lord Thomas and his family approached the gate, Harlan turned to the defender preparing to escort them and said, 'I've got this one.'

The defender looked slightly confused but nodded before moving his horse to the side of the road.

'Commander Wright,' Lord Thomas said as the cart

drew near. 'I heard you have been enjoying some downtime.'

Harlan's disdain for the man was written all over his face. 'The walls still need guarding, my lord.'

Thomas nodded as his cart rolled beneath the archway. 'I suppose so. We cannot have the king's killer escaping. He must be brought to justice for his horrendous crime.'

Lady Victoria and Lady Kendra were seated opposite him, swaying slightly with the movement as they listened in on the conversation.

'Aren't you going to ask me how your family is holding up in there?' Harlan said.

Victoria looked up from her lap. 'Have you seen them?'

Harlan saw genuine concern on her face. 'Only from afar, my lady.'

'And did they seem well?' Kendra asked, clearly not comprehending the severity of the situation.

His gaze slid to her. 'As well as one can be when starved of food and basic human rights, my lady.'

She settled back in her seat with a relieved expression. 'That is pleasing to hear. We have been so worried.'

Harlan's eyes met Lady Victoria's before facing forwards again.

'It is a pity the place was not locked down *before* my niece weaselled her way into the nobility borough and splashed herself around,' Thomas said.

Victoria closed her eyes. 'Thomas, please.'

'Of course you will defend them,' he replied. 'It is your sister.'

Harlan narrowed his gaze on the man. 'Blake didn't weasel her way in. I invited her.'

Thomas scoffed. 'But a proper lady would decline such an invitation. It is all right for her. She does not have a reputation to protect.'

'If you truly care about your family's reputation, then might I suggest you stop being the primary source of the rumours.'

Thomas's face hardened. 'You are lucky I did not have you removed from your post for your part in it.'

'You don't have that kind of power, so you can save your empty threats.' He continued to stare at Thomas. 'And the next time you swing that hand of yours, make sure it's aimed at me. Because if you ever lay a hand on any of the Suttone women again, I'll be paying you a visit.'

Thomas sat forwards in his seat, mouth open. 'How dare you lecture me when you are the man who ruined her future.'

'What future, exactly? You had the chance to help that family and you left them in that shithole to starve.' He saw Victoria flinch at his words. 'Breathe deeply, my lord. Can you smell it? The bodies are decomposing.'

Kendra reached out and took her mother's hand.

Thomas leaned towards Harlan, who was trotting alongside the cart. 'My wife's sister *chose* that life. She is lucky we still speak to her, let alone support her.'

They were nearing the gate, so Harlan pulled his horse up before he said or did something he would regret. 'Ladies,' he said with a nod. Then he turned his horse away.

'I know it was a funeral, but the mood was darker than anything I've attended before,' Astin told Harlan the next day. 'The nobility want justice, but I don't think many support the lockdown. They're just not brave enough to admit it aloud.'

They were leaning on the wall looking out at the merchant borough. There was hardly any movement.

'I hoped Borin would wake up to himself once he saw what was happening in the borough,' Astin continued, 'but I fear his mood is only building to something far worse.'

'Worse than this?' Harlan asked, nodding towards two men carrying a corpse to the wall.

The merchants did not have the space or energy to dig that many graves.

'I've served as the prince's bodyguard since he came of age,' Astin said. 'This isn't about justice anymore. This is a matter of pride.' He turned to Harlan. 'I heard him whining to his father's advisor this morning that everyone was laughing behind his back at the funeral.'

'And were they?'

'Probably. That's not a new thing. Borin's just sensitive to it suddenly.' Astin crossed his arms. 'You still watch for her every day.'

Harlan did not have to ask who he was referring to. 'I do.' It had been nearly nine weeks since he had seen her close up.

'This must be a form of slow torture as you watch the bodies stack up.'

Harlan was silent a moment. 'I keep thinking up ways to get her out, but there's nowhere to send her.'

'*That's* your concern? Where to send her?' Astin shook his head. 'You'd be sacrificing yourself in the process. Borin would make an example of you.'

'She wouldn't leave her family anyway' was Harlan's response. He straightened. 'I don't think anyone in there knows who the killer is any more than we do.'

Astin nodded. 'They should lay blame on one of the corpses.'

'We both know it wouldn't be enough for our new king.'

'He's no fool, despite appearances. God help us all after the coronation.'

'Has a date been set?'

'He'll wait until the queen and Prince Becket return.' Astin gave him a knowing look. 'You know how much he needs his mother's approval.'

If there was ever a boy desperate for his mother's attention, it was Borin.

Approaching footsteps made them both fall silent. They turned as Shapur emerged from the fog lingering atop the wall. He looked between the men before his eyes settled on Harlan.

'Prince Borin has called us to the throne room.'

Astin cast a knowing glance at Harlan and whispered, 'Brace yourself.'

~

Prince Borin had grown very attached to his father's throne in the weeks since his death. King Oswin would have held such a meeting around a table, in a less formal environment, but Borin liked his platform, plush chair, and everyone standing while he sat in comfort.

King Oswin's advisors stood to one side, looking like their best dog had just died. That did nothing to help the unease in Harlan's gut as he stood beside his father on the lavish rug, bracing for what would spill from the prince's mouth.

'I am receiving a lot of complaints regarding the odour coming from the merchant borough,' Borin began.

Harlan was careful to keep his expression nice and neutral. 'The dead are decomposing, Your Highness.'

'You know it is bad when the farmers are the ones complaining,' Borin said with a small smile. 'They live and breathe shit for a living.' He glanced at the advisors, who were not smiling. 'Why are the merchants not burying the dead? It is not as if they have anything else to do.'

Harlan's fingers curled at his side. 'There's no cemetery in the borough. They would have to bury them in the forest, and they would struggle to dig graves quick enough.'

Borin looked to Shapur. 'Is there really no cemetery in the merchant borough?'

'No,' Shapur replied. 'Normally the funerals are held in the borough before the dead are taken to the lazaretto borough for burying.'

Borin thought for a moment. 'I think it is time to put an end to this insanity.'

Relief swelled in Harlan. He bit the inside of his cheek to stop from verbalising it.

'I would like you to round up the merchants and bring them to the square so I might address them.'

'Round them up?' Harlan could not keep the irritation out of his voice. The merchants were not sheep, and his men were not dogs.

Borin rose. 'I will be there within the hour.'

Shapur cleared his throat. 'What is your objective, Your Highness?'

Annoyance flashed in Borin's eyes. 'It is your job to ensure my wishes are carried out, Warden, not question my motives.'

Harlan glanced at the advisors for clues and found them staring at the ground. Borin probably wanted to make one of his famous speeches, be the hero who declared the gates be opened and freed the merchants from the clutches of death. Harlan would let him have his moment if it meant they could all move on and begin the necessary healing.

'The merchants will be in the square within the hour,' Shapur said, bowing.

Harlan bowed also and followed his father from the room.

CHAPTER 41

'Eda, wake up,' Blake said, rubbing her sister's back. 'There are defenders in the borough.'

Eda's eyes fluttered open, red-rimmed and void of life. She immediately began coughing. Blake pressed her palm to her fevered forehead.

'There's a notice,' Lyndal said, entering the room and grabbing her cloak. 'Birtle just returned from the square. It says every merchant is to be in the square within the hour.'

Candace entered with a cup of water. 'She needs to drink something.'

'She can't walk,' Blake said.

And no one had the strength to carry her.

'Birtle gave us a few cloves of garlic,' Lyndal said, walking over to the bed. 'Perhaps we can boil it up in some water.'

Blake wiped damp hair back from Eda's face and helped her sit up. 'It's going to take more than a few cloves of garlic to get her walking.' She kneeled in front of her sister. 'I'm going to carry you.' But announcing it and doing it were two very different things.

Eda swallowed and nodded.

'Put two cloaks on her,' Candace said, flitting about the room grabbing items. 'We must keep her warm.'

Lyndal studied Blake. 'Are you sure you can carry her? You barely got yourself off the chair earlier.'

That was true. Blake was growing weaker by the day. 'I'll be fine.' She did not have a choice.

A horn sounded in the distance, announcing the arrival of royalty. The women stilled and looked between each other.

'Are we to endure one of Prince Borin's speeches before they'll open the gate?' Lyndal asked. 'More people will die while waiting for him to finish.'

Blake attempted a smile. 'How else will we know who to thank when that portcullis goes up?'

Candace walked ahead of them. 'Let us hope this speech does not end in bloodshed like last time.'

'We still have Father's bow,' Blake mumbled, lifting her sister into her arms with a groan.

Candace tutted her remark.

They left the house and stepped down onto the street, joining the slow trickle of people emerging from hibernation. No one looked up anymore. People had disconnected from each other out of necessity. Better not to notice the bodies being carried from the houses. Better not to see their own desperation mirrored back at them.

Better not to feel anything at all.

Up ahead, Blake saw two defenders walking towards them. They were easy to spot amid a sea of walking corpses, their frames solid and their heads impossibly high. They entered the houses on either side of the road, no doubt checking to ensure everyone was accounted for. Apparently Prince Borin wanted a big audience.

Blake's breathing grew laboured. Every time Eda coughed, it would throw her balance.

'Do you want me to take her for a bit?' Lyndal asked.

Blake looked at her ghost of a sister. Her hair was a mess of brassy strands around her wasting face. She knew Lyndal would not make it five steps. 'I'm fine.'

'I see Commander Wright,' her mother said, pointing ahead.

Blake almost tripped at the mention of him. She searched the growing crowd, her chest tightening when she caught sight of him. It was the closest she had been to him in over two months. He had always been atop the wall, completely out of reach. Now if she continued straight, she would be face to face with him.

'Are you all right?' Lyndal asked. 'Can you not continue?'

Blake looked at her sister, then down at her feet. She had not even realised she had stopped walking. Her eyes returned to Harlan, fearing he would disappear if she lost sight of him. She need not have worried, because those bronze eyes of his were fixed on her as he headed towards them. She reminded herself to breathe, to remain calm, to not cry.

She most definitely would not cry.

She tried to think of some sensible first words, but he was in front of her before she could gather her thoughts, eyes moving over her at a frantic pace. She could feel his relief and heartbreak all at once. It would have been a shock to see her so thin. He blinked away his pity, eyes settling on Eda, whose feverish face rested against Blake's collarbone.

'What's wrong with her?' he asked, stepping closer.

His scent took over the air for a moment. It was such a welcome relief from the stench of death that had settled in the borough.

Blake inhaled deeply. 'She has a fever and a cough.'

'It's sounding like pneumonia,' Candace added.

Harlan took Eda from Blake's arms and settled her against his chest. The sudden absence of weight made Blake tilt, but Harlan managed to grab hold of her.

'Can you walk?' he asked.

She nodded.

The women followed slowly behind Harlan, whose steps were too fast and strides too long for them. Blake's eyes never left him. She drank in the sight of him, strong and healthy. It was unfathomable given the state of the merchants surrounding him. She was grateful though. It felt like one small win after months of losses.

When they reached the square, Blake looked up at the defenders evenly spaced along the wall. It took her a moment to spot Prince Borin because he was so heavily guarded. Astin stood directly in front of him, hand on the hilt of his sword and eyes moving in all directions.

Harlan tried to place Eda on her feet, but her knees buckled and the coughing started. People around them took a step away.

'Put her on my back,' Blake said.

Harlan shook his head. 'She's too heavy for you. Put her between the two of you.'

Blake touched his arm, and he stilled. 'Lyndal can't hold her.'

Harlan's mouth flattened into a thin line. He hesitated, then carefully placed Eda on her back. Blake made sure not to buckle under the weight.

'Don't venture too far into the crowd in case there's panic,' Harlan said, voice low.

She searched his eyes. 'Why would there be panic?'

He tucked the cloaks around Eda. 'This will all be over soon. Just try to be invisible until then.' He marched off before Blake could reply.

She watched him until he disappeared into the turret, then looked around. Defenders had formed a circle around them. Dread swirled in her empty stomach.

Candace rubbed Eda's back and gestured to the prince, who had emerged from his guards and was preparing to speak. 'Here we go.'

All eyes were on him now, except Blake's. Her gaze travelled the length of the wall, looking for Harlan.

'It is time to bring an end to the suffering of my people,' Prince Borin began. 'I have been very patient, praying those responsible for the death of my father, *your* king, would be handed over so we could all move forwards together.' He paused, eyes sweeping the crowd. 'But it seems you are quite determined to protect the identity of those responsible.'

Blake and Lyndal exchanged a look of concern. Did he really think people would say nothing while their loved ones died?

'Look at the bodies piled beneath me,' the prince continued. 'That is the cost of your deceit.'

The crowd remained silent. Not one person standing before him had the energy to disagree. They just blinked against the rain. A servant stepped forwards with a piece of stretched canvas and raised it above the prince, shielding him from the weather.

'Since you all seem intent on wallowing in your own suffering, it falls to me to move the process along and get the answers we all seek.'

Blake adjusted her grip on her sister.

'What's he doing?' Lyndal whispered when the prince gestured to one of his guards.

'I don't know.'

The defender loaded his bow, approached the embrasure, and took aim at the crowd. Astin shifted beside the prince, appearing uncomfortable. No one in the crowd moved, because no one was expecting what happened next.

The prince nodded once, and the defender released the arrow, shooting a middle-aged man through the chest. The woman standing at his side screamed into her hands as he collapsed to the ground. Nearby merchants reared back as if his death were contagious. A ripple of panic surged through the crowd, people knocking into one another. Blake gripped Eda tighter and looked around. The line of defenders surrounding them meant there was no way out.

'One death every minute until the killer is brought to me,' Prince Borin shouted, his face turning red. 'How many of your friends and family are you prepared to watch die for this treasonous cause?'

People looked between one another with helpless expressions. No one knew what to do.

Lyndal positioned herself in front of their mother, fighting back tears.

'He can't just kill people,' she said, head shaking with denial.

But the prince gestured again, and the archer shifted his bow to another part of the crowd. Screams rang out when another arrow whistled through the air and struck a woman in the neck. The crowd surged towards the port gate this time, which was still closed.

'God save us,' Candace cried, pressing her eyes shut.

Lyndal's grip tightened on her. 'He's going to kill us all.'

Blake watched as the archer drew another arrow and aimed it at the centre of the square. At any moment it could be one of them. Was Blake just supposed to stand there and do nothing?

'*Be invisible*,' Harlan had told her.

Had he known what was about to happen?

Blake lowered Eda to the ground and passed her to Lyndal and her mother. 'You have to take her.'

More screaming as another arrow was released into the crowd.

Lyndal tore her gaze from the archer. 'What?'

'Take her!'

Lyndal and Candace both reached for Eda, sharing the weight between them.

'What are you doing?' Lyndal asked. There was no disguising the fear in her voice.

Blake took hold of Lyndal's face. 'Do not move from this spot. You hear me?'

Lyndal searched her eyes. 'Tell me what you're going to do.'

Blake let go of her sister's face. 'I'm going to put an end to this insanity.'

CHAPTER 42

When the first arrow hit, Harlan knew the prince would not stop until he had what he needed. The fact that the prince had not shared his plan with the commander of the borough spoke volumes. Following orders without question was no longer an option for Harlan. With blood pounding in his ears, he marched over to his father, who was standing outside the turret on the nobility wall. The one person who stood a chance at ending the madness playing out in front of them was remaining silent.

Shapur looked in his direction as he approached. 'Return to your post, Commander.'

Harlan continued straight up to his father. 'You're just going to stand there while defenders use innocent merchants for target practice?'

Shapur's eyes narrowed on him. 'I said back to your post, Commander. One more word from you and it will be the tower instead.'

Adrenaline coursed through Harlan at such a high

speed he was dizzy from it. He raked a hand over his head and looked back at the crowd just as another merchant was shot, this time a few rows in front of Blake. God help that archer if an arrow touched her.

He searched for her as the crowd rose and fell with panic, but she was no longer standing with her sisters and mother. Candace and Lyndal now held Eda between them —barely.

Where the hell is Blake? His eyes moved over the crowd, searching.

'Commander Wright,' his father hissed. 'This is your final warning.'

Harlan barely registered what he was saying as his eyes landed on Blake. She was pushing her way through the crowd towards the front.

What are you doing?

A cold sensation crawled up his spine.

His distress must have shown on his face, because instead of having Harlan dragged off to the tower as he had promised, Shapur said, 'What is it?'

Harlan did not reply. There was no time. Rushing past his father, he re-entered the turret, taking the steps three at a time. He burst through the door at the bottom, startling the two defenders guarding it, and took off at a sprint towards the square just as Blake reached the front.

'I did it!' she shouted. 'I shot the king!'

Harlan's feet slowed as he imagined all the ways the prince was going to hurt her.

He was too late.

The damage was done.

'Stop shooting,' Blake shouted to the archer atop the wall.

'Please. It's me you want.' She was out of breath and even paler than when he had left her earlier, if that were possible. How she was even standing in her condition, let alone carrying her sister around the borough, was beyond him.

Harlan stopped, ran a hand down his face, and turned in a circle as he tried to figure out his next move.

Prince Borin's hand went up, stopping the archer in his tracks. Then he moved closer to the edge so he could get a better look at his father's killer.

Harlan took a few steps in Blake's direction, fearing arrows would rain down on her at any moment. He had to be careful from that point. He was of no use to her locked up.

'You?' Borin asked, sounding amused.

That was good. It meant he did not believe her. Maybe he would dismiss her confession.

Blake stood tall and strong—just like the warrior her father told her to be. 'Yes.'

The prince pressed his hands against the embrasure. 'You expect me to believe you shot the king from that distance, with that level of accuracy?'

'Desperate people can do incredible things.' She swallowed. 'I know you understand that.'

Harlan was at least fifteen yards from her. Even if he reached her before the other defenders did, then what? He was one man against an army.

'I do not appreciate being lied to.'

'I have the longbow,' Blake said, stepping closer to the wall. 'It's hidden in a mattress in our house.'

Harlan's blood turned to ice.

'Search her house and bring me the weapon,' the prince said.

Harlan knew they would find one. He had seen the opening in the mattress with his own eyes. Why had he not confiscated it when he had the chance?

Blake looked in his direction, her face falling when her eyes met his. There was no remorse, only quiet determination. She had done what she could to end the killings, to protect her sisters and mother. That was the kind of warrior she was.

And it was one of the many reasons he loved her.

He was about to go to her when Lyndal pushed through the crowd, stopping beside her sister.

'I am the king's killer!' she called to the prince. 'The bow belongs to me.'

'What are you doing?' Blake whispered, eyes filled with panic.

Borin looked Lyndal up and down. 'I have to assume you are trying to make me laugh, but I should warn you, I am not in the mood for jokes.'

'I assure you I'm not here for your entertainment, Your Highness.'

The prince did not appreciate her tone. 'Have it your way, boor. Arrest them both.'

Harlan's feet were moving then.

'It was me!' a man shouted a few rows back, pushing forwards. 'I killed the king.'

The prince's eyes narrowed on him.

Another woman stepped forwards. 'It was me!'

'I did it!' called a young man. The people standing with

him looked between themselves, then up at the prince. 'It was all of us!'

Harlan's feet slowed. He watched more and more merchants shuffle forwards to confess to a crime they had not committed. Blake and Lyndal turned, shock and awe on their faces as more people risked what little life they had left to protect one of their own.

Soon every merchant was shouting, 'I did it! I killed the king!' The chorus of voices bounced between the walls before drifting up to open sky.

'Enough!' Borin shouted, slapping a hand on the embrasure.

The crowd fell silent, but their stoic expressions remained.

Harlan's eyes met Blake's as he waited to see what would happen next.

'If you insist on playing these games,' Borin said, 'then you can all pay for the crime! Every person who confesses gets an arrow!' The prince threw his hands up in frustration. 'Defenders ready!'

Harlan's hands shot up. 'Hold!' He moved towards Blake, looking around at his men. 'Hold!'

Blake shook her head as though warning him back. He was about to cross a line that could not be uncrossed. But he stepped over it willingly, pulling her into his arms and crushing her wasted frame to his chest. 'The only way an arrow is getting to you is through me,' he said into her ear.

Blake covered her face with her hands.

'Both of you behind me,' Harlan instructed the girls before turning to face the prince.

Borin leaned over the edge, eyes narrowing on Harlan. 'Something you want to say, Commander?'

Harlan glanced at his father, who was gripping the embrasure, watching him intently. That was not admiration on his face. 'This is not justice, Your Highness. This is genocide.'

'Words of a traitor!' the prince boomed.

'Words of truth!' Harlan looked around. 'Not one of my men wishes these people dead, yet every man will kill if you tell them to.'

Borin was practically hanging over the edge. 'Except you, Commander?'

This was his opportunity to self-correct, step aside, follow orders, but Roul's words stuck in his mind. 'I became a defender to protect the kingdom, not contribute to the suffering. I will not shoot arrows at people who have committed no crimes.'

The prince slapped his hand on the stone again. 'Then you will die along with them. Not one of your men will think twice about shooting a *traitor*.'

Blake pressed her forehead to his back.

'Your commander has deserted you,' Borin shouted to the defenders below. 'What do we do to deserters?'

Blake's bony arms went around his middle, as if she could shield him somehow. She was trembling. Harlan drew his sword and anchored his feet firmly in front of the sisters. Six months earlier, he could not have fathomed drawing a weapon against his own men, his king. His father.

So this is how it ends for me?

His eyes went to Astin. His friend. His brother

through this miserable existence. Astin gave him the smallest nod. A tiny gesture of understanding, of forgiveness. Harlan would be labelled a traitor. Slaughtered by his own men. Shot down by his own king. Yet his only regret in those final moments was that he had stayed silent for as long as he had.

None of the defenders on the ground made a move towards him.

'Draw your weapons!' Borin shouted, agitated by the lack of movement below.

Roul stepped into sight and drew his sword. Harlan was surprised that he was first to act, but he was also one of the best defenders he had ever had the privilege of training. He would do the job he was trained to do.

Every muscle in Harlan's body tensed as he drew closer. He could win that fight, but it was just one fight. Every defender he cut down, another would replace him.

But Roul did not raise his weapon at Harlan. Instead, he turned and looked up at the prince. 'I too refuse to contribute to the suffering any longer, and I stand with my commander.'

Harlan exhaled. While he did not want to be responsible for the young defender's death, he knew in his gut Roul probably would have arrived at the conclusion on his own anyway.

One by one, the other defenders drew their swords and closed in on the merchants. Blake's arms tightened around him.

'I'm sorry,' she whispered.

He did not want those to be her final words. His hand

went over hers, the tension so thick in the air it was difficult to breathe.

The defenders did not use their weapons on the merchants. They turned to the wall, as Roul had done, in an act of defiance.

Prince Borin's mouth twisted. He pushed back from the wall and looked in Shapur's direction. 'Take charge of your men, Warden! Every defender with a bow should have it nocked, drawn, and pointed in that borough!'

Shapur blinked slowly. 'Your Highness—'

'This is not a discussion! This is an order.' Borin spun around. 'Archers ready!'

Shapur stood motionless, torn between duty and love for the second time in his life.

The men atop the wall did as Prince Borin had ordered, but their actions were not the sharp, authoritative movements of a defender. They were slow and hesitant. Still, if instructed to shoot, they would shoot.

'Your Highness!' Shapur said, taking a step towards Borin. There was a harshness in his tone he had never used with a member of the royal family before.

The prince spun to face him, finger pointed in accusation, but the sound of a portcullis rising stopped him in his tracks. He rushed to the edge of the wall and peered down at the port gate just as a circle of defenders marched through. They split apart, and Prince Becket and Queen Fayre entered the borough, coming to a stop and looking around.

Silence was heavy in the air as the merchants stared at their returned queen. Her sharp eyes took in the scene before her: the pinched faces, the corpses stacked against the walls, the defenders standing between the merchants and the arrows pointed at them.

Her spine lengthened, and her mouth flattened into a disapproving line as her gaze travelled up to her son. 'What in God's name is going on here?' She was the kind of woman who could instil fear with just a few carefully selected words.

'Mother,' Borin said, suddenly sounding ten years younger.

She shook her head, her disappointment palpable. 'Your father is barely cold and you stand there stoking the flames that caused his death.'

The prince's face contorted. 'I do this *for* him.'

'You do this for your own childish pride!' She took a few steps towards him, her guards moving with her like shadows. 'Look at these corpses piled at your doorstep. Look at them!'

Prince Becket watched on, saying nothing.

'They only have themselves to blame,' Borin replied, pointing at the merchants.

Fayre's expression fell. 'You sentenced every merchant standing before you, every merchant *dead* before you, without any evidence.'

Borin leaned over the edge. 'They have blocked me at every turn—'

'Enough!'

Borin straightened, his mouth closing.

Blake emerged from behind Harlan, keeping a hold of her sister's hand as she eyed the queen.

Fayre turned to the defenders standing in front of the merchants. 'Never in Chadora's history have defenders taken a stand *against* their king.' The anger in her voice vibrated within the walls.

'I am dealing with it,' Borin called out to her.

She raised a hand to silence him. 'You are the cause of it. Do you have any idea how far a man has to be pushed to disobey a direct order? To point an arrow at the men they eat, sleep, and train with every single day of their lives?' She looked at the archers along the walls. 'Weapons down! There is no enemy before you!'

The archers lowered their bows.

'I give the orders now!' Borin shouted.

The queen eyed him coolly. 'Did I miss the coronation too?'

He did not reply.

'Given the way you have handled things since your father's death, I question whether you are worthy to wear his crown at all.'

Borin shook his head slowly. 'I am the Crown Prince of Chadora. Even *you* cannot change that.'

She turned away and faced the defenders on foot in the borough. 'Stand down, defenders. We are all on the same side.'

The defenders slowly returned their swords to their sheaths. Merchants sank to the ground or held tightly to loved ones. They were exhausted, depleted. *Saved.* Silent tears were brushed away as they murmured their gratitude.

'And open the port gate,' Fayre instructed, turning to it.

Those with enough energy cheered.

Harlan looked over at Roul. 'Thank you, defender.'

The young defender nodded before walking away.

'I'm going to find Mother and Eda,' Lyndal said, squeezing Blake's hand before letting go.

'I'll be there in a moment,' Blake said. She looked up at Harlan and let out a long breath. 'I really thought that was the end.'

He nodded. 'Me too.'

She reached out, fingers brushing the back of his hand. 'How am I supposed to adequately express the level of gratitude I feel right now? I still have no idea what I did to deserve my own personal defender.' Her hand fell away. 'Do I just thank you and go about my day?'

'Thank Queen Fayre. She saved us both.' Harlan pushed hair back from Blake's pale face. 'Today has proven something I've long suspected.'

She closed her eyes at his touch. 'What's that?'

'There's nothing I wouldn't do to keep you alive.' His eyes went to the wall, where his father was watching them.

Blake followed the direction of his gaze and let out a breath. 'I should go.'

'I'm going to send you food—proper food.'

Sadness passed over her face. 'It's what you do.' She looked away. 'Nothing's changed between us, has it?'

'Did you want it to change?'

Her eyes returned to him. 'Yes. I prayed every day for the strength to turn it off. Please God, release us both from this strange hell.'

He knew she was not talking about the lockdown.

'Commander!' Shapur's voice cut through the borough. 'Throne room—now.'

Harlan and Blake stared at one another.

'Go,' she said when he did not move. 'We'll be fine.'

'What about Eda?'

Blake shrugged. 'I'll carry her. You must know by now that I draw strength from you.' Hugging herself against the cold, she turned away.

'You're wrong,' he said. 'It's me who draws strength from you.'

She looked back, some of that old light in her eyes. 'Stand tall and strong in that room, defender. I want to see you back on that wall.'

Harlan had expected to be brought before Prince Borin. Instead, Queen Fayre was seated on the throne where her husband had once sat. She filled the space much better than her son. Her long back rested comfortably on the plush fabric, one elegant hand draping the arm while the other turned an arrow. It was the one defenders had taken from the king's neck.

'Made of Serbian spruce, I believe,' she observed.

Harlan nodded. 'Yes, Your Majesty.'

'Certainly not grown in the merchant borough. And the fletching…' She ran her finger along it. 'Feathers from a ruddy shelduck. Also not found locally.'

'Made from imported materials,' Harlan said.

She continued to study it. 'Imported by a fletcher?'

'That's one possibility.'

She nodded slowly. 'So it is plausible that a merchant purchased these materials, produced an arrow, and killed my husband during the unveiling?'

Harlan glanced over at his father, who stood to the side intently watching the exchange. 'Yes, Your Majesty.'

'Is it not also plausible that the raw materials were sold to someone in another borough? *Any* borough, for that matter?'

Finally some sense. 'Yes.'

'And is it possible that the materials were imported years earlier, before the walls were built? Perhaps for another purpose entirely?'

Harlan nodded. 'Again, yes.'

'So many possibilities indeed.' The queen looked around the room. 'I do recall Lady Brighton wore a head-piece made from these gorgeous orange feathers at last year's festival. Her dress was equally as beautiful. But I digress.' Her sharp eyes returned to Harlan. 'I have been informed that you were the first defender to stand against my son today. Is that correct?'

Harlan felt like he was on trial. 'Yes, Your Majesty. My men followed my lead because I'm their commander. I assure you every one of them is a trustworthy defender. If you want to lay blame, lay it squarely on me.'

There was amusement in her eyes. 'You are a lot like your father. All grace and honour.'

'I shall take that as a compliment, Your Majesty.'

'Do. It was intended as one.' She let out a breath. 'My son's pride has been severely wounded by recent events, and he wishes to see you disciplined.' She tilted her head. 'What do you suppose would appease him, Commander?'

Harlan blinked. 'You want *me* to suggest something?'

'You know Prince Borin fairly well by now.' She tapped one finger on the arm of the throne. 'Perhaps we could have you assigned to night duty in the farming borough for a few months.'

'I doubt that will suffice,' Harlan said. An idea took shape in his mind. 'Perhaps you should demote me.'

The queen's eyebrows rose, and Shapur looked up.

'Demote you?' the queen asked. 'You have earned the title of commander. I have no desire to take it from you. What would you do without it?'

This was turning into an opportunity. 'Defenders are often placed in training roles as a form of discipline.'

Fayre's gaze slid to Shapur. 'Go on.'

'The warden oversees the training, but it falls on different defenders to supervise and teach the new recruits. I think the men will benefit from a more consistent and structured approach.'

'And you want to be that person?'

Harlan felt his father's eyes burning into him. 'Yes.'

Fayre leaned to one side. 'If the training role is undesirable, then why do you want it?'

'I believe foundation-level training shapes a soldier for the rest of his service. I think there's more to teach than fitness, discipline, and obedience.'

'Such as?' she asked.

'Such as courage, decency, conviction of purpose'—he paused, feeling his father's eyes on him—'and compassion.' He dared a glance at Shapur and saw him swallow.

'What do you think, Warden?' the queen asked. 'Is that what is missing from our military? And more importantly, is your son the one to implement such change?'

Shapur stood with his weight evenly distributed through his feet and hands behind his back. Always a pillar of respectability. He looked at Harlan when he said, 'I think we could all benefit from a little more compassion. And I cannot think of a better defender to teach it.'

The queen gave Harlan a tight-lipped smile. 'Then it is done. Harlan Wright, you are hereby stood down as commander of the merchant borough, effective immediately. Moving forwards, you will be responsible for the recruitment and training within the military.' She rose from the chair. 'Now you must excuse me. I must break the news to my son.'

Harlan walked along the edge of the training field, sizing up five new recruits running laps. His father walked next to him.

'Do you think Queen Fayre has a suspect in mind?' Harlan asked.

Shapur stared straight ahead. 'If she does, she has not shared her suspicions with me yet.'

'I'm relieved she's back.'

Shapur nodded. 'I believe it will be a good thing for everyone.'

Harlan watched his father. 'Are you ever going to look at me again?'

Shapur glanced sideways at him. 'What are you talking about?'

'Better to air your disappointment than hold it in.' Harlan stopped and turned to him. 'Out with it.'

Shapur turned to him but looked out at the field. 'I am not disappointed in you. I am oddly proud.'

Harlan frowned. 'Are you drunk?'

Shapur's mouth lifted in a rare smile. 'Not yet, but give me a few hours. It has been a heck of a day.'

'It has.'

They watched the recruits in silence for a few moments.

'This clever suggestion of yours,' Shapur said. 'Is it really about training the recruits? Or is this about the merchant girl?'

'Both.' Harlan swallowed. 'I can't command that borough properly with her in it.'

Shapur nodded and crossed his arms over his chest. 'That girl has bigger balls than most of the men I know.'

Harlan smiled. 'She sure does.'

'She's a fighter, a survivor.'

'Yes.'

Shapur looked at him. 'Was it wrong of me to step in the way I did?'

Harlan met his eyes. 'I understand why you did. But I can't see past her, even now. Especially now.'

'I could not see past your mother either.' Shapur faced forwards again. 'If you are a fool like me and decide to go against good sense and terrible odds, I will not stand in your way.'

Harlan's breathing slowed as he comprehended what his father was saying.

'That house is just going to sit there empty,' Shapur went on. 'I plan on dying on my feet within these walls.'

Harlan swallowed against his thickening throat. 'Probably while barking orders at me.'

A low chuckle came from Shapur.

'Thank you,' Harlan said, unable to look at him this time.

'Do not thank me yet.' Shapur clapped him on the back. 'You still have to pay your good friend Lord Thomas a visit.'

~

'You want to *what*?' Lord Thomas asked, sitting forwards in his chair.

Harlan sat opposite him in the library, unsurprised by his reaction. 'I'd like to buy your shop in the merchant borough.'

Thomas sat processing this request for a moment. 'The shop has not turned a profit in months, so my next question to you is *why*?'

Harlan did not want the Suttone family's financial future to be dependent on Lord Thomas's whims. If Harlan owned the shop, the women would be free to run it as they pleased as well as hold on to all profits. He said none of this aloud. 'Does it matter why?' He placed a piece of paper on the desk with the amount he was prepared to pay.

Thomas picked it up and opened it, eyes on Harlan the whole time. When he read it, his eyebrows rose. 'It will take you twenty years to earn your money back, and that is assuming business returns to normal.'

Harlan shrugged. 'I'm a very patient investor.'

'Did Blake set you up to this? She is a cunning girl.'

Harlan was careful not to bite. There was more he needed from the man. 'Blake has been too busy trying to keep herself and her family alive. She knows nothing of this.' He paused. 'So what do you say to the sale?'

Thomas continued to stare down at the piece of paper. 'All right. The shop is yours. Just do not come complaining to me when those women send you spiralling into debt.'

Harlan rose and offered his hand.

Thomas eyed it suspiciously before standing and taking hold of it. 'I'll have the agreement written up and sent to you at the barracks.'

'You can send it to my home, here in the borough.'

Thomas's eyebrows rose. 'Your home?'

'I'm moving into the old house.'

'Do not tell me the warden kicked his own son out of the barracks.'

Harlan forced a smile. 'No, nothing like that. There's one more thing I wanted to talk to you about.'

Thomas gestured for him to sit again. 'Go on.'

'It's about Blake.'

Thomas all but rolled his eyes. 'If you are going to lecture me about providing for the family—'

'I'm not here to lecture you about anything.' Harlan sat forwards and drew a slow breath. 'I would like to ask you for Blake's hand.'

CHAPTER 44

Blake removed her boots and stepped into the icy water. When the foaming waves rolled in to meet her, she did not bother lifting her skirt. She let it twist around her legs as she stared out to sea. The fishing boats had gone out, and Blake wanted to be waiting at the port when they returned.

Queen Fayre had organised food to be delivered to each household, including a portion of ox bones that could be boiled up to make broth. She also had the lazaretto gate opened and a cart brought in to remove and bury the dead.

It was time for life in the merchant borough to restart.

'Waiting for Odo?' came a familiar voice.

Blake turned and found Harlan standing at the edge of the water. Relief rolled through her. He was still in uniform with all his limbs intact, so that was a good sign. 'Looks like Prince Borin went easy on you yesterday.' She made her way over to him.

'Actually, he wasn't even there. I think Queen Fayre

sent him to his quarters to have a good, hard think about what he'd done.'

Blake laughed, but it died quickly. 'Thank you for the food parcel you sent last night. Eda was sitting up eating when I left this morning.'

'Good.' He nodded. 'Sorry I didn't make it to see you in person. I had a rather eventful day.'

'I can only imagine.'

They stood two feet apart with their hands at their sides.

'What are you doing in the port borough by yourself?' Harlan asked.

She blinked up at him. 'My bodyguard was indisposed.'

'You could have waited for me.'

'I was referring to Eda.'

He chuckled and looked away. 'I've been demoted.'

Blake's face fell. 'Oh. I'm sorry.'

'Don't be.' His eyes returned to her. 'It's a good thing. As I told my father, I can't command the merchant borough with you in it.'

She bit her lower lip. 'What will you be doing instead?'

'Training new recruits at the barracks.'

She could not hide her disappointment. 'I'll never see you. Though I suppose that's a good thing.'

'Is it?'

'No,' she replied immediately.

He tucked her hair behind her ear, but the breeze blew it forwards again. 'I don't want you to suffer anymore, and I don't want to be separated by walls.'

'Those are some big wants.'

'And I want to see you every day.'

She watched him with a cautious expression. 'We're Chadorians. We don't get what we want, we get what we're given.'

Harlan took hold of her face with both hands. 'I want you, all the time.'

She swallowed. How was she supposed to respond to that without coming apart?

He dipped his head, eyes searching hers. 'Marry me.'

She pulled free of his grip and retreated into the water. 'You can't say things like that.'

'Why not?'

'You know why.'

He stepped into the sea, his boots filling with water. '*Marry me.*'

She threw up her hands. 'We can't.'

'We can't or you can't?'

Her eyes never left him. 'You can't marry below you, and I can't leave my family to suffer in that place without me.'

'Marry below me? I barely deserve you.'

'You know what I mean. You were born in the nobility borough.'

He shook his head. 'Who cares about that shit?'

'Everyone who isn't us.' She reminded herself to breathe. 'And I can't leave my family behind.'

'I'd never expect you to.'

Laughter escaped her, despite there being nothing funny about their conversation. 'What's your plan, then? Are you going to come live with me? Sleep in my tiny bed with my sisters in the same room?'

He pulled her to him until she tipped forwards, head

resting on his chest. He pressed his lips to her hair. 'Your sisters and mother will come live with us in our home, in the nobility borough. No one you love will suffer under my watch. Understand?'

A sob rose in Blake, but she covered her mouth before it could escape. 'What about all the other reasons?'

Harlan's arms went around her, his chin resting on her head. 'They're not reasons. They're just noise we must block out.'

There was no holding back the tears then; they soaked the front of Harlan's uniform.

'Tell me that's a yes,' he said when her shoulders finally stilled. 'Because I'm done being apart.'

She looked up at him. 'Are you sure about this?'

His mouth tilted up. 'Very sure.' He took hold of her face again. 'I love you.'

She pushed herself up onto her toes to kiss him, tears rolling freely down her cheeks. Harlan brushed them away until they stopped coming, and then Blake's heels returned to the sea floor. 'What if my uncle says no?'

His eyes were penetrating. 'He's already agreed.'

'What if he changes his mind?'

'If you think I'm going to let that man weasel his way between us, you're crazy.'

Her toes were going numb from the cold. 'Your father said—'

'I know what my father said. Stop worrying about everyone else.'

She nodded. 'It's just that everything good gets taken from us eventually.'

'Not this. Not me. Understand?' He kissed her again,

his mouth soft and reassuring. He lowered his forehead to hers. 'Just say yes and let me worry about the rest.'

Blake wiped her face. 'Is there by any chance room for a duck in the house?'

'How is that thing still alive?'

'It turns out he is a *she*.'

'So?'

She shrugged. 'So better to have eggs for several years than stew for a week.'

'Christ.' He took her hand and led her out of the water. 'The duck lives outside.'

'We don't have to decide that now.'

Laughing, he said, 'If you think we're having that thing in our bed, you're crazy.'

She smiled up at him. 'Yes.'

He stilled. 'Yes to the duck living outside, or yes you'll marry me?'

'Yes, I'll marry you.'

Then he was kissing her again, unfazed by the people glancing in their direction. They broke apart at the sound of a fishing boat docking and looked over to where a crowd of people were already gathering.

'Let's go get you a fish,' Harlan said, taking her by the hand.

Blake shoved her feet into her boots, and Harlan led her along the beach towards the dock.

If someone had told her six months earlier that she would marry a defender, she would have thought them mad. If someone had told her six months earlier that she would marry for love, she would have laughed in their face. Now her entire body sang with the realisation that

Harlan would soon belong to her. Hers to fuss and cry over, to argue and play games with. Hers to protect with her life, run through arrows for, wake up beside.

He would be hers to love as she pleased.

Water sloshed in her boots, and her wet skirt caught on her bare legs. She tried not to let it slow her, but Harlan missed nothing. He slowed his pace, his hand tightening around hers. He had a way of making her feel invincible.

When they reached the dock, they joined the queue of merchants waiting to buy fish. Blake held Harlan's arm and resisted the temptation to rest her head on him.

'Tired?' he asked as though reading her mind.

She had been exhausted for months. 'I'm fine.'

His arm went around her, guiding her head to his side. 'Liar.'

Her eyes sank shut. She knew even if she fell asleep in that moment, the defender standing at her side would never let her fall. 'Sorry,' she whispered.

He moved them forwards in the line and kissed the top of her head. 'You don't have to stand tall and strong when I'm around. I've got you.'

The faintest smile played on her lips as her mind drifted.

EPILOGUE

*L*yndal closed the shop door and leaned against it. 'I think that was our busiest day yet.'

Blake had already counted the day's coin and was seated at the table filling in the ledger. The first few months of her marriage, she had taken the ledger home to Harlan each night but quickly realised he had no interest in seeing it—or any of the profits, for that matter.

Rising from the table, she wandered into the back room where Birtle was eating. 'We're leaving for the day. Eda will be in to help tomorrow. Do you need anything before we go?'

He smiled. 'No. All sorted here.'

It had made sense to have Birtle move in when he was forced to sell his own home. He lived expense free in exchange for keeping an eye on the shop while they were away. It also meant they did not have to come in every day, because he was more than capable of managing things in their absence.

'Eda will bring you some eggs in the morning,' Blake said, waving and disappearing back into the shop.

'The cart's out front,' Lyndal whispered, gathering her things.

Blake's eyebrows came together. 'Why are you whispering?'

'Because Astin's driving it.' She rolled her eyes at Blake.

The defender had a special knack for winding Lyndal up, and her normally level-headed sister always took the bait.

Lyndal opened the shop door and breezed past Astin, who had just stepped up onto the veranda. 'Don't you ever work?'

'And good afternoon to you too,' he replied to her back.

Blake gave him an apologetic smile as she stepped past him and followed her sister. 'Defender.'

He nodded a greeting. 'I'm having dinner at the house, so I offered to collect you.'

'Great,' Lyndal said, settling herself on the bench. 'Now we get to listen to your jokes for the entirety of the journey *and* through dinner.'

Blake shook her head.

Astin climbed up into the driver's seat. 'I had no idea you were paying such close attention to everything I say.'

'I'm still refining my ability to tune you out.'

Astin chuckled and slapped the reins on the horse's back, and the cart lurched forwards.

At the gate, the women presented the letter they carried, written and signed by the warden. It ensured they could move between the two boroughs for the purpose of work. The defenders had gotten so used to them coming and going, they often waved them through without even checking it.

Blake looked up at the sky as the portcullis lowered behind them. The clouds were high, giving the illusion that they might dissipate and let the sun through. She would do anything to feel the sun on her face.

When they pulled up at the house, the groom came out to tend the horse, and Candace wandered out front to greet her daughters. Their mother had taken to her old life like a fish to water. She had even rekindled a friendship from her youth. While Blake would never wish away the years they spent in the merchant borough, she was glad her mother could live out the rest of her life in comfort.

'Where's Harlan?' Blake asked, looking to the windows above.

Her mother touched her cheek. 'It's so good to see the weight back on you and all that colour in your face.' She kissed Blake's forehead. 'He's out back with Eda.'

'Sparring again?'

Her mother let out a resigned sigh. 'She never stops.'

Blake walked around the side of the house and spotted them working with training swords near the stables. She watched them out of sight for a while. Eda was hungry to learn every skill Harlan could teach her. He never said no to her, no matter how tired he was.

He never said no to any of them.

Blake watched them for a while, enjoying the sight of her sister healthy and full of energy again. Her fire was back and her confidence growing with each passing day.

She had not spoken yet, but that would come—Blake was sure of it.

'Plant that back foot,' Harlan said, poking Eda's leg with his wooden sword.

She whacked his sword away as he passed, and he chuckled. Blake's heart was so completely full in that moment. Eda needed good men in her life to replace all the ones she had lost too soon.

'Aren't you tired yet?' Blake called out, stepping into view.

Harlan's eyes shot to her, his shoulders dropping slightly. She was home safe for another day. He watched her approach and pulled her to him the moment she was within reach.

'Good day?' he asked, brushing hair back from Blake's face and kissing her.

It was always a good day when it finished with him. 'Very good day.' She looked at her sister. 'Was he being gentle?'

Eda shook her head. *If I wanted gentle, I'd ask someone else to teach me.*

'I got "gentle" and "me",' Harlan said.

Eda was teaching him things too.

Blake patted his chest before stepping back. 'Very good.'

Eda took the sword from Harlan's hand and wandered off in the direction of the house.

'How was your day?' Blake asked. 'Send those recruits down the cliff yet?'

'Not yet.' He kissed her cheek, then the top of her

head, before slinging an arm around her. 'Need to build up their fitness a little more first.'

They began walking slowly. Blake pulled away when she spotted Garlic running towards them. She gathered her skirts and crouched down.

'Hello, you. Did you lay me an egg?'

'Yes,' Harlan said. *'In the house.'*

Blake rose. 'She must have sneaked in when—'

'When your mother opened the back door and invited her inside?'

She scrunched up her nose and decided to go with a subject change. 'Who else is coming for dinner tonight?'

'My father said he'd try to make it, and your mother invited your uncle.'

Blake took his hand and squeezed it. 'Look at your pouty face. He's well behaved when you're around.'

'He doesn't have a choice.'

She smiled at the ground. 'It's the cost of time spent with my aunt and cousin.' It had taken a while, but their new life was starting to find a rhythm. 'I should go help with dinner.'

Harlan pulled her in the direction of the stables. 'I want to show you something first.'

She angled her head. 'I'm not falling for that again.'

'What do you mean?'

'Last time you said that, you locked us in a stall and did unspeakable things to me. We missed dinner completely.'

'I don't recall you complaining at the time.'

Her cheeks heated. 'Well, I'll complain this time because I'm in the process of winning over your father. A good start is to be present when he comes for dinner.'

Harlan squinted down at her. 'You've already won him over.'

'How can you tell?'

He walked her towards the stables. 'He doesn't come to the house to see me.'

'It's probably Lyndal's cooking.' Stepping inside, Blake looked around. 'Well? What am I looking at?'

A soft bleating noise came from the stall at the far end, and her head snapped in that direction. Harlan guided her up to the door, and they both looked inside. Huddled in the far corner were two small goats.

'Meet Ginger and Clove,' he said.

A wide smile spread across Blake's face. 'Oh my goodness.' She opened the stall door and walked over to them, crouching down.

'I hear they're good for keeping the weeds down,' Harlan said behind her.

Blake stroked their soft backs. 'I can't believe you remembered.'

'I remember every detail of that visit.'

Her smile widened, and she rose and wandered back over to him. 'Six months ago, I was certain I was going to lie down one evening and never get up again. Death followed me everywhere.' She wound her arms round his neck. 'Now I have you, and all of this'—she gestured around her—'my sisters are healthy, and I've not seen my mother this content since my father was alive.'

Harlan watched her closely. 'And now you have goats.'

'Goats with *names*.'

He looked in their direction. 'God help us.'

'My point is'—Blake turned his head so he was looking

at her—'I love you. I love our life and the home we've made together. And I love that I caught you petting Garlic in the kitchen two days ago.'

'I was cleaning something off my boot.'

'What about the day before that?'

'I was picking up a feather. That thing moults all over the house.'

Blake gave him a sceptical look, then released a contented breath. 'I keep waiting for it all to just disappear.'

He gripped her waist with his large hands. 'Well, stop. I can't speak for the goats, but I'm not going anywhere.'

She pressed a hand to his face. 'Thank you for loving me so completely.'

'Thank you for giving me the chance.' He kissed her lips, cheek, forehead. 'I suppose I should let you go inside now.'

Blake's arms slid off Harlan as she turned to the goats. 'Come along, ladies. Time to go inside.'

Harlan grabbed her around the waist and hoisted her up in the air. She squealed and kicked her legs out.

'I swear to God,' he said, 'if I ever find those goats inside…'

She tipped her head back as she laughed. 'I was joking.'

'Swear it.'

'I swear before Belenus.' The words came out on breaths of laughter.

He lowered her to the ground, turned her, and kissed her deeply. Her eyes sank shut, and heat pooled in her belly.

Harlan broke away first. 'You stand no chance of making that dinner if you keep that up.'

Blake patted his chest. 'Stand down, defender.' With her hand wrapped in his, they exited the stables and strolled towards the house.

ACKNOWLEDGMENTS

I would like to express my gratitude to the many people who contributed to this book. My biggest thanks goes to my readers. Without you guys, I wouldn't get to do what I love. Next, a huge thank you to my rock star husband who supports and encourages me even though my writing takes time away from him. I love you to bits. A big thank you to McKinley, Kristin and the team at Hot Tree Editing for polishing the manuscript into something beautiful. A shout out to Katy for beta reading, and to my proofreader, Rebecca, for catching everything I missed. A round of applause for my cover designer, Stuart Bache, for another gorgeous cover. And finally, a huge thank you to my Launch Team for your encouragement, honest reviews, and being the final set of eyes on my work. You guys are amazing.

ALSO BY TANYA BIRD

You can find a complete list of published works at

tanyabird.com/books

www.ingramcontent.com/pod-product-compliance
Lightning Source LLC
Chambersburg PA
CBHW030231120726
47903CB00005B/1442